The Phony Reformer

*Greed, Status, and Patronage
in Late Qing China*

A translation of Dieming (Anonymous),
Xindang shengguan facai ji (1906)

Translated with an introduction by
Luke S. K. Kwong

ROWMAN & LITTLEFIELD
Lanham · Boulder · New York · London

Executive Editor: Susan McEachern
Editorial Assistant: Katelyn Turner
Senior Marketing Manager: Kim Lyons

Credits and acknowledgments for material borrowed from other sources, and reproduced with permission, appear on the appropriate page within the text.

Published by Rowman & Littlefield
A wholly owned subsidiary of The Rowman & Littlefield Publishing Group, Inc.
4501 Forbes Boulevard, Suite 200, Lanham, Maryland 20706
www.rowman.com

Unit A, Whitacre Mews, 26-34 Stannary Street, London SE11 4AB, United Kingdom

British Library Cataloguing in Publication Information Available

Library of Congress Cataloging-in-Publication Data Available

ISBN: 978-1-5381-1239-7 (cloth : alk. paper)
ISBN: 978-1-5381-1240-3 (pbk. : alk. paper)
ISBN: 978-1-5381-1241-0 (electronic)

♾™ The paper used in this publication meets the minimum requirements of American National Standard for Information Sciences—Permanence of Paper for Printed Library Materials, ANSI/NISO Z39.48-1992.

Printed in the United States of America

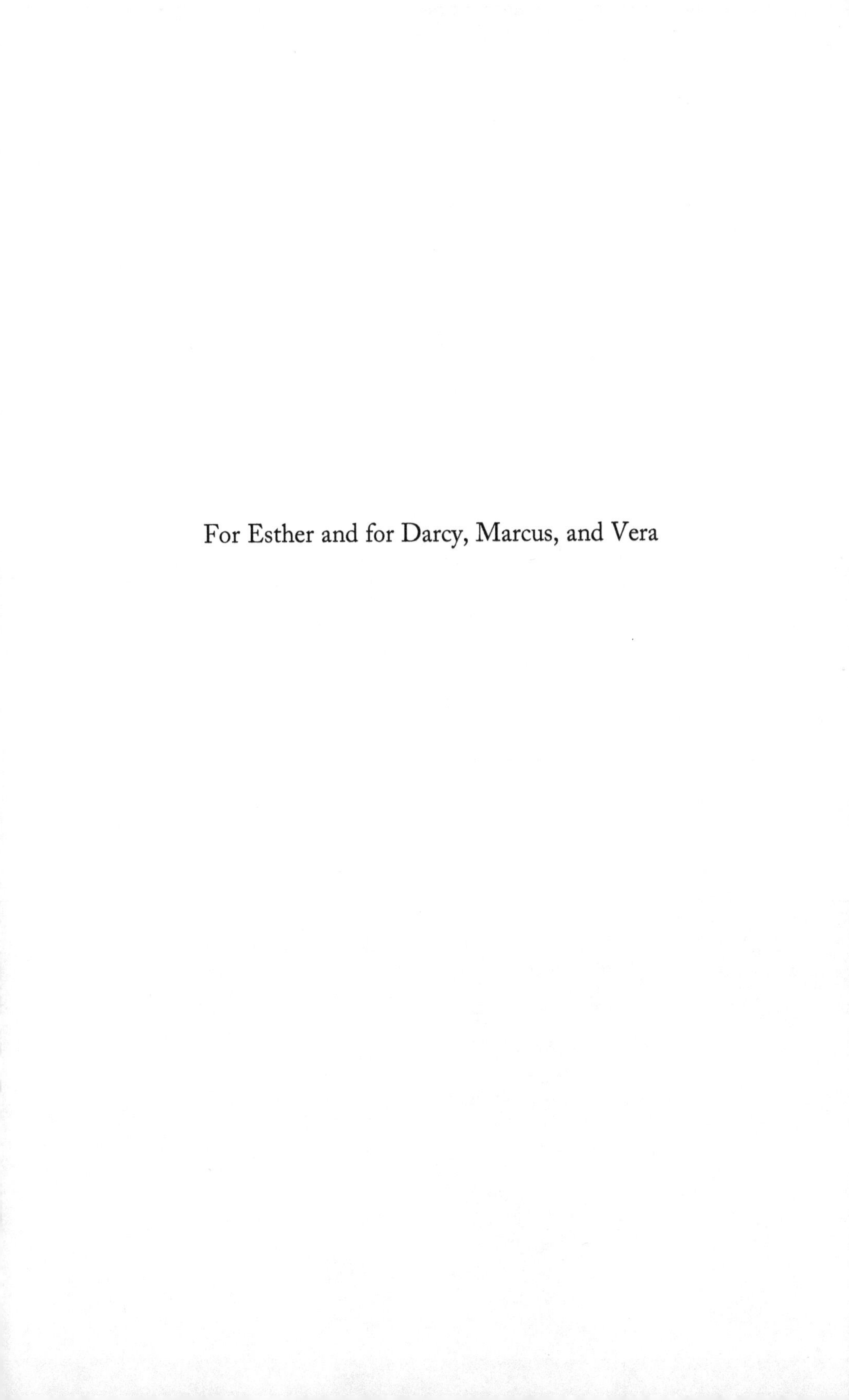

For Esther and for Darcy, Marcus, and Vera

Contents

Chapter 6   61
Mining shares are peddled on Fuzhou Road to attract investors;
A company is set up in Guangxin prefecture to produce camphor.

Chapter 7   69
New rules are drafted to forestall school education's harmful effects;
Preemptive action is the key to success in handling foreign relations.

Chapter 8   77
An old friend's cooperation helps resolve a Sino-foreign dispute;
A police surcharge is enforced in the name of policy innovation.

Chapter 9   85
An old flame cannot reignite as the nestled bird is scared away;
The heartache lingers as the male fox sets out to look for a mate.

Chapter 10   93
A superior's favor incurs add-on duties at the correctional center;
In search of marital bliss, a letter is sent with a marriage proposal.

Chapter 11   101
The dress-up embrace of Great Universality dazzles every eye;
Vengeance over a private feud goes public in the newspapers.

Chapter 12   109
Harsh words in heated argument cause affection and fortune to vanish;
Endurance through hardship yields fruits of fame and riches in the end.

Chapter 13   117
Commendation for the intendant status fulfills a long-standing career desire;
Supervision of school affairs calls for implementation of authoritarian rules.

Chapter 14   125
Deft skills in making money are applied to maximize mining profits;
Army duties become a concurrent job when no other deputy is found.

Preface and Acknowledgments

From beginning to end, my goal here has been to provide a primary source reading for courses with an emphasis on modern or late imperial China. I also hoped that the general reader might find this translated novel both informative and entertaining. At no time during the long process was it my intention to branch out, in terms of academic pigeonholing, from "history" to "literature." I am well aware that this attempt to straddle the two disciplines may have fallen short of the rigorous standards of both. My apology, then, at the close of a humbling experience, is due for all the inadequacies of technique, language, and substance that may remain in these pages. I alone am responsible for them.

For instructors who look beyond the textbook for supplementary materials in teaching the past, primary sources are a valuable tool. Government documents and literati writings are the obvious choices, but the effort to make sense of truncated selections can be a challenge to students. Novels are arguably different. Notwithstanding authorial biases and limitations that mar all written sources, novels have a story to tell, a moral to impart, and a collage of human images to evoke empathy that enhances understanding. Novels are not, of course, substitutes for government documents and literati writings but can help to illuminate many of the selfsame situations that these other sources were meant to depict.

By tracing the path of one man's career progress under the guise of reform, *The Phony Reformer* spins an edifying tale of personal ambitions, elite follies, and the Qing court's last-ditch effort in the post-Boxer years to revitalize the country. The novel ends when the protagonist, Yuan Bozhen, is offered his choice of several government positions in Beijing. These are middle-ranking leadership positions in newly established, reform-oriented administrations. Much to the envy of his peers, these positions are basically low-risk, if not risk-free, and potentially lucrative. The chain of command would allow Yuan Bozhen to shift the dreaded responsibility for critical decisions to his superiors without jeopardizing his own chances for promotions and illicit profits (such as bribes). Soft-pedaling the roles of ideas and politics in reform, but not oblivious to them, *The Phony Reformer* focuses on human agency in explaining the mixed results of late Qing reform. Such a focus is hardly surprising. In Chinese traditions, the humanistic strain had long upheld "finding the right men" (*deren*) as the key to successful government. The "right man," simply put, was preferably a moralist rather than a legalist, a scholar rather than a technocrat, although conscientious rulers through dynastic times always looked past the dichotomy for candidates who were distinguished in both areas—in ethical principles and practical action. The great irony, to the author of *The Phony Reformer*, was that the high demand for reform personnel opened up career opportunities that attracted not this ideal type of human talent but the likes of Yuan Bozhen, who were more devoted to self-interest than to public good.

If Yuan Bozhen was a fictional character subject to critical assessment, the scrutiny extended to real-life reformers as well. In Huang Xiaopei's *The Big Cheat* (Da mabian, 1909), for instance, Kang Youwei (1858–1927) of Hundred Days Reform (1898) fame was portrayed as a complete fraud, unworthy of his reputation as a reform leader. Huang's novel, while certainly open to criticism for its polemical overtones and factual inaccuracies, may serve as a needed reminder that Kang's historical significance in 1898 has continued to be misread. The warped perspective began early, almost as soon as Kang became a wanted criminal in the wake of the Hundred Days Reform. Largely ignorant of Kang's role in Chinese politics, foreign leaders such as US president Theodore Roosevelt and Canada's prime minister Sir Wilfred Laurier received Kang as if he were a VIP political fugitive from China. The foreign press did no better, calling Kang the "Vice Minister of War," "Prime Minister," "ex-Counsellor of State," "Secretary of His Imperial Majesty," "General," "Prince," and "His Excellency." Kang Youwei was none of those things. It would be instructive to take a close look at *The Big Cheat* not only for a possible corrective to the skewed image of Kang but also, alongside *The Phony Reformer*, for insights into a relatively neglected aspect of late Qing reform: its human dimension. But that will have to wait for another time and another book.

The publication of this book owes a multiple debt to colleagues, friends, and family. My gratitude goes to the anonymous readers of the manuscript for their thoughtful comments; to Brian Hill and Rebeccah Shumaker at Rowman & Littlefield for their kind support; to Susan McEachern, whose editorial acumen has immeasurably improved the quality of the finished work, and to her assistant Katelyn Turner, who ably and cheerfully helped along the way; to Helen Subbio for her meticulous attention to detail that saved me from many infelicities of expression; to Alden Perkins, whose professionalism guided the production of this book to a gratifying finish; to Wen-hsin Yeh for her exemplary scholarship and encouragement; to Nap-yin Lau for his friendship and for sending reference materials; to Ruihan Wu at Beida, who promptly agreed to lend a hand amid her busy preparations for her visit to Ann Arbor; and to Kathleen Wright, who read the first draft and made valuable suggestions.

Finally, Esther and our little ones, two generations removed, Darcy, Marcus, and Vera, have been an unfailing source of inspiration. To them this slim volume is dedicated.

Translator's Introduction

If "awakening" (*xingjue*) was a favorite Chinese metaphor for China's hoped-for reconstruction during and after the late Qing period (c. 1862–1912),[1] the wait for it to happen was like a long night of interminable sleep. Reconstruction required power, which, in words made famous by Mao Zedong, "comes out of the barrel of a gun."[2] The blunt dictum aptly summed up the violence that ravaged the country for much of the nineteenth and twentieth centuries. Mao personally witnessed and took part in many of the later occurrences. What had come before was a manifold crisis that culminated in the fall of China's last Qing dynasty (1644–1912). Grassroots discontent had given rise to massive rebellions, such as the Taiping (1850–1864), the Nian (1851–1868), the Boxer (1898–1900), and, with long-simmering ethnic grievances added to the fray, the Muslim Hui (1856–1877). Late in the century, the discourse of race helped refuel the anti-Manchu sentiment, which had never completely dissipated since the Manchu conquest of Ming China and its Han population in 1644. It was now rekindled with ideological flair and intensity as Chinese revolutionaries set forth their anti-Manchu agenda in the name of Han nationalism.

Internal upheaval aside, turmoil also issued from clashes with enemies at the gate. The Qing defeat by Britain and other Western powers in the Opium Wars (1839–1842, 1856–1860) is by now a well-documented story. The humiliating terms of peace that Qing China was forced to accept foreshadowed further losses and concessions in later decades. Stripped of its pretense as the self-proclaimed Celestial Dynasty (*Tianchao*), the Qing court had to recognize, at long last, its perilous plight.

Rebellion, revolution, and neo-imperialism were high drama that captured historical headlines. However, the bloodshed, the dispute over Qing legitimacy, and the thunderous roar of cannons, to pursue the metaphor, did more to highlight the nightmarish quality of China's deep sleep than to end it.

Less spectacular but no less significant in the long run were the individual voices that sounded the wake-up call. The rise of the modern press during the last Qing decades did much to facilitate their articulation. The great number of Chinese periodicals and newspapers that mushroomed from the 1890s on—many, admittedly, experimental and short-lived—furnished a platform (or a "middle realm" or "public sphere") for these voices to be heard, shared, and contested.[3] Still accessible only to a minority, primarily the literate, the new print culture nonetheless registered a defining characteristic of China's modernity.[4]

THE NOVEL: PUBLICATION, THEME, AND AUTHOR

The short novel translated here was a product of the times. Both in publication and in theme, *The Phony Reformer: Greed, Status, and Patronage in Late Qing China* (Xindang shengguan facai ji) exhibited some of the common characteristics of the nascent press. Like many contemporary works of fiction, whether original or translated, it first appeared as a serial in a periodical; in this instance, in the semimonthly *Continent* (Dalu bao) during the second half of 1905.[5] In April 1906, it came out as a separate volume under the imprint of Zuoxin she,[6] which published the *Continent* and boasted of an elaborate printing facility in Shanghai. A second printing followed six months later. The story reveals, through the main character's exploits, many of the ills that were plaguing the late Qing state and society. The protagonist Yuan Bozhen started out as a small-time community leader in his native district in Jiangxi province and went on to realize his career ambitions by seizing opportunities that opened up as a result of the Qing court's decision after the Boxer Rebellion to implement countrywide reform. Yuan Bozhen achieved what was, to his peers, much-envied success while he raked in cash from his official posts and assignments. To the author, Yuan Bozhen epitomized a new breed of self-seekers who maximized personal gains by exploiting the government's initiatives of change.[7]

The novel is said to be an "unfinished" work.[8] Internal evidence suggests otherwise. Not only does the final chapter provide a diagram that sums up Yuan Bozhen's progress as a "reform" official, but it also spells out, in plain language and in a lyrical poem (*ci*), the author's overall assessment of opportunists like Yuan Bozhen. There is no hint, on the other hand, that the author was contemplating a continuation of the story or a sequel. The completion of the novel may also be plausibly dated. In chapter 16, there is mention of some provincial officials' plea with the throne to adopt constitutional monarchy and to send a mission abroad to observe firsthand the political practices of foreign governments. The twofold request was prompted by Japan's astounding victory in the Russo-Japanese War (1904–1905)—proof to Chinese observers of the superiority of Japan's imperial constitutionalism over Tsarist autocracy. The author alluded to the proposal but not to the throne's decision not long after, in mid-July 1905, to send a delegation of ministers abroad for the purpose. It is highly likely that when the author was drafting the final chapter of the novel, he only knew of the officials' dual request but not its final outcome. The completion of the novel may, therefore, be tentatively dated to a time shortly before the throne's July 1905 announcement while the novel was being serialized in the *Continent*.

All modern editions of the novel do not identify the author but use Dieming (Name unknown or missing) in place of a name. The anonymity may well have been a disguise for Ji Yuancheng (1878–1908), who founded Zuoxin she and published its organ, the *Continent*. There are episodes in the story that cross-reference aspects of Ji's life.[9] Much of the story unfolds in Wuchang, a political and economic hub in Hubei province in central China, where Ji had spent his early years. Scattered remarks in the novel refer to study in Japan and the translation of Japanese works into Chinese. These, again, resonate with Ji's personal experiences, as he had gone to Japan as a student and later worked as a translator of Japanese before starting his own publishing business in 1902. The repercussion of the Wealth Voucher (or Independent Army) Rebellion, a concurrent sideshow in central China in 1900 to the main Boxer event in the north, in which Ji was allegedly involved, explains a character's travels and fear of government reprisal. Ji later worked for a time in the Ministry of Foreign Affairs in Beijing. His familiarity with the tendency of all levels of government officials to evade responsibility by routinely referring cases of foreign demand or dispute to Beijing and, ultimately, to the throne found its way into the dialog. In short, if Ji had authored the novel and serialized it in his semimonthly *Continent* before publishing it again by his Zuoxin she,[10] he had reason to opt for anonymity. Cynics might otherwise have had a field day with his repeated efforts to promote his own work.

Fiction, like art, imitates life. The truism is especially applicable to the "exposé novel" (*qianze xiaoshuo*), a popular subgenre of late Qing fiction to which *The Phony Reformer* belongs. While many works of this subgenre favor the use of caricature and overwrought strokes,[11] *The Phony Reformer* stands out for its polished prose, moderate tone, and subtle (and not-so-subtle) satire.[12] This does not mean that *The Phony Reformer* is a flawless work. Yuan Bozhen's extraordinary rise, for example, is compressed into the short span of a few years that seems too tidy and neat—that is, overly expedited. The appeal of the novel, therefore, lies not in its literary merit but in its descriptive realism. The frequent references to the time elapsed between events and to travel itineraries that corresponded with actual geography betray the author's determination to convey a sense of the familiar and real. Yuan Bozhen's experiences shed light on the kinds of toil and trouble that an ambitious upstart in late Qing officialdom had to go through in hopes to get what he wanted, and his interactions with superiors and friends and with those below his station showcase some of the prevailing norms of elite behavior. Also credible are opium smoking and brothel visits as favorite pastimes to illustrate the unsavory side of elite life.[13] By packing social and political critiques into self-contained plots, *The Phony Reformer* injects materiality and details into situations that historians, for lack of evidence, cannot freely depict. More than an extant work of fiction from the period, *The Phony Reformer* is a social, cultural, and historical document in its own right.

Despite the author's disclaimer that the story was contrived out of thin air, it can be safely assumed that the novel's characters and episodes were modeled on contemporary personalities and events. While Yuan Bozhen was, in all likelihood, a composite profile from diverse sources, some of the secondary characters can be readily traced to contemporary figures. For instance, the prince who helped Yuan Bozhen advance his career bears an uncanny resemblance to Prince Qing (1838–1917), who emerged as the most powerful Manchu leader at the imperial court after the Boxer Rebellion. The governor-general of Hubei (and Hunan), who appointed Yuan Bozhen to special assignments and thereby afforded him opportunities to consolidate his credentials, is arguably a spitting image of Zhang Zhidong (1837–1909). Zhang's steadfast sponsorship of reform projects as governor-general was legendary, as was his quirky temperament, which made for a favorite morsel of elite gossip. In chapter 4, the governor-general suddenly walks out of an interview with Yuan Bozhen and never returns to finish it—all for no obvious reason except, perhaps, a moment's whimsical distraction. The historical Zhang Zhidong was entirely capable of such erratic behavior.

INTERSECTING: PAST AND PRESENT

The story unfolds within the main timeframe of the early years of the twentieth century (to mid-1905) and maps the path of the "phony" reformer's rise to prominence. The contemporary focus, however, gains full clarity only against the social and political patterns that had formed long before. Where the past and present intersect, the novel spins a tale about late Qing China's woes and its need for deliverance.

By virtue of his degrees obtained through civil service examinations, Yuan Bozhen established himself as an elite member of society.[14] In one form or another, examinations as a recruitment method for government service had been in place in China for more than one thousand years. The Qing dynasty basically followed the Ming system and emphasized, above all, the skills of composing the highly formalized, complex "eight-legged" essay.[15] It took long years for candidates to master its intricate techniques, which often proved an insurmountable hurdle. As much as the "eight-legged" essay had been criticized for encouraging imitation rather than originality and for its sheer irrelevance to practical statecraft,[16] it remained a crucial requirement until it was abolished in 1902, and the examination system that had fostered it came to an end in 1905.

There were three main levels of competition. Yuan Bozhen passed the prefectural and provincial levels but not the third, or metropolitan level, held in Beijing.[17] He stayed in his home district, where he served as a community leader. His degrees entitled him to some measure of social prestige and influence. Even local officials showed him respect and occasionally turned to him for help with troublesome situations. Yuan Bozhen's life up to this point was hardly rare or unique. He was merely one of many degree holders who had little or no prospect of an official career because of the saturation of government bureaucracies with active and wait-listed ("expectant") personnel. Even his two degrees had by now lost much of their importance for entry into civil service. Ever since the mid-nineteenth century, the Qing court had allowed a steady increase in the sale of official titles and government posts.[18] Such sales were, again, nothing new. As a quick way for the dynastic state to raise revenues, the practice had been known in China since the Warring States period (453–221 BC). When the Qing government resorted to it, which soon increased to an unprecedented scale, it was in dire need of emergency funding to offset expenses such as those incurred by the military campaigns against rebels like the Taipings.

As a result of the credential sales, elite society vastly expanded. New entrants got in not through the narrow portal of examinations but through purchase. The two constituencies, broadly defined as those with or without the hard-earned degrees, were not clear-cut or mutually exclusive. It was not unusual for lower-degree holders to improve the chances of their upward mobility, or simply to enhance the social prestige of self, family, and clan, by acquiring additional titles or ranks with cash. While status gained through the examinations entailed lifelong ties with examiners and fellow candidates of the same year (*tongnian*), purchased ones came in handy when appointment to a government job favored the flexibility of experience or seniority, or both.

All this factored in Yuan Bozhen's climb up the ladder of success. As a degree holder, he had access to the elite network of patronage and social connections that stood him in good stead when he needed a helping hand. With his purchased credentials, he was able to go where opportunities or his opportunistic hunches beckoned. The author singled out the "expectant intendant" as the most desirable status for a career seeker to possess and concluded the story when Yuan Bozhen, in that capacity, had the luxury to choose from three attractive jobs that were offered him in Beijing. The "expectant" status was indeed a very popular category of the late Qing credential sales. It produced, over time, an unwieldy mass of aspirants, many of whom flocked to provincial capitals or administrative centers for their chances. Since jobs were few, most ended up as little more than stalkers, so to speak, of would-be patrons, or sycophantic hangers-on in official circles, desperate but going nowhere.

With well-coordinated moves and opportune timing, Yuan Bozhen was able to squirm his way through this human jungle. Patronage and gifts enabled him to tap into the Qing demand for utility personnel to fill a spate of reform-related jobs. During the crisis-laden decades of the late Qing, reform became a topic of discussion not only among officials whose sense of duty did not let them turn a blind eye, but also among members of the educated elite who were similarly troubled by the country's deteriorating conditions.

It is now a commonplace to compare and contrast reform and revolution as representing the two dominant positions on change in the late Qing political spectrum: one "moderate" and the other "radical." The distinction, however, can be overdrawn, and the assumption of both being of similar strength, in diametrical opposition to one another, can be misleading. In fact, reform as an attempt to advocate change short of repudiating Qing rule offered a far more diverse field of thought and action than the specific, narrow focus of revolution. Consider, for instance, the Qing initiative in the post-Boxer period to restructure many of its economic, social, and political institutions to be in line with those of advanced nations.[19] If these changes had been allowed a chance to reach fruition before revolution broke out to shatter the Qing throne as a rallying point or focus of loyalty, China might have gone through a more peaceful, constructive overhaul in many aspects of society and life than the political disarray that set in at the inauguration of the Republic in 1912.

The end of the Qing dynasty, therefore, does not warrant a retrospective dismissal of all its earlier reform efforts as "insincere" or futile. In short, reform delineated a vast gray area for the retreat of educated Chinese who vacillated between moderate and radical courses of action or who were simply unsure of the benefits of the Qing collapse or the republican experiment.

Reform, in this sense, broadly comprised the preferences not only of known reformers but also of the silent majority who held out hope for China's uplift through gradualist change.

INTERSECTING: PRESENT AND FUTURE

While critical of the "phony" reformer, the novel was not a partisan effort to promote revolution. If Ji Yuancheng had indeed authored the novel, as suggested earlier, his ties to revolutionaries would have to be more closely reassessed.[20] Both his publishing business and his employment in the Ministry of Foreign Affairs would seem to indicate, rather than a mere cover for his subversive intent, his willingness to engage in the status quo for the country's betterment. In any case, while poking fun at self-seeking individuals like Yuan Bozhen, the author (whether it was Ji Yuancheng or not) concluded on a hopeful note: Selfish motives could translate into public good through government service, and incidental gains from the half-hearted efforts of phony reformers were better than no gain at all. Yuan Bozhen and his ilk could still redeem themselves by doing what they did.

Reform (as an attempt to modify policies or put new ones in place to improve the quality of government) and revolution (as an attempt to overthrow the existing regime and replace it with a new one)[21] attested to some of the late Qing responses to the deepening crises. Similar efforts at change had been documented through China's dynastic history, but historical precedents and traditional patterns alone do not adequately explain the late Qing experience. Forces of flux and contingency, often unique in kind and magnitude, were also at work to fashion the late Qing variations on these familiar themes.

A telltale sign comes early in the story. In chapter 1, the Chinese assistant of a foreign missionary gets into an altercation with peasants of a local village. Violence breaks out, resulting in the assistant's injuries and the missionary's loss of belongings. The missionary's adamant demand to provincial authorities for compensation and the officials' ready compliance, more out of concern for a quick closure of the incident than for justice, are reminiscent of a familiar scenario in late Qing foreign relations that readers during that time period would easily recognize.[22] The novel features other foreign characters as well, and foreign opinion was cited approvingly in several places in scathing criticism of the Chinese character. In the late Qing context, foreign presence signified one of the most powerful factors conducive to change,[23] one that generated controversies and elicited a wide array of Chinese reactions, from confusion to wonderment, from hostility to accommodation, from xenophobia to nationalism.

There is no question that the author appreciated foreign achievements, which were, to him, demonstrated primarily by Western countries and, to a less extent, by Meiji Japan. Through a character's monologue in chapter 1, he rehearsed what was an idealized version of Western society (in the singular) that late Qing Chinese often construed in lamenting their country's decrepitude. Yet he was not a xenophile with an infinite enthusiasm for foreigners and foreign things. He made fun of Chinese, who, like Yuan Bozhen, were ever so eager to please or ingratiate themselves with foreigners, and he even waxed nationalistic in episodes in which resistance to foreign encroachment on China's natural resources became a refrain. With some understanding of Western and Japanese feminist thought, he decried its extreme manifestations.[24] Yuan Bozhen's second wife, Miss Kuan, a self-avowed adherent of "civilized" standards, engaged in extramarital affairs in the name of her inviolable rights and freedom. The author portrayed her as no more than a manipulative, licentious woman.

Nor did the several foreign characters in the novel necessarily exemplify higher morals or wisdom. They were, if anything, a reminder of the treaty privileges that foreign governments had wrested from Qing China. Shanghai, the quintessential bundle of cultural contradictions, was the destination of Yuan Bozhen's official trips.[25] To be precise, his preferred venues for business and pleasure were located in the foreign-controlled sections to the north and west (the British Concession or International Settlement and the French Concession) rather than in the Chinese district seat in the southeast. The differences in physical layout, in architectural style, and in amenities were striking and demarcated two distinct but adjoining worlds. The author depicted the foreign areas of Greater Shanghai in deserving terms: They were a gateway to Western lifestyle, culture, and technology but also a haven for the proliferation of Chinese vices, like prostitution and opium sales.

It is worth noting that the author identified foreigners and foreign objects in unadorned language, shorn of the usual tidbits like eye and hair colors that animated contemporary caricatures of the "barbarian" and "son of the devil" or of extraordinary features that made a horse-drawn carriage ride or a Western restaurant dinner a marvel. The lack of embellishing details, whether in admiration or mockery, betrayed the author's acclimatized familiarity with these objects of his reference. All were taken for granted, as if they were naturally juxtaposed alongside their native counterparts in the Qing environment.

Juxtaposition is an apt word that describes the proximity of the cultural parallels and options available. In this mix of the old and new, of resilience and fluidity, Yuan Bozhen found an opening for his maneuvers and thrived. Leather shoes, sunglasses, and cigarettes were pricey foreign imports but provided comic relief when Yuan Bozhen displayed his bizarre sense of avant-garde fashion by parading these with his traditional gown and mandated Qing hairstyle.[26] A fitted Western dress accentuated the contours of a woman's body. The sensuality was a far cry from the ideal of feminine beauty that Chinese men had long invested in the petite "lotus feet."[27] Yuan Bozhen may be described as infatuated with both, but, if forced to choose, his fine-honed instincts would probably still dispose him to favor the foot fetish over the seductive bustline and slim waist.

AUTHOR'S VISION

With choices and options came a sense of empowerment that threatened existing authorities, values, and practices. The boundary between traditions and innovations, between Chinese and foreign, became less rigid. In places like treaty ports that were carved out of Qing territory but outside of Qing control, a reversal of fortune actually took place to privilege the foreign and new. There was, in short, an in-between ambiguity about the author's perspective, which, when writ large, may be said to have also characterized the Chinese outlook since the late Qing decades. The contrast of juxtaposed elements, like Yuan Bozhen's long gown and leather shoes, his shaven head and sunglasses, has etched an awareness of bicultural possibilities in Chinese consciousness. It has since yielded a mix of acceptance, tolerance, and denial of the Sino-Western binary in Chinese thought and behavior.

In the final chapter, the author alluded to Jean-Jacques Rousseau (1712–1778) and Saigo Takamori (1828–1877) as inspiration for China's quest for change.[28] Both are iconic figures in modern Western and Japanese history, respectively. The author's appeal to external references included a crude, if hilarious, "scientific" overview of the evolution of humans from dogs and monkeys, a tripartite process analogous to the formation and ranking of nations. China was compared to the second stage of monkeys, which had yet to evolve fully into humans (modern nations). It was biological Darwinism and Social Darwinism rolled into one.[29] These pseudoscientific overtones not only echoed contemporary Chinese interest in Western theories of race and comparative society but, more pointedly, affirmed universality as that which bound all human groups to the same developmental path and struggle for survival.[30]

Universality implies the whole world. The world that late Qing China inherited was far more complex than any of its dynastic predecessors had known, although the forces that had shaped it had been at work for several centuries. With the steady arrival of Europeans to late Ming and Qing China after the "voyages of discovery," there was also the coming of New World food crops like potatoes and maize along with Peruvian and Mexican silver.[31] Slowly but surely, the hardy crops and precious metals coalesced with indigenous factors to transform China's demographic and fiscal profiles. When, in the late eighteenth century, India opium was found to be the only commodity capable of balancing the British tea trade with China, the stage was set for a confrontational approach. Both long-term trends and interim clashes occurred in the context of what we now call "globalism." Qing China thus found itself thrust into a new world system, euphemistically called the "family of nations," for which it was ill prepared.

The global vision was indeed an intriguing one.[32] However, as much as the author celebrated universality—a shared space and time for all countries and peoples—he could hardly envision China's future outside of the Western and Japanese paradigms. Between the particular and universal, the national and global, China and the world, there was, again, ambiguity. The author navigated through it by holding fast to an ancient Chinese principle. In taking the phony reformer to task, he invoked authenticity as the corrective. Authenticity as a core human virtue harks back to early Confucian teachings. It begins with the moral self and extends through social and political institutions, like the family and the state, to the entire world.[33] Where statecraft is concerned, authenticity prescribes attributes such as purity of purpose, the unity of motive and action, and selfless dedication to the common good.

It was a tall order, but it was in the revival of this ancient ethic that the author saw a glimmer of hope in China's long, dark night. Indeed, so he believed, when dawn came and China awoke, darkness would be there no more.

NOTES

1. See John Fitzgerald, *Awakening China* (Stanford, CA: Stanford University Press, 1996).

2. Mao employed this expression in a speech given in August 1927. See Mao Zedong, *Mao Zedong junshi wenji* (Mao Zedong's writings on military affairs), 6 vols. (Beijing: Junshi chubanshe and Zhongyang wenxian chubanshe, 1994), I:2.

3. The "middle realm" is Joan Judge's term in her *Print and Politics: "Shibao" and the Culture of Reform in Late Qing China* (Stanford, CA: Stanford University Press, 1997). The essays in Rudolf Wagner, ed., *Joining the Global Public: Word, Image, and City in Early Chinese Newspapers, 1870–1910* (Albany: State University of New York Press, 2007) make cautious use of the concept "public sphere," originally coined by the German philosopher Jürgen Habermas for Europe in the seventeenth to nineteenth centuries, to describe the late Qing print media as constituting a comparable domain

for rational-critical opinions. The application of this concept to China, however, remains a controversial one.

4. "Modernity" is used here in a very broad sense to denote a cultural propensity for innovative change against time-honored values, practices, and institutions, or what is collectively called "tradition." It is now commonly accepted that there is not only one kind of modernity based on the Western experience but multiple kinds. See Shmuel N. Eisenstadt, "Multiple Modernities," *Daedalus* 129, no. 1 (2000): 1–29. David Wang examines more than sixty late Qing novels and discusses how they already displayed a "creative, innovative" modern literary form, despite the dismissive view of them by a later ("May Fourth") generation of writers. See his *Fin-de-Siècle Splendor: Repressed Modernities of Late Qing Fiction, 1848–1911* (Stanford, CA: Stanford University Press, 1997).

5. It would appear that the *Continent* began as a monthly and became a semi-monthly after the first two issues. The novel was serialized in issue numbers 8 to 20 (June 12 to December 6, 1905). See publisher's remarks in Dieming (Anonymous), *Xindang shengguan facai ji* (The phony reformer), in the combined volume with *Hou guanchang xianxing ji* (A sequel to *Guanchang xianxing ji*, An exposure of the officials' world), and *Lengyan guan* (Observations with an impartial eye), in the series, *Zhongguo jindai xiaoshuo daxi* (A comprehensive collection of novels published in the modern period) (Nanchang: Baihuazhou wenyi chubanshe, 1991), v-vi.

6. For a discussion of the title and edition of the novel, see "Notes on the Translation," no. 5.

7. The term *xindang* (reform faction) in the title requires a word of explanation. *Xin* means "new," as opposed to *jiu* (old), and *dang* has a long history of use that runs the gamut of meanings, from an informal grouping of like-minded individuals around an interest or principle to a political clique and party with distinct leaders and followers. During the late Qing, *xindang* and *jiudang* were in use as identifiers, and often self-identifiers, by educated Chinese who championed or rejected foreign-inspired change. *Xin* is also a shortened reference to *weixin* (reform). In the context of the story, it seems more fitting to translate *xindang* as "reform faction," though the author intended it to mean individuals who supported reform rather than a formal political organization.

8. See publisher's remarks in Dieming (Anonymous), *Xindang shengguan facai ji* cited in note 5.

9. For Ji's life, see Zou Zhenhuan, "Ji Yuancheng ji qi chuangban di Zuoxin she yu *Dalu bao*" (Ji Yuancheng and the Zuoxin she and the *Continent* that he established), *Anhui daxue xuebao zhexue shehui kexue ban* (Journal of Anhui University: Philosophy and Social Sciences) 6 (2012): 106–16; also, Fan Tiequan and Kong Xiangji, "Keming dangren Ji Yihui zhongyao shishi shukao" (Investigation into important aspects of the life of the revolutionary Ji Yihui), *Lishi yanjiu* (Historical research) 5 (2013): 173–82.

10. A piece of circumstantial evidence may be cited. On the copyright page of the edition used for this translation, under "author and distributor," the name Zuoxin she is given. See Dieming (Anonymous), *Xindang shengguan facai ji* (The phony reformer), 2nd printing (Shanghai: Zuoxin she, 1906). This would seem to imply

that someone working at or for the Zuoxin she had composed the work. No one, in this sense, would have been more qualified to carry the name Zuoxin she than Ji Yuancheng himself.

11. Lu Xun's brief critique of the exposé novel is found in his *Zhongguo xiaoshuo shi lue* (A brief history of Chinese fiction) (Beijing: Dongfang chubanshe, 1996), 231. His work is available in an English translation, *A Brief History of Chinese Fiction*, trans. Yang Xianyi and Gladys Yang (Beijing: Foreign Languages Press, 1959).

12. Qian Xingcun (A Ying), a pioneering researcher on the late Qing literary output, calls it "one of the better crafted works" about the reform faction. See his *Wanqing xiaoshuo shi* (A history of the late Qing novel) (Beijing: Renmin wenxue chubanshe, 1980), 84. As Zhao Jingshen points out, some of the characters' names in the novel are a play on words with sarcastic or derogatory connotations. Yuan Bozhen sounds like *yuan bu zhen* that means "unauthentic from the start." Cheng Rixian (chapter 3) sounds like *cheng ri xian* that means "idle all the time." Wu Guixiang (chapter 8) sounds like *wu gui xiang* that means "a turtle's smell." Fuzhongting (chapter 9) sounds like *wu zhong ting* that means "never a truthful word." Zhao Yesheng (chapter 10) sounds like *zao nie sheng* that means "the man who brings on retribution." See Dieming (Anonymous), *Guanchang weixin ji* (The phony reformer) (Shanghai: Zhonghua shuju, 1959), preface, 2.

13. For opium smoking, see Jonathan Spence, "Opium Smoking in Ch'ing China," in *Conflict and Control in Late Imperial China*, ed. Frederic Wakeman and Carolyn Grant (Berkeley: University of California Press, 1975), 143–73; also, Yangwen Zheng, *The Social Life of Opium in China* (Cambridge: Cambridge University Press, 2005). For prostitution that thrived in a treaty-port city, see Gail Hershatter, *Dangerous Pleasures: Prostitution and Modernity in Twentieth-Century Shanghai* (Berkeley: University of California Press, 1997).

14. China scholars have mostly discarded the term "gentry" for Qing examination degree holders because of its association with landowning in the European context. "Elite," on the other hand, is free of this aspect of the socioeconomic connotation.

15. For a comprehensive study, see Benjamin Elman, *A Cultural History of Civil Examinations in Late Imperial China* (Berkeley: University of California Press, 2000).

16. See David Nivison, "Protest Against Conventions and Conventions of Protest," in *The Confucian Persuasion*, ed. Arthur Wright (Stanford, CA: Stanford University Press, 1960), 177–201.

17. Successful candidates who passed the metropolitan examination were required soon afterward to attend the "palace examination" (*tingshi* or *dianshi*), known by its venue inside the Forbidden City. This final round of competition was not for screening purposes but for determining the candidates' ranking and posting to various levels or branches of government service.

18. An interesting study of the practice is Elisabeth Kaske, "Fund-Raising Wars: Office Selling and Interprovincial Finance in Nineteenth-Century China," *Harvard Journal of Asiatic Studies* 71, no. 1 (2011): 69–141.

19. Mary Wright, ed., *China in Revolution: The First Phase, 1900–1913* (New Haven, CT: Yale University Press, 1968) explores many important themes during the last decade of the Qing dynasty, including the rival approaches to change.

20. The article by Fan Tiequan and Kong Xiangji cited in note 9 above tends to be one-sided about Ji Yuancheng's political commitment. Even the Qing court did not cite proof of Ji's subversion, which would have been punishable by death, when he was dismissed from the Ministry of Foreign Affairs in 1907. He was condemned instead for his association with the "criminal kind" (*feilei*) and sentenced to live under the supervision of local authorities in his native place. While the "criminal kind" can indeed be interpreted to include revolutionaries, his "association" with them could not have been a deep or extensive one without dire consequences.

21. The working definition here broadly includes the term *revolution*'s ancient meaning. The Chinese term *geming* is as old as *The Book of Changes* and refers to dynastic turnover as a result of the *shift* of "the *mandate* of heaven" from one ruling house to another. The term acquired modern connotations, via Japanese usage, during the late Qing to denote violent or profound changes in any area of human life. In this as in other instances, Meiji Japan, viewed by many Chinese as a land of the "same language and same race" (*tongwen tongzhong*), exerted an influence on China that cannot be overstated. See Douglas Reynolds (with Carol T. Reynolds), *East Meets East: Chinese Discover the Modern World in Japan, 1854–1898* (Ann Arbor, MI: Association for Asian Studies, 2014).

22. Alan Sweeten uses Jiangxi in his case study and explains the administrative chain of command in the settlement of antimissionary incidents in *Christianity in Rural China: Conflict and Accommodation in Jiangxi Province, 1860–1900* (Ann Arbor: University of Michigan Center for Chinese Studies, 2001).

23. As Tu Wei-ming astutely pointed out more than twenty years ago, China's forced diplomatic contact with Western nations in the nineteenth century "fundamentally redefined the *Problematik* for the Chinese intellectual." See his "Cultural China: The Periphery as the Center," *Daedalus* 120, no. 2 (1991): 4.

24. For Chinese feminist thought in the early twentieth century, see, for instance, Lydia Liu, Rebecca Karl, and Dorothy Ko, eds., *The Birth of Chinese Feminism: Essential Texts in Transnational Theory* (New York: Columbia University Press, 2013).

25. A classic study of Shanghai is Rhodes Murphey, *Shanghai: Key to Modern China* (Cambridge, MA: Harvard University Press, 1953). Wen-hsin Yeh, *Shanghai Splendor: A Cultural History, 1843–1945* (Berkeley: University of California Press, 2007) is a more interesting read.

26. The mandated Qing hairstyle for men was a single braid, or queue, at the back of the head, with a shaven top. It was originally a Manchu hairstyle and became a symbol of subjugation when it was imposed on Han Chinese men after the Manchu conquest in 1644.

27. By the late Qing, foot-binding for women had existed in China for more than one thousand years. It commenced early in a girl's life, the object being to stunt the natural growth of her feet by tightly wrapping a long bandage around each. Tiny feet were upheld as a measure of a woman's feminine beauty and sensuality; the smaller they were, the better. Dorothy Ko's two works enhance our understanding of this abomination against the female body: *Cinderella's Sisters: A Revisionist History of Footbinding* (Berkeley: University of California Press, 2005) and *Every Step a Lotus: Shoes for Bound Feet* (Berkeley: University of California Press, 2001).

28. Saigo Takamori was a legendary leader turned rebel in early Meiji Japan. Jean-Jacques Rousseau was an influential Enlightenment thinker and writer. Both were highly respected by educated Chinese as they pondered the fate of their country during and after the late Qing.

29. For the introduction of Darwinism and Social Darwinism into China, see James Pusey, *China and Charles Darwin* (Cambridge, MA: Harvard University Asia Center, 1983) and Benjamin Schwartz, *In Search of Wealth and Power: Yen Fu and the West* (Cambridge, MA: Harvard University Press, 1964).

30. For a relevant discussion, see Luke Kwong, "The Rise of the Linear Perspective on History and Time in Late Qing China (c. 1860–1911)," in *Past & Present* 173 (2001): 157–90.

31. The treatment of the High Qing in Susan Naquin and Evelyn Rawski, *Chinese Society in the Eighteenth Century* (New Haven, CT: Yale University Press, 1987) provides insights into important social and economic patterns that had a profound impact on China's later developments.

32. Rudolf Wagner uses the "global imaginaire" in his "Joining the Global Imaginaire: The Shanghai Illustrated Newspaper *Dianshizhai huabao*," in Wagner, *Joining the Global Public*, 105–73.

33. The representative statement of the interconnectedness between the moral self and the world is found in *The Great Learning*, in Confucius, *Confucian Analects, The Great Learning & The Doctrine of the Mean*, trans. James Legge (New York: Dover Publications, 1971), 355–59.

Notes on the Translation

1. The romanization or transliteration of Chinese terms follows the *pinyin* system. Institutional names are rendered according to their commonly accepted English equivalents in the study of Qing China, like governor-general for *zongdu* and Grand Council for Junjichu.

2. Like many publications of the late Qing period, the early edition of the novel used for this translation did not employ modern punctuation and paragraph breaks, with the pages looking like rectangular blocks of printed characters throughout. Modern editions have used punctuation symbols and paragraphing to enhance readability. This translation follows this practice.

3. Instead of a title, each chapter opens with two verse-like lines, each eight characters long, to highlight the chapter's contents. On occasion, these lines do not closely reflect the story that follows, possibly suggesting the author's deviation from the outline after he started writing. Each chapter also ends with two verses, each seven characters long, that are meant either as a summary of the chapter or as a transition to the next. Again, they do not always serve their intended purpose.

4. The forms of social address in the dialog indicate the Chinese practice, common in traditional times but still prevalent today, to apply kinship terminology to people outside the family, even total strangers. It would mitigate the awkwardness somewhat, for example, to call a passerby "uncle," "aunt," "elder brother," or "elder sister" before asking for directions. Similar relational terms were more often applied between friends and acquaintances than pronouns like "you" and "I." Respectful designators were required when meeting a superior or a dignitary or someone in a position to grant a favor, in

order to acknowledge disparity in rank, age, seniority, and/or power. There were many such designators, and their application could be flexible, except in settings bound by strict formal etiquette. The party of the higher status, however, might elect to show cordiality with a more casual form of address. An attempt is made in this translation to convey the literal meanings of these social labels (like Elder Brother in instances where no blood tie actually existed and Your Esteemed Person to demonstrate respect for a superior or someone of a higher status), except where such renditions might seem too distractive or cumbersome. The common pronouns in English or some other substitutes will then be used.

5. A word on the novel's titles and editions is in order. Since the *Dalu bao* (Continent), where the novel was first serialized in 1905, is not available, it is impossible to verify whether the novel had been revised before it came out as a separate volume in 1906. The following, in sequence of their publication dates, are the editions consulted for this translation, which is based primarily on the earliest (1906). As noted below, the novel has been known by several titles, but they are all subsumed under the English title *The Phony Reformer* in this translation:

(1) Dieming (Anonymous), *Xindang shengguan facai ji*, 2nd printing (Shanghai: Zuoxin she, 1906). Two titles appear in this edition: the first, *Xindang facai ji*, on the cover page, and the second, *Xindang shengguan facai ji*, preceding both the table of contents and chapter 1. In chapter 16, the author confirmed *Xindang shengguan facai ji* as the title he gave his novel, but he did not explain why a different title appeared on the title page.

(2) Dieming (Anonymous), *Guanchang weixin ji* (Shanghai: Shanghai gudianwenxue chubanshe, 1956). According to the publisher's remarks, this edition is based on a two-volume, thread-bound edition of the novel, where this third title appears. Nothing more, however, is known about this early edition with this title.

(3) Dieming (Anonymous), *Guanchang weixin ji* (Shanghai: Zhonghua shuju, 1959).

(4) Dieming (Anonymous), *Guanchang weixin ji* (Taibei: Shijie shuju, 1976). This edition is clearly based on (2) above and quotes verbatim its publisher's remarks regarding the novel's title.

(5) Dieming (Anonymous), *Xindang shengguan facai ji*, in the combined volume *Xindang shengguan facai ji, Hou guanchang xianxing ji* (A sequel to *Guanchang xianxing ji*, An exposure of the officials' world), and *Lengyan guan* (Observations with an impartial eye), in

the series *Zhongguo jindai xiaoshuo daxi* (A comprehensive collection of novels published in the modern period) (Nanchang: Baihuazhou wenyi chubanshe, 1991). This modern edition is based on an early printing of the novel with a copyright page showing April 16, 1906, to be its distribution date.

$$\bullet \quad 1 \quad \bullet$$

An antimissionary case funnels
public funds into private pockets;

Old-school folks break down
prejudices to go after new measures.

Since the beginning of time, two kinds of people have inhabited this universe. There is the authentic kind, and there is the phony kind. By some natural process, the phony and the authentic have always come together to form a pair so deceiving to the public eye that no one could tell them apart. Occasionally, the phony even gets the better of the authentic. This is truly one of the unfathomable mysteries in all of heaven and earth.

It follows, then: There was Confucius the Great Sage, and there was the moral hypocrite. There was Yi Yin, and there was Huo Guang.[1] There was the Duke of Zhou, and there was Wang Mang.[2] King Yao and King Shun abdicated in favor of virtuous successors, and there were the likes of Cao Cao and Sima Yen, who put on masks to mimic them.[3] Examples of this kind are too many to be enumerated.

This holds true for animate and inanimate things as well. Fish eyes resemble pearls; exquisite pebbles resemble jade; a fuba[4] resembles a lion; poisonous weeds resemble lifesaving herbs. Generally speaking, the impostor is always there. Qiu the Enlightened One, who wrote *Journey to the West*, understood this principle best.[5] In *Journey to the West*, every one of his characters, whether the Buddha, the Goddess of Mercy, the Monk of Tang, the Monkey King, the Pig-Man Monk, or Monk Sandy, has its phony counterpart.

We can infer from this that imitation of others, however shabbily done, happens everywhere in this world—nothing to marvel at. Foreigners have said it well: Chinese are born with superior imitation skills. Consequently, Chinese excel in passing falsehoods off as truths. Take, for instance, the trendies of our time who love to talk about reform. The topic of reform is constantly on their lips, and an earnest plea for reform is written all over their faces. Only a plaque sporting the two characters for reform is missing from their foreheads.[6] If you say they are not really committed, they will protest and cry, "Unfair." In the final analysis, however, they are only interested in the appearances of reform. If we want to find those who are truly committed to practical action, we may only find one or two in a hundred among those who are currently engaged in reform projects.

Still, one must not judge phony reformers to be totally worthless in our current state of affairs. Given the way things are, it should be clear that, without changes in fits and starts that are initiated by phony reformers, China would still be that grand, old empire that it has always been, ten thousand years from now. Therefore, phony reformers are absolutely indispensable. If readers are skeptical, this fiction writer will tell the tale about a big talker of reform in officialdom, whose life experiences can be cited to illustrate the point. Let all hear it.

This man was born in the district seat of Xinyu in Jiangxi province. His family name was Yuan, his given name, Weixian, and his courtesy name, Bozhen. His parents died early. He started out as a scholar living in poverty. Luckily for him, he had studied under reputable teachers since his youth and learned the techniques of writing the invincible "eight-legged" essay.[7] Shortly after he turned thirty, he tackled the provincial examination successfully in just one attempt and obtained the provincial degree.[8] He had an older paternal cousin, Xixian (courtesy name, Yangchai), who had passed the examination for the metropolitan degree and was serving as a supernumerary secretary in the Board of Revenue in Beijing. Yuan Bozhen did not pass the metropolitan examination and stayed home in the district seat to serve as an elite leader of the community.[9]

Xinyu was a small district with few celebrities. Since his family had produced a Board of Revenue official, this community leader was very well known to the locals. After the district magistrate, he counted as the second most powerful man around. In his everyday life, he abhorred, above all else, the so-called new measures and new policies and all branches of foreign learning.[10] Only because of his fondness for a puff or two of opium, to his close friends he often said, "I care for none of those foreign things. Only Indian opium and the Mexican silver dollar tickle my fancy a little."[11]

Those good-for-nothing prefectural degree-holders in the area marked his words like absolute truth. They imitated his behavior as if they breathed through the same nostrils. Needless to say, the low-life elements in society simply followed suit.

It happened that year that a foreign missionary came to Xinyu to preach the gospel. While passing through Huang Village in the eastern section of the district, his Chinese assistant went up to a peasant to buy eggs and got into an altercation. Before long, the whole village was aroused. Some three or four hundred villagers came pouring out and beat the Chinese assistant half to death. Spurred on by their superior numbers, they made away with the missionary's luggage. Sensing danger, the missionary seized a tight instant to run for his life. He traveled that night on the same route back to Jiangxi's provincial capital.

Once there, he went immediately to see the governor to recount in detail the indignities that he had suffered in Huang Village. He demanded that the governor send instructions to local officials with a deadline for apprehending the culprits and punishing them to the full extent of the law. In addition, there must be full compensation for his lost luggage, and the people of Huang Village must provide medical treatment for his Chinese assistant, whom they had injured, until he fully recovered. The missionary was adamant in all his demands.

After hearing the missionary out, the governor did not dare drag his feet. He sent orders to Xinyu that very night to instruct the magistrate to look into this serious antimissionary incident and settle it by a certain date. Failure to get all this done would result in his impeachment to the imperial throne, as stipulated in procedural regulations.

It so happened that Magistrate Hu of Xinyu was new to his job, with no prior experience in handling a case that involved foreigners. Totally without warning, he received the governor's order. Reading it, he was terrified out of his wits, like being struck by a thunderbolt out of the clear blue sky. He discussed the matter immediately with his private secretary and decided to order the commander of the city garrison to dispatch soldiers to Huang Village to make arrests.[12] At the same time, he sent a message to Yuan Bozhen to invite him to his office to find a way to compensate the missionary for his lost luggage.

Seeing that it was the magistrate's invitation, Yuan Bozhen made haste to his office. Magistrate Hu asked him to come into the reception room. Showing him the governor's message, he said, "I haven't been at this job long and never thought the villagers could have gotten into such a mess. As I see it, it won't be cheap to compensate the missionary for his luggage. It'd take at least eight thousand to ten thousand *taels*.[13] It's not even clear at this time whether the perpetrators can be apprehended. One thing is for sure, though. For the compensation, we can't divert funds from our regular budget. This is why I asked Elder Brother to come over to figure out a solution.[14] This is community business. I trust Elder Brother would not turn a deaf ear to this call of duty."

Only then did Yuan Bozhen realize that an antimissionary incident had occurred. But how could such a large sum of money be found on such short notice? He hesitated for a while before replying to Magistrate Hu, "The only public resource that's available and could be used as a temporary loan is the grain reserves. But once the matter is settled, it'll be hard to pay it back."

Thereupon, Magistrate Hu said, "As long as the case is settled quickly, it shouldn't be too difficult to find money to pay back the loan. We could, say, raise the current surcharges on meat, wine, and businesses by ten to twenty percent."

At this point, the doorman at the gate came in to announce, "The Grand Venerable Master of the city garrison is here." Hearing this, Magistrate Hu raised his teacup. The servants attending him on both sides saw the signal and called out at once, "Our guest is leaving." Magistrate Hu stood up and walked Yuan Bozhen all the way out the reception room, saying, "Could Elder Brother please get the grain reserves funds ready as soon as possible? There's no need to look elsewhere for the money."

After he went home, Yuan Bozhen summoned all the grain reserves directors to his house and repeated to them what Magistrate Hu had just said. The Xinyu district had always kept thirty to forty thousand *shi* of grain in reserve,[15] divided up among a number of directors for safekeeping. Knowing that the reserve grains would not be used unless there was a flood, a drought, or a famine, some of the directors had sold their consignments and used the money in private business and profit-making ventures. Others, quietly and little by little, took the grains home that ended up, day after day, in the bellies of their wives and children. After a year or two, there was not a grain left.

Now, on being told that they were to convert the stored grains into cash, they panicked and had no choice but to tell Yuan Bozhen the truth. They added that there would not be enough time for them to replenish their consignments through purchase. Besides, such a great, sudden demand would jack up grain prices, and they could hardly afford to take the losses. They begged Venerable Master Yuan to find a way out for them.

Yuan Bozhen could not very well ignore the directors' plea. He agreed to allow them to pay back in cash in ten days half the value of their consignments according to the current market price. They could then work on the other half. The directors were extremely grateful. They thanked Yuan Bozhen before going home to get the money ready. We will leave this for now.

Two days went by, and Yuan Bozhen heard widespread rumors that the Grand Venerable Magistrate had personally led a group of rural braves and several tens of militiamen to Huang Village to make arrests, scaring all the villagers—men and women, young and old—into hiding.[16] The Grand Venerable Magistrate had no choice but to summon the headman of neighborhood security, have him spanked one thousand times with a flat bamboo, and tell him to hand over the offenders. Desperate, the headman led the way to a nearby village, where a dozen or so people were rounded up willy-nilly and brought back to the district seat. It appeared that the chief offenders were still at large. Only an accomplice or two were apprehended. As to the missionary's Chinese assistant, there was no trace of him anywhere.

Several days later, Magistrate Hu sent another invitation. Yuan Bozhen went and met Magistrate Hu in the same reception room as before. Magistrate Hu began, "I've been busy for days on end because of this antimissionary case. There hasn't been a spare moment. Yesterday, I got another order from the governor for the immediate transfer of the arrested criminals to the provincial capital. After extensive negotiation between the director of the Foreign Matters Bureau[17] and the missionary, compensation is now set at eight thousand taels. Fortunately, the Chinese assistant didn't die and made his way back to the provincial capital. The missionary insists that his assistant has been seriously injured and demands one thousand taels for his medical compensation. It'll probably cost a total of ten thousand taels for all of this to end. I've in custody now two of those who had a hand in beating up the assistant. I've interrogated them twice as ringleaders and took their statements. They'll be transferred tomorrow. I wonder if Your Esteemed Person has collected all the money from the grain reserves yet."

It so happened that Yuan Bozhen had by then received more than seventeen thousand taels from the grain reserves directors. On hearing Magistrate Hu say that he would only need about ten thousand taels, he instantly came up with an idea. To Magistrate Hu, he spun a tall tale: "The reserve grains have been in storage for three to four years and have gone stale. Both their color and scent have turned bad. All the grocery stores refused at first to buy any of them. Only after Your Humble Subordinate pleaded repeatedly with them did they agree, still reluctantly, to buy half and only at seventy percent of the market price. The amount collected so far is just a little more than eleven thousand taels, deposited at the two large money shops. It can be taken out any time with an official withdrawal voucher."

Anxious as he was to close the case right away in order to avoid his superiors' reprimand, Magistrate Hu failed to notice holes in Yuan Bozhen's account. He thereupon saluted Yuan Bozhen by cupping one hand in the other, saying, "It's all because of Elder Brother's help! I shall think of some reason in due course to call a meeting of all thirty-six trades in the area and have them discuss how to put together a monthly contribution of one thousand taels or so. We'll replenish the grain money with it."

Deep down, Yuan Bozhen was delighted that Magistrate Hu believed every word he said. As soon as he returned home, he worked out a detailed plan. He would remit the money he had just pocketed to Beijing, to ask Yangchai to purchase an "eighty percent cash magistrate's post" for him.[18] This would ensure an endless source of income for him for the rest of his life.

A few days later, rather unexpectedly, the streets were buzzing with rumors that the Boxers had started an uprising in Beijing.[19] They wanted to kill all foreigners and all missionaries to avenge China's grievances. Yuan Bozhen thought to himself, "Marvelous! I've always hated those new policies and new measures. They can now be wiped out once and for all."

From this day forward, Yuan Bozhen watched closely for news about the Boxers. At first, he heard all about the great power of the Boxer Elder Brothers' spells and charms and the supreme potency of the Yellow Lotus Saintly Mother's magic. But a month or so later, news suddenly came that the eight-nation Allied expeditionary forces had captured Tianjin and that the empress-dowager and emperor had fled Beijing for safety in a westerly direction to Taiyuan prefecture in Shanxi province. Yuan Bozhen was skeptical about the report. With the Boxers' magnificent skills, he thought, how could they have failed so miserably?

Several more days passed. As he was about to leave home one day to get more news about the situation in Beijing, a servant came from Yangchai's household with the message that the Grand Venerable Master had just arrived home after journeying from the capital to the south; he wished to ask Venerable Master to come over for a visit. Yuan Bozhen was taken aback: Yangchai was well established in his career in Beijing. Why did he come home all of a sudden? Did he get into some serious trouble that cost him his credentials and career? As he was puzzling over this, he rushed off with the messenger to Yangchai's house.

Many relatives and friends had already gathered in the study—a noisy and disorderly scene. Yangchai was sitting in their midst, making animated gestures as he talked about the Boxers. As soon as he saw Yuan Bozhen, he stood up to grab his hand, "Brother, greeting you now is someone who has just turned back from the Gate of Hell!"

Yuan Bozhen found Yangchai looking very tired and dejected and his words quite perplexing. "Elder brother, what do you mean?" he inquired in earnest.

"Why don't you sit down? I'll explain," replied Yangchai. Yuan Bozhen sat down as he was told. Yangchai began recounting how the Boxers had started their uprising; how they slaughtered people and set fire to buildings; how they laid siege to the Legations and made trouble for foreigners; how the princes and ministers at the imperial court had trusted them; how the Allied forces took Tianjin; how the empress-dowager and emperor left for safety elsewhere; how he himself had been manhandled by the Boxers, then slipped out of Beijing, and gone from Dezhou on land to the south; how he had faced extreme danger, time and again, along the way. It took him more than two hours to go from beginning to end.

Yuan Bozhen was fascinated by what he heard. He waited for Yangchai to finish before asking, "Were the foreign soldiers really so powerful that they got the better of the Boxers?"

Yangchai let out a sigh and said, "Hey, brother, you never would have guessed. Those countries in the West pay closest attention to two things: government and culture.[20] Their finances; military training; colonization; protection of valued beliefs; and various industrial, agricultural, commercial, and mining policies are as properly regulated as they are perfectly executed. They enforce laws in their countries after the Upper and Lower Houses formulated them jointly. If a loophole is found, it'll be amended right away. Ruler and ruled can truly be said to become one. It never happens that the imperial court will take arbitrary action, with no concern for its people's well-being.

"As to their learning, it's particularly advanced. Almost all their people are school graduates. Every branch of learning, whether higher education, agriculture, industry, commerce, or some other like astronomy, geography, law, military science, music, arts, writing, and language is set up with its own area of specialization. Of these, the greatest emphasis is placed on philosophy, which is similar to our Song scholars' discourse of Nature and Principle. From this philosophy they derive guidelines on how to live life and how to cultivate the patriotic spirit. Government and culture are, therefore, the basis of foreign wealth and power.

"China, our own country, can hardly match them in any of this. Even the new policies and new measures implemented in recent years are no more than superficial imitation of what foreigners do. For example, those mongers of foreign things and foreign fashion may have their braids cut off and change into foreign-style clothing,[21] but their faces are still Chinese faces, their hearts and guts still Chinese hearts and guts. No matter how hard they try, they could never turn into something else. So, what's the point?

"As to the Boxers, they were the most ignorant, dumbest lot who didn't care about life or death. They came barefisted, too, clueless about the power of rapid guns and modern cannons. How could they have stood a chance fighting foreign soldiers? Come to think of it, when they died at the hands of foreigners, they simply became muddle-headed ghosts, truly pathetic and pitiable!"

At heart, Yuan Bozhen had been a most stubborn man. No matter what new policies and new measures he came across, he had always been dismissive of them. He often said that foreigners were able to oppress Chinese people not because they possessed real abilities but because they had help from a conniving Chinese government. Now, listening to Yangchai, he was like waking from a dream or becoming sober after a drunken stupor. His usual slights for foreigners changed into adulation of them. There and then, he wanted to change his ways completely and commit himself wholeheartedly to reform.

Again, he asked Yangchai, "Does it mean that after the Boxers, all the new policies and new measures that have been implemented so far will have no use anymore?"

"Why not?" Yangchai asked back. "When the forces of reaction go up a notch, reform will go up a notch. This is what the law of nations has demonstrated in the past. As I see it, there'll be more new policies and new measures to be adopted in the future."

"Elder brother," continued Yuan Bozhen, "you sound like you'll get serious about reform, don't you?" Reader, at this very moment, Yuan Bozhen was all fired up about reform and showed keenness in his unguarded words. But he was far from set in his view, which could still go in any direction, either north or south. If, let us suppose, Yangchai had caught the drift of what Yuan Bozhen was saying, gone along with it, and encouraged him to take proper steps to become a model reformer, would it not have been wonderful?

Instead, to everyone's surprise, Yangchai broke into a hearty laugh. He followed with words that could only corrupt one's mind and lead one astray. As a result, the highly motivated Yuan Bozhen immediately modified his thinking and changed his goal. He who could have become an authentic reformer turned instantly into a phony one. And so it goes:

Words of advice awaken the dream of a third-watch slumber;[22]
An instant is all it takes to fashion a different sort of man.

If you want to know what Yangchai said to Yuan Bozhen, read on to find out in the next chapter.

NOTES

1. Yi Yin rose to be a prominent minister at the court of the Shang dynasty (c. 1500–1045 BC) and assisted a few young kings in government. He had one of them banished for three years for arbitrary rule and served as regent until the king changed his ways. Huo Guang, a powerful statesman of the Early Han dynasty in the first century BC, deposed a young emperor for incompetence and had another emperor enthroned. Political intrigues led to the decimation of his clan after his death, and his role in government has since become controversial in historical assessment.

2. The Duke of Zhou was the legendary regent and statesman of the early Zhou dynasty (c. 1055–250 BC) and a much revered culture hero to posterity. Wang Mang (45 BC–AD 23) was the most powerful figure at the Former Han court. His intrigues led the child heir to the Han throne to renounce his claim, so Wang Mang could set up his own Xin dynasty, which subsequently became the interregnum between the Former and Later Han dynasties.

3. King Yao and King Shun were legendary culture heroes known for their political wisdom and virtue. Cao Cao (155–220) was a powerful military leader turned ruler at the end of the Later Han dynasty, with Emperor Xian as a puppet under his control. Sima Yen (236–290) was the dominant court minister during the Wei dynasty; he forced the last emperor to abdicate so he could establish his own Jin dynasty.

4. According to ancient Chinese accounts, a *fuba* is a central Asian animal that looks like a deer or a female unicorn without the horn.

5. First published in the sixteenth century, *Journey to the West* (Xiyou ji) has been hailed as one of the four great Chinese classical novels. Its authorship, often attributed to Wu Cheng'en (1501–1582), remains a controversy.

6. The Chinese expression for reform comprises the two characters *wei* and *xin*.

7. A key requirement in these examinations was the ability to compose the "eight-legged" essay according to strict rules of structure, language, and contents. Candidates could spend long years trying to master the techniques but still fail to acquire them.

8. There is no mention here of Yuan Bozhen's first (prefectural) degree, also called "licentiate" (*xiucai* or *shengyuan*), but it is understood that he would have obtained it before moving on to the provincial examination.

9. With credentials obtained through civil service examinations, even at the first or prefectural level, one became a member of the educated elite (*shenshi*), with a corresponding degree of social prestige and influence. The term *shenshi* used to be translated as "gentry" but is now more commonly translated as "elite." See "Translator's Introduction," note 14.

10. "New measures" and "new policies" were general terms for the reforms that had been adopted by the late Qing government or proposed by educated Chinese along Western or Meiji-Japanese lines.

11. The (Spanish) Mexican silver dollar, also called by the Chinese "the eagle silver dollar" (*yingyang*) because of the eagle image on it, was a widely used currency in international trade at the time. Its standard shape and value appealed to the Chinese, whose silver as a legal tender and medium of exchange lacked these features. For a discussion of the silver coins in circulation in China, see Richard Von Glahn, "Foreign Silver Coins in the Market Culture of Nineteenth Century China," *International Journal of Asian Studies* 4, no. 1 (2007): 51–79. For a broader perspective on Chinese money, see Niv Horesh, *Chinese Money in Global Context: Historic Junctures Between 600 BCE and 2012* (Stanford, CA: Stanford University Press, 2014), especially chapter 3.

12. A "private secretary," who offered his patron help and advice in areas of his expertise, like litigation, was not on a government payroll but paid a salary or fees out of his patron's own pocket. This kind of patron-client relationship, known as the "tent friends" (*mufu* or *muliao*) system, goes back to ancient Chinese history. A wealthy patron could have dozens or more of such tent friends. Later in the novel, there are more instances in which a "private secretary" made decisions on his patron's behalf. Two works enhance our understanding of tent friends during the late Qing: Kenneth Folsom, *Friends, Guests, and Colleagues: The Mu-fu System in the Late Ch'ing Period* (Berkeley: University of California Press, 1968) and Jonathan Porter, *Tseng Kuo-fan's Private Bureaucracy* (Berkeley: Center for Chinese Studies, University of California, 1972).

13. A *tael* was a unit of silver used as a legal tender during the Qing period. Its value fluctuated over time. In the early twentieth century, one tael was worth about three shillings.

14. For expressions like Elder Brother, see "Notes on the Translation," note 4.

15. One *shi* is one picul, about 133.3 pounds or 60.5 kilograms.

16. "Rural braves" were peasants recruited to work for the local government at the magistrate's discretion. For a discussion of the militia, its origins, developments, and importance for the state, see Philip Kuhn, *Rebellion and Its Enemies in Late Imperial China: Militarization and Social Structure, 1796–1864* (Cambridge, MA: Harvard University Press, 1970).

17. The Foreign Matters Bureau (*Yangwuju*) was a government office created at the provincial level during the late Qing to deal with Westerners.

18. According to the late Qing system of credential sales, a discount like 20 percent off the stipulated price for a title or post was often allowed. If the cash payment was made in full at the time of purchase, there could be, in addition, the priority of appointment to an actual government job over others who paid in installments.

19. For the Boxer Rebellion, see Paul Cohen, *History in Three Keys: The Boxers as Event, Experience, and Myth* (New York: Columbia University Press, 1998); Joseph Esherick, *The Origins of the Boxer Rebellion* (Berkeley: University of California Press, 1987); and Robert Bickers and R. G. Tiedemann, eds., *The Boxers, China, and the World* (Lanham, MD: Rowman & Littlefield, 2007).

20. "Culture" is a broad translation of *jiao*, which has a wide range of meanings in Chinese, from personal cultivation to established religion to education. In light of Yangchai's elaboration, a general meaning is preferred.

21. As explained in "Translator's Introduction," note 26, the braid or queue on a man was a symbol of Han Chinese submission to Manchu control. Cutting it off was seen as a gesture of cultural and political defiance.

22. "Third watch" refers to the time around midnight.

Admirable words of advice focus on
promotions up official ranks and making riches;

Patronage and gift-giving are shortcuts
to career success for which people scramble.

*A*s we were saying, after listening to Yuan Bozhen, Yangchai let out a big laugh and said, "My old buddy, aren't you being silly! Did you know that those gallant reformers in the history of Western countries behaved like they had swallowed the madness pill? They gave all of themselves, heedless of the danger to their lives. Whether there was the executioner's blade or saw in front or a boiling cauldron behind, they knew only lunging forward to their goal. In the end, they either shed blood or had their heads chopped off while causing numerous innocent people to die by the sword. There are examples of authentic reformers, like Yoshida Shoin and Saigo Takamori of Japan, Madame Roland of France, and Garibaldi of Italy.[1] So, I say, the true bliss of reform is secured, in fact, at the cost of countless, rolling heads.

"Just think, my brother, why must a person, kicking and alive, be led on this path to death? Besides, in times like these, even if you and I wanted to start real reform, we might not be able to make a single move. You may say, 'We'll do it for the country, for the people,' but what does the country, the people, matter to you? Why would you want to pick up the one-thousand-catty burden of others and load it on your own shoulders?[2] If you should get in trouble someday, shed blood, and get your head chopped off, would you be called a loyal official or a filial son?

"Living this life on earth as humans, I believe, we'll pass muster as long as we gain a measure of social prominence and wealth and have a chance to enjoy them in peace for ten to twenty years. Even if we want to get into reform now, we'll do so simply as a shortcut to promotions and riches. We must never get serious about it. Never! Brother, you are a smart man. Why did you say such a dumb thing all of a sudden?"

Yuan Bozhen took in every one of these words. "Every bit of his long speech has the ring of truth," he thought. As he was about to ask other questions, he saw Yangchai's servants come out from the inner chamber with two opium pipes, an opium lamp, and a large pot of opium paste. They placed them on the couch-bed and lit the lamp. Opium smoking was an old habit of Yangchai's. When he got home earlier that day, he only had a puff or two in the main living quarter—hardly enough to satisfy his craving. He had to stop because visitors were arriving to see him. Now, his servants figured that both the host and his guests had been sitting around long enough; it was time to bring out the opium-smoking accessories.

Pointing to the pot of opium paste, Yangchai said to all, "I bought this Pure Paste at Guangchengxin while passing through Shanghai.[3] Why don't you all come over to have a puff?" They all laughed, insisting that Yangchai should have the first go at it.

Yangchai grabbed Yuan Bozhen's hand to walk over to the couch-bed. They both lay down, one on each side of the lamp. Yangchai started first. After seven or eight puffs to ease his urge, he let Yuan Bozhen satisfy his, adding with a grin, "If you, my brother, should ever get serious about reform, you'd have to give up this stuff. You couldn't even take concubines as you please."

His mouth puffing opium, Yuan Bozhen carefully went over in his mind what Yangchai had just said. Though some of his words were meant to tease, they contained great truth. After a few puffs of the Pure Paste, he was still not satisfied but did not feel right about going on. On the excuse of some errand to run, he asked to leave and went home.

A couple of days later, he had his servants prepare several seasonal dishes and sent a messenger to invite Yangchai over for a homecoming dinner. Before Yangchai arrived, someone showed up unexpectedly at the front door, wearing a straw hat and a pair of leather shoes and speaking with a Hunanese accent. Yuan Bozhen told his servant to ask him for a calling card. It was a snow-white, glossy piece of foreign paper, about 2 inches by 3.5 inches in size. Printed horizontally on it were the three characters, Zeng Shi Shi, with Songsheng in smaller print below.

Yuan Bozhen was puzzled. On meeting him, he then found out that the caller was a native of Liuyang district in Hunan province. His uncle Zeng Guohuai had passed the provincial examination in the same year as Yuan Bozhen. He had just returned from studies in Japan and heard about the Wealth Voucher rebels in Xinti of Hubei province.[4] Since he was a distant relative of the rebel leader Tang Caichang, he feared he would be incriminated. To ensure safety, he crossed the provincial border into Jiangxi. He also wanted to take the opportunity to check out the mineral and coal ores in the Linjiang area in Yuanzhou prefecture. With the information collected, he was hoping someday to persuade some foreigner to put up the capital to start a mining business. Passing through Xinyu today, he recalled his uncle's "same year" connection with Yuan Bozhen and decided to drop by to pay his respects.[5]

After inquiring into his comings and goings, Yuan Bozhen knew that Zeng Songsheng belonged to the reform faction. As Yuan Bozhen was about to ask him about his studies in Japan, a servant announced, "The Grand Venerable Master is here!"

Yuan Bozhen looked up and saw Yangchai already entering the living room. Yangchai and Zeng Songsheng greeted one another and exchanged names. They all sat down. Yuan Bozhen gave Yangchai a detailed account of Zeng Songsheng's background. With emphasis, he added that Zeng Songsheng was a nephew of his "same year" from Liuyang. He then turned to Zeng Songsheng, "Please don't mind the simple fare and stay for dinner in my humble home. You can tell us about the sights and sounds of foreign countries."

Zeng Songsheng found that he could not very well decline and agreed to stay. A short time later, the servants brought out wine and dishes and set them down on the table. Yuan Bozhen accompanied his guests to their seats. In the course of dinner, Yangchai chatted away with Zeng Songsheng and found him to be an open-minded man. Both enjoyed the conversation very much. All the while, Yuan Bozhen listened intently with a great deal of interest. Finally, he could not hold back and interjected, "About the new policies and new measures that you two are talking about and also, about the social conditions and customs of foreign countries, what books have the information that I can look up?"

"I don't recall offhand," Yangchai replied. "The books that I bought were printed and bound in foreign style. I was afraid that the Boxers might find them and mistake me for a Secondary Hairy Man.[6] So, I burnt them all."

"Young Nephew does have a few in his luggage," said Zeng Songsheng. "If Elder Uncle wants to take a look at them, Young Nephew will send them over tomorrow."

"That'd be wonderful!" Yuan Bozhen quickly replied.

Meanwhile, Yuan Bozhen noticed that Yangchai had already yawned twice. So he told his servants to set up the opium tray to let Yangchai have a smoke. Zeng Songsheng waited while Yangchai took his time with the opium before returning to the dinner table. They had another round of drinks before finishing off the meal.

The servants handed them towels. They wiped their faces. The sky had already turned dark. As Yangchai stood up to say good-bye, he took Zeng Songsheng's hand and offered him lodging for the night. Yuan Bozhen could not persuade them to stay longer and walked them to the front door to see them off.

Next day, Zeng Songsheng asked one of Yangchai's servants to deliver several books to Yuan Bozhen. Yuan Bozhen took a look at them and found four titles [translated as]: *A complete guide to Western learning, A new treatise on current affairs, Warnings to a prosperous age,* and *A history of nations.* They were not available in Xinyu for sale. From that day on, Yuan Bozhen stayed home and, with determination and a focused mind, studied those books.

Time flew. Very soon, the remains of the winter season came to the end, and it was New Year again. Zeng Songsheng had by then returned to Hunan for the festivities. Yuan Bozhen had only Yangchai to chat with about New Learning.[7] Sometimes they strolled together down to the town center for news about the imperial capital. Yangchai was obsessed with the prospects of career and riches. It was hard, therefore, for him to stay idle in his hometown for several months.

Finally, word came that a peace settlement had been reached with the Allied powers and that preparations were being made for the empress-dowager and emperor to return to Beijing. Another month or so went by, and it was reported that the governors-general and governors in the southern and eastern provinces had responded to the throne's call for change and submitted proposals on a wide range of reform topics, like the abolition of the civil service examinations, the founding of schools, military innovations, the promotion of business and industry, the establishment of banks, and the adoption of the police system. All of this, it was emphasized, would be implemented.

Yangchai said to Yuan Bozhen, "How about it? I told you before: With every force of reaction against reform, reform will go up a notch. This has now come true." Yuan Bozhen was greatly impressed. He inquired when it would be convenient for Yangchai to return to Beijing.

Yangchai replied, "I got a letter yesterday from a friend in Beijing. He said that the provisional Six Boards set up at the temporary court in Xi'an are short-staffed.[8] If I could make haste to Shaanxi province to serve on the return journey of the empress-dowager and emperor, there'd no doubt be some kind of commendation for me later. So I plan to take off in a few days."

These words rekindled Yuan Bozhen's earlier desire for government service. He told Yangchai his intent to obtain an official post through purchase and asked him for advice. Yangchai asked, "Brother, how much money are you prepared to put up?"

"If I really try," answered Yuan Bozhen, "I can probably come up with six thousand to seven thousand taels."

Yangchai went on, "Since you have that kind of money, you can come with me on a trip to Hubei province. I'll show you a way of getting a government post without going through purchase." Yuan Bozhen lost no time in pressing for details. Yangchai disclosed none. "It's not time yet to say anything more. You'll know when we get to Hubei."

Yuan Bozhen could only assume that Yangchai must know what he was talking about. He felt very pleased. After he went home, he discussed the matter with his wife, Woman Wu. They put together what he had pocketed from the grain reserves the year before and what he had skimmed off over the years as a community leader. In addition, they borrowed more than one thousand taels from friends and relatives, making a grand total of eight thousand taels.

Yuan Bozhen was packing his luggage when Yangchai sent someone over to say that they would leave in five days. Yuan Bozhen quickly took his money to a reputable money shop for remittance to Hankou.[9] He then went with Yangchai on farewell visits to relatives and friends. They made arrangements for hiring a riverboat. Each accompanied by a servant, they left home four days later and boarded the riverboat.

They sailed past Linjiang and Nanchang prefectures to Hukou, where they transferred to a steamer. Crossing Lake Boyang, they reached the pier at Jiujiang, where they again switched to a steamship. It took them over ten days to get to Hankou. Yangchai and his party got on a ferryboat with their luggage across the Yangzi River to Wuchang, where they found lodging in a large inn in the busy quarter of the city.

When Yangchai got up the next day, he told his servant to hire a sedan chair suitable for someone with official rank. Wearing a large cap and travel clothes, he set out on the sedan chair to make visits, which lasted a whole day. On returning to the inn at dusk, he told Yuan Bozhen, "I've asked a friend of mine to look into your affairs. He was my 'same year' from the metropolitan examination. His family name is Huang. He was serving as an expectant intendant in Zhili province when the governor-general here, who was his teacher, requested in a memorial to the throne his transfer to this jurisdiction. He's also very close to the prefect of Wuchang and the governor-general's confidant, Chief Commander Li.[10] I've asked him to bring your matter up with the prefect and Chief Commander Li. There'll be advice forthcoming soon." Yuan Bozhen was glad to hear this. He could only hope that Intendant Huang would send good news before long.

Sure enough, two days later, Intendant Huang came to the inn to pay his return visit. Yangchai told Yuan Bozhen to stay away. He spoke with Intendant Huang alone for a long time. After Intendant Huang left, Yangchai said to Yuan Bozhen, "Things are looking up! Old Huang asked me just now when you passed your degree examinations. I told him. He said your examiner was a student of the governor-general's. Two days ago, Old Huang did the prep work by asking Chief Commander Li for help to get in on the inside track.

"Now, this is what you should do tomorrow: Write up a calling card as Intendant Huang's student; request a meeting with Chief Commander Li and bring him a greeting gift of two hundred taels on your first visit. Next, prepare a second calling card as a student of the governor-general's student and pay the governor-general a visit.

"The governor-general is now committed to reform. He's currently planning to set up a Japanese language school but hasn't found the money for it. You should draft a memorandum on the need for such a school and ask Old Huang to polish it for you. Take it with you and hand it to the governor-general when you see him. You'll volunteer to donate five thousand taels toward the school's start-up fund. Your reward will come soon enough.

"But, first, you must purchase an honorific title of a subprefect or department magistrate. With something like this in hand, it'd be far easier to get what you want. Again, according to Old Huang, the governor-general is very particular about prose style. Your memorandum must not stick to any rigid literary form. To please him, it would have to exude between the lines a touch of ancient prose. This is the most important. If you get this right, even a smaller contribution will not matter much."

Yuan Bozhen took this all in. He thought for a while before saying to Yangchai, "I can do what Intendant Huang suggested. Some years ago, I found having merely a metal button on my cap rather petty-looking and purchased a subprefect title.[11] Only the memorandum is the hard part!"

"Just go ahead and scribble something up," said Yangchai. "We'll show it to Old Huang to see what he can do with it." Yuan Bozhen had no choice but to agree. After supper, reclining on his opium couch-bed, he racked his brains and probed his guts to come up with things to say in the memorandum. He worked through the night but still did not finish it. It was past two o'clock when he woke up the following afternoon. Since he had to get the money ready, he took out his remittance voucher and made a special trip across the river to Hankou, where he found a money shop to redeem it and arranged for the funds to be transferred to Wuchang. Sooner or later there would be need for the money, and it should be there at the ready. By the time he got all this done, it was already dark. He could only accept lodging offered by the money shop for the night.

It was past the noon hour the next day when he crossed the river back to Wuchang. As he was entering the city gate, he bumped into a young man wearing a straw hat and leather shoes. The young man lifted his head to glance at Yuan Bozhen and uttered a cry of surprise, "Oh my!" And so it goes:

> The sea of officialdom reveals unexpected horizons of a new world;
> Old friends cross paths by chance on the road to vainglorious quest.

It is not clear who this young man was. Read on to find out in the next chapter.

NOTES

1. Yoshida Shoin (1830–1859) was a Japanese scholar of "Dutch Learning" (Western studies), whose pro-emperor stance contributed to the eventual overthrow of the Tokugawa shogun and restoration of power to the Meiji emperor in 1868. Before all this came to pass, however, he had been executed for implication in a plot to assassinate the shogun's representative in the imperial capital, Kyoto. Saigo Takamori (1828–1877) was a leader in the Meiji Restoration but left government after colleagues disagreed with his aggressive policy toward Korea. He led a rebellion against the government and, as legend has it, committed *seppuku* (ritual self-disembowelment) when his rebellion failed. Madame Roland (1754–1793), along with her husband, was at first a supporter of the French Revolution but got in trouble during Robespierre's "reign of terror." She died on the guillotine. Together with Giuseppe Mazzini (1805-1872) and Camillo Benso di Cavour (1810–1861), Giuseppe Garibaldi (1807–1882) was known to the Chinese as one of the three great architects of the Italian Unification.

2. One catty is about 1.33 pounds.

3. Guangchengxin, located in the British Concession or International Settlement in Shanghai, was best known for the superior quality of the opium paste that it sold.

4. This refers to the uprising of the Independence Army (1900) led by Tang Caicheng (1867–1900). The "wealth voucher" was the paper proof of membership of his insurgent organization.

5. Passing a major examination together in the same year was another important link in the social network of the educated elite. See "Translator's Introduction."

6. Secondary Hairy Man (*Erh maozi*) was a Boxer term for Chinese Christians. Primary Hairy Man (*Da maozi*) was reserved for foreigners, and Tertiary Hairy Man (*San maozi*) referred to Chinese with an interest in foreign things. Since there was no mention of Yangchai's conversion to Christianity, he would have been more properly called a Tertiary Hairy Man. "Hairy" may have come from the profusion of Western men's facial and body hairs and the sharp contrast between their hairstyle and the Qing style with a braid and shaven top for men.

7. New Learning was a late Qing term for information and knowledge of Western or Japanese origins.

8. The Six Boards—Appointments, Finance, Rites, War, Punishments, and Public Works—had formed the core administration of the imperial court since the late sixth century. They were in the process of being abolished or reconstituted in the post-Boxer years.

9. Hankou (Hankow) was a treaty port on the Yangzi River and, together with Wuchang across the river and Hanyang to its southwest, formed a major political,

economic, and cultural region in central China. Its great importance is explored in two volumes by William Rowe, *Hankow: Commerce and Society in a Chinese City, 1796–1889* (Stanford, CA: Stanford University Press, 1984) and *Hankow: Conflict and Community in a Chinese City* (Stanford, CA: Stanford University Press, 1989).

10. This is a broad translation of Li's title *tongling*, which should be distinguished from *tidu,* usually translated as "provincial commander-in-chief" under the governor-general and used in chapter 14 to identify one of the corrupt high officials in Guangxi province. There is no higher military official than Li identified in the novel as responsible for the military affairs in Hubei and Hunan.

11. It was a decorative piece on the front of the cap to indicate one's official status. The higher the status, the more elegant or exquisite were its design and material.

$$\cdot \; 3 \; \cdot$$

The job of machine procurement comes
as a reward for the cash contribution;

In the name of civilization is the effort
made to join the Natural Feet Society.

As mentioned previously, Yuan Bozhen ran into a young man at the city gate. It was none other than Zeng Songsheng, who had visited Jiangxi province the year before. When Zeng Songsheng looked up, he uttered, "Oh my! Venerable Elder Uncle, what brought you here today?"

Yuan Bozhen recognized Zeng Songsheng and felt a special affection to see a familiar face so far away from home. They stood there chatting, recounting what each had done since they last met. Yuan Bozhen found out that Zeng Songsheng now worked as a translator of Japanese at the Translation Bureau in the city. He took him back to see Yangchai and also told him about his plan to submit a memorandum to the governor-general. Showing Zeng Songsheng the unfinished draft from two nights ago, he asked him to revise it for him. Being young and eager, Zeng Songsheng was not about to refuse. He took out his pencil and quickly rewrote more than half the draft. Yuan Bozhen saw that he had finished and wanted to keep him for a late supper.

"I still have work to do," replied Zeng Songsheng. He then left in a hurry. Yuan Bozhen took a close look at Zeng Songsheng's corrections and found them rather abstruse. He copied the revised draft on a fresh sheet of paper and gave it to Yangchai, who had a servant deliver it to Intendant Huang.

Two days later, coming home from the outside, Yangchai said to Yuan Bozhen, "Why did you use so many strange new terms in your memorandum?[1] Old Huang told me today that as much as the governor-general favors reform, he dislikes strange new terms. Old Huang revised the draft thoroughly and gave it back to me. You'll make a fair copy of it using the proper memorandum paper and take care of this tomorrow."

Yuan Bozhen spent all night copying out the memorandum and reading through it together with Yangchai. Yuan Bozhen said, "The memorandum sounds so comprehensive and thoughtful. I'm afraid the proposal will be easier said than done. What are we going to do?"

"Old brother, here you go again!" replied Yangchai. "In official circles, all memoranda, regulations, et cetera, relating to policy always sound comprehensive and thoughtful. But when the time comes to implement them, they never work the way they are drawn up." Nodding, Yuan Bozhen listened but did not say anything.

The next day, Yuan Bozhen put on formal attire, complete with cap and gown. He prepared a student's written request to meet and placed a money draft for two hundred taels in a small pouch for tucking away in his boot. With his servant close behind, he set out to pay homage to Chief Commander Li. It turned out that Chief Commander Li was extremely busy with work that day and only had time for a few words. Next morning, Yuan Bozhen was again all dressed up. With the memorandum and his student-of-a-student's calling card in hand, he went to the governor-general's office to request an interview.

One of the guards at the gate took his calling card inside. He came out after a long time to say, "His Highness has to go outside the city today to inspect troops trained in foreign drills and has no time for guests. Please come again tomorrow." For the next seven or eight days, he went every day but did not get to see his host. He started having doubts.

He again waited until dusk one day. As he was about to leave to go back to the inn, a guard unexpectedly came out to announce, "His Highness said, 'Please, come in.'" Yuan Bozhen followed him and hurried into the reception room. There he again waited for a long time before seeing the servants raise the curtain partition to escort the governor-general into the room. Yuan Bozhen dashed forward to perform salutation. The governor-general had barely sat down when he asked Yuan Bozhen when he passed his examination and who his examiners were. Yuan Bozhen duly answered. Then he stood up and presented his memorandum to the governor-general with both hands. The governor-general put his glasses on and read the first few lines before laying it down on the table, saying, "This is something I want to get done, too. But there's the problem of finding the money for it."

Standing erect, Yuan Bozhen replied, "This student of your student's is willing to make a contribution of five thousand taels toward the project. He wonders, would Great Grand Teacher do him the favor of accepting it?"

The governor-general smiled and said, "This is Hubei business. It would make us look ridiculous to accept a contribution from a Jiangxi man."

To this Yuan Bozhen replied, "In the humble opinion of this student of your student's, this is China setting up a Chinese academy. There is no room for selfish motive or provincial boundary. This is why I make the brash offer of a contribution." The governor-general listened and nodded.

At this point, a guard came in again to announce, "The prefect of Wuchang is here on urgent business." Yuan Bozhen knew it would not be convenient for him to stay. He stood up to take leave and made haste to the exit. The prefect was already entering the room.

Back at the inn, he gave Yangchai a detailed account of his meeting with the governor-general. "As I see it," Yangchai remarked, "the governor-general will most definitely accept your money, and you'll get your reward."

Sure enough, in the early morning two days later, Intendant Huang came to the inn and spoke with Yangchai, saying, "Congratulations to your younger brother! Yesterday the governor-general issued an order for his guard to relay this message to your younger brother soon: 'He will make payment of the said contribution at the prefect's office and will submit his resumé for purpose of commendation to the throne.'"

On hearing this, Yangchai quickly asked Yuan Bozhen to come out to thank Intendant Huang. He noted, emphatically, that Intendant Huang should be more adequately compensated in the future for the great trouble he had gone through on Yuan Bozhen's behalf. He also told Yuan Bozhen to write up his resumé right away and give it to Intendant Huang, along with a five-thousand-tael money draft, for forwarding to the prefect of Wuchang. Yuan Bozhen immediately did what he was told, adding that he would pay a visit to the prefect later. Intendant Huang took the money draft and the resumé and left after chatting some more.

Seeing that the matter was off to a good start, Yangchai said to Yuan Bozhen, "You'll probably have to wait a month or two before any good news comes, but I can't wait any longer. I've asked Old Huang to look after your affairs. I plan to leave either tomorrow or the day after."

Knowing that Yangchai could not really stay longer, Yuan Bozhen had a two-hundred-tael money draft placed in an envelope as a gift to Yangchai for all his help. Next day, Yangchai made his round of farewell visits before boarding a boat with his servant on River Xiang to go directly to Shaanxi. We will leave this for now.

For the next few days, Yuan Bozhen kept busy. He met with the prefect of Wuchang and sought another interview with the governor-general. He then waited patiently at the inn for news. When bored, he called at the residences of Intendant Huang and several of his fellow Jiangxi sojourners to learn about the dos and don'ts of entering the world of officials.

More than a month went quietly by. Then one day, the governor-general sent a guard over to congratulate him, saying that his name had been included in the commendations to the throne for a different project. His honorific title of subprefect had been upgraded, as recommended by the Board of Appointments, to a substantive one that qualified him for job placement. He was instructed to remain in Hubei to serve in a post to be specified shortly.

Yuan Bozhen was delighted at first. But when he thought of the mere eligibility for a Board appointment as a subprefect in return for the large sum of money he had spent, he felt shortchanged. As he was weighing his gains and losses, Intendant Huang and several friends dropped by in turn at the inn to congratulate him.

What happened was, as he later found out confidentially from Intendant Huang, that the governor-general had been inclined at first to cite him for meritorious service because of his cash contribution. Chief Commander Li countered that such a commendation would only qualify Yuan Bozhen for the award of an imperial plaque of merit and nothing more. To make it worth Yuan Bozhen's while, it would be better to cite him for some other completed project so as to allow him an opportunity to land a substantive post or cushy job. This was why the matter had been handled this way. Yuan Bozhen then understood that the governor-general had meant well.

He was busy through the day. As he was about to leave the next day on a visit to thank the governor-general, a letter came from the provincial treasurer to appoint him procurer for the Silver Dollar Mintage Bureau. Official salary aside, the post could generate, off the record, an annual perk of several thousand taels. Yuan Bozhen quickly changed into formal attire and went to the offices of the provincial treasurer and the governor-general to thank them for the appointment. On this occasion, the governor-general received him right away.

After performing salutation, Yuan Bozhen broke into a torrent of grateful words for the opportunity to serve and so on. In response, the governor-general said, "There has been a shortage of copper cash. I plan to produce copper coins at the Mintage Bureau and need someone to go to Shanghai to purchase two machines for the purpose. That's why I gave you the job. You'll discuss this with the bureau director tomorrow before going to Shanghai to find out which foreign firm is fair to deal with. Send us a telegram. The matter can then move forward without a hitch."

Yuan Bozhen uttered affirmatives in quick succession and left after the governor-general had finished. He next went to see Chief Commander Li and thanked him for his kind intercession with the governor-general on his behalf. Nothing else transpired that evening.

The next day was the first of the lunar fifth month. Yuan Bozhen called at a couple of government offices before going off to see the director of the Mintage Bureau, partly to report to duty and partly to discuss the governor-general's instructions. Sensing that Yuan Bozhen had some kind of special connection with the governor-general, the director appeared exceptionally courteous. He merely said, "We'll leave the whole matter to Elder Brother's discretion. Whichever machines you think would be useful, just place an order for them." Only after Yuan Bozhen pressed for specifics did he go on to explain that as long as production reached four hundred thousand to five hundred thousand copper coins a day, it would do. Having extracted this information from the director, Yuan Bozhen then met with several of the bureau's assistants.

Back at the inn, he started packing. Time slipped by swiftly, like the blink of an eye. The Dragon Boat Festival came and went.[2] On the seventh day of the fifth month, Yuan Bozhen, having bidden farewell at various places and obtained a three-month advance on his salary, checked out of the inn and boarded the Jiangfu steamship to go downstream on the Yangzi River. On the third day, he arrived at the harbor of Shanghai and found a room to settle into at the Changfa Inn along the Yangjingbang.[3]

The next day, Yuan Bozhen went into the Chinese city to pay a visit to the intendant and the magistrate of Shanghai.[4] His arrival stirred up quite a bit of excitement among those who worked for foreign firms. Knowing that an agent had arrived from Hubei to purchase copper cash production machines, they scrambled hard for an entry point to get close to Yuan Bozhen to fetch the deal. They entertained him lavishly in turn: a Western dinner one day, a sightseeing ride on a horse-drawn carriage the next.

Ever since Yuan Bozhen made the acquaintance of Zeng Songsheng, his outlook had broadened considerably. On this visit to Shanghai, after a few encounters with foreigners, he even managed to say "yes" in English. He also read a few books with new theories on topics like sex between man and woman. Indeed, he was becoming more open-minded.

At first, he was wary of scandals that might stigmatize his official mission, so he decided to stay away from the pleasure quarters. Then he was told that, as far as those grandees most given to reform talk were concerned, drinks with prostitutes were as ordinary as a daily meal and the brothel was as fitting a place for overnight accommodation as home. Besides, one would never understand the principle of equal rights between man and woman without setting foot inside these establishments. Excessive circumspection would merely enslave one to old standards of behavior. Ideas like these allowed Yuan Bozhen's horizon to broaden even more. Previously, nine times out of ten, the mention of strange new terms like "association," "bonding," "strategy," and "agenda" would have baffled him. Now, they were his catchwords, which he enunciated with great fluency.

Yuan Bozhen stayed a full two months in Shanghai. After comparing the prices quoted by various foreign firms, he found one that seemed the most reasonable and signed a contract for the purchase of a sixty-horsepower copper coin machine. In order to cut back the foreigners' profit margin, he had the price double-checked and demanded, in addition, a 10 percent payoff for himself. The comprador of the firm, who hoped to get his future business, reluctantly agreed.[5] Yuan Bozhen reckoned that with this as a done deal to conclude his mission, he would recover the exact amount of five thousand taels that he had earlier laid out. He was very pleased with himself. While waiting for the authorizing telegraph to arrive from Hubei, he went to the brothel every afternoon for fun.

Meanwhile, some fellow provincials from Jiangxi and promoters of reform had established a Natural Feet Society in Shanghai.[6] Because Yuan Bozhen was known to be enlightened, they got him involved as an honorary member. They met every day at the brothel to discuss the project.

Yuan Bozhen, so engrossed now in pleasure, had no idea that sadness awaited him. One day, a letter from home broke the news that his wife, Woman Wu, had died of dry cholera.[7] She had borne him no children. Being childless made him feel all the more sorrowful. Friends who heard the news came to the inn the following day to offer their condolences. His two closest friends, Cheng Yixian and Guan Xiangbin, invited him to the brothel for the distraction of women and wine.

There was a prostitute at the brothel called Golden Emblem,[8] who had been a "pheasant" in Yangzhou before coming to Shanghai and could speak a few sentences in a foreign language.[9] Yuan Bozhen went to Golden Emblem's chamber and took a close look at her from head to toe: She had a skinny, oval face with a shapely figure. Below her skirt, there was a pair of petite feet that could be no more than a few inches in length. Their small size was an absolute delight to behold.

As soon as Yuan Bozhen saw those tiny feet, all the grief that had earlier filled his chest was tossed away to faraway Java. He immediately asked Golden Emblem to come to him. Holding her hand, he chatted nonstop with her, his stare constantly returning to those feet below. Not until wine and food were served on the table did he let go of her hand. After briefly refusing the seat of honor in favor of Cheng Yixian, he took it, still absorbed all the while in chatting with Golden Emblem. He did not even hear them when others asked him to taste the dishes.

Seeing what was going on, Cheng Yixian whispered a few words in Golden Emblem's ear. Then he called out to Venerable Uncle Yuan and said something. With this, things began to take shape. And so it goes:

> One's better half can iron out personal differences inside the home;
> Behavior outside the home suddenly lays claim to personal freedom.

It is not clear what Cheng Yixian had to say. Read on to find out in the next chapter.

NOTES

1. The "strange new terms," mostly adapted from Japanese translation of Western concepts, often became a controversial issue in the 1890s and 1900s between traditionalists and reformers. Even supporters of reform, like the governor-general in the story, would frown on these as constituting polluted language.

2. It is a major Chinese festival to commemorate the suicide by drowning of Qu Yuan (c. 340–278 BC), the famous poet and statesman of the ancient Chu state in central China. It falls on the fifth day of the lunar fifth month. The Dragon Boat race, now an international event, is an integral component of the festival.

3. It was initially a tributary of the Huangpu River in the Shanghai area that served as the boundary between the British Concession (i. e., the International Settlement) and the French Concession. The businesses on its banks formed the center of foreign trade in the area, which was famous, among other things, for its garbled language (pidgin English) that enabled Chinese to communicate with foreigners. It was reclaimed for land use in the early twentieth century to become a thoroughfare.

4. Greater Shanghai now comprised the original Chinese city (district seat of Shanghai) under Qing jurisdiction and the treaty port of the British and French Concessions.

5. A comprador was a Chinese agent of a foreign firm. See Yen-p'ing Hao, *The Comprador in Nineteenth Century China: Bridge Between East and West* (Cambridge, MA: Harvard University Press, 1970).

6. One of the projects of the late-Qing reformers was to liberate women from the age-old practice of foot-binding. For foot-binding, see "Translator's Introduction," note 27.

7. Dry cholera (*jiaochangsha*) occurs when bacteria cause intestinal obstruction in the patient without the symptoms of vomiting or diarrhea.

8. Her Chinese name Jinyu consists of two characters. *Jin* refers to "gold," either the precious metal or the color. *Yu* means, literally, "to reside," "to imply," "to contain," "to embody," etc. Its rendition as Golden Emblem, though a bit awkward, seems to suit the context best.

9. "Pheasant" was a term for a drifting prostitute who, according to the contemporary classification of the sex trade, ranked lower than one attached to a brothel.

• *4* •

Mockery is what motivates the
effort to study the English primer;

The social circle broadens to lead
to making friends with Wilkes.

As we were saying, Cheng Yixian saw how Yuan Bozhen chatted and flirted with Golden Emblem and knew that Yuan Bozhen had ensnared himself in the web of seduction. He called out to him, "Venerable Uncle Yuan, if you fall for this lady, I can be the go-between to get her to become your second wife. She used to enjoy the 'right of self-determination.' She's trapped in this fiery pit only because she owes a debt of more than one thousand silver dollars. If you pay it off for her, she's yours."

Yuan Bozhen listened and felt that the words struck a sensitive chord in his heart. He blushed and, with difficulty, muttered, "Nonsense. A friend's sweetheart . . . How could I?"

"No, she's no sweetheart of mine," declared Cheng Yixian. "I've only played card games twice with her and had her for company several times. She's quite open-minded and studies English every day. When Venerable Uncle deals with foreigners in the future, she'd be one better half you can't do without."

Yuan Bozhen did not know what to say and could only quickly change the subject. He tasted several dishes and then retired to the couch-bed for a few puffs of opium. Making up some excuse for leaving, he went back to the inn.

He recalled Cheng Yixian's words the following day and thought to himself, "Cheng Yixian is a friend I made at the brothel. Even if I took Golden Emblem for myself, he shouldn't get jealous." He waited until evening before sending Golden Emblem an invitation to dinner at the House of Spring, a Western-style restaurant, to ascertain her feelings.

It so happened that Golden Emblem was indeed Cheng Yixian's mistress. Both had worked out a plan the night before to swindle money from Yuan Bozhen to pay off her debt. As soon as she heard what Yuan

45

Bozhen had to say, she wasted no time in giving her consent. Yuan Bozhen was beside himself with joy and asked her not to utter a word about this to Cheng Yixian.

The next day, Yuan Bozhen had his closest friend handle Golden Emblem's buyout at the brothel. He rented a house for the two of them to live in. Since Golden Emblem and several of her prostitute friends were learning English, he, too, found himself a teacher and studied the English primer every day. He also decorated their home with pieces of foreign furniture, just like they did at the brothel.

It was not even a half month later when Cheng Yixian colluded with Golden Emblem's parents and coaxed them to make a big fuss at the house. They threatened to take their daughter away. Yuan Bozhen was furious. He bellowed that there was no right in this world; only might. He made use of his connections with the Shanghai magistrate to have Golden Emblem's parents arrested and locked up.

To continue her affair with Cheng Yixian, Golden Emblem resorted to her usual excuse of visiting her girlfriends. When Yuan Bozhen tried to stop her from going out, she shot back, "You are the one who likes to talk about reform. You shouldn't interfere with my right to freedom!" There was nothing that Yuan Bozhen could do except let her come and go as she pleased.

A few days later, Golden Emblem left home. Like the yellow crane that had flown away,[1] she never returned. Yuan Bozhen quickly checked around the home. Nothing was missing except all the jewelry, money vouchers, and silver dollars. He was so enraged that he could not speak a word. He was also worried that he might become a laughingstock if news of what happened should leak out. After weighing the pros and cons through the day and the night, he still could not figure out what to do. He had to give up. By this time, he had finished reading only half the English primer but had already squandered all the money that he had pilfered from the machine deal. Brooding, Yuan Bozhen stayed home all the time to smoke opium and did not go out at all for social calls.

Over a month later, the machine that he had ordered from abroad finally arrived. The purchase money had also been remitted from Hubei, and the machine's components, all accounted for. He handed the money over, paid the import duty at the Imperial Maritime Customs, and had the machine loaded on a steamship going up the Yangzi River. He also bought a few gas lamps and several gramophones as presents for Intendant Huang, Chief Commander Li, and others. After a round of farewell visits, he went back to Hubei with his servant.

It was already the lunar eighth month. Yuan Bozhen spent four days on the way before reaching the harbor of Wuchang. He arranged for the machine to be put in storage at the warehouse of the China Merchants Steam Navigation Company and for his luggage to be transferred inside the city.[2] That same evening he found accommodation in a rented house.

The following day, he took the gifts he bought in Shanghai with him to visit Intendant Huang, Chief Commander Li, and the Mintage Bureau. He did not see Intendant Huang, who was away on a mineral prospecting mission to Yunyang, and met only Chief Commander Li and the bureau director. To them, he talked about his experience of purchasing the machine in Shanghai. Then he left for the governor-general's office to request an interview with him to report on his mission. The governor-general happened to be busy and did not have time to receive Yuan Bozhen. He only sent word for the bureau director to go with the bureau's foreign engineer to inspect and take possession of the machine.

After the inspection was over, Yuan Bozhen went again to see the governor-general. He wanted to give an account of what he had accomplished. The governor-general invited him in and inquired what he did in his spare time in Shanghai. Yuan Bozhen was desperate and knew not what to say. He managed to mutter that he did not do much of anything except learn to speak and read a little English.

"This is something urgent, too," the governor-general nodded in approval, "something we can't do without." As he was saying this, he suddenly stood up and walked back into the inner chamber. Yuan Bozhen waited alone in the reception room for a long time but did not see him come out again. It was getting dark; soon the night lanterns would be lit. A guard then emerged to say, "His Highness is caught up in another matter. Please feel free to leave." Yuan Bozhen did accordingly.

Going back to his house, Yuan Bozhen found Zeng Songsheng already waiting for him in the living room. Zeng Songsheng had heard that Yuan Bozhen had come back from Shanghai. With him was a young man who was dressed in foreign-style clothing and had his hair cut short. Yuan Bozhen chatted with the young man and found out that he was called Xiang Guomin (alternate name, Tianlei), the son of an expectant intendant. When he spoke, he sounded remarkably open-minded. But when his father was mentioned during the conversation, he snorted, "He's a pig-headed enemy of the people! Let's not talk about him." Yuan Bozhen was taken aback by this response but admired him deep down for his broad knowledge. They spoke for a long time before the two visitors took leave. From then on, Yuan Bozhen met with Xiang Guomin frequently, and they became fast friends. We will leave this for now.

Soon after Yuan Bozhen completed his mission and returned to Wuchang, there was a certain Wei Baoji, one of the many hangers-on in official

circles, with the title of expectant magistrate, who submitted a memorandum
to the governor-general's office. The gist of it argued that given the current
state of financial stringency, it would be advisable to eliminate waste by abol-
ishing or combining some of the government bureaus and offices and to let
the surplus staffs go. It was high-sounding and persuasive.

After the governor-general read it, he indeed took it up with the prefect
of Wuchang and decided to abolish, in one stroke, the posts of several tens
of junior deputies and secretaries of the bureaus and offices. Yuan Bozhen's
was among them. As soon as Yuan Bozhen heard the news, he panicked. He
visited Chief Commander Li that same night, pleading for his intercession.
Several days later, Chief Commander Li sent a messenger over to say that
he had brought the matter up with his teacher, the governor-general, and
secured his permission for Yuan Bozhen to serve as a secretary in the Valiant
Defense Army under Li's command. On hearing this, Yuan Bozhen figured
that the job was not going to be a lucrative one but carried the prospect of
very generous commendations for promotion or transfer. Before reporting to
duty at the army office, he went to see the Mintage Bureau director to conclude his procurement duties.

As strong as it was, the Valiant Defense Army did not have standard
drills for its troops and only a nondescript program that was neither Chinese
nor Western. Yuan Bozhen had seen the drill exercises of foreign troops in
Shanghai, which he found well synchronized and orderly. He therefore persuaded Chief Commander Li to convince the governor-general of the benefit
to switch completely to foreign drills. The governor-general asked whose idea
it was. Chief Commander Li answered it was Yuan Bozhen's. "That suits me
just fine," said the governor-general.

The next day, the governor-general had a discussion with a Western
consul in the area. The consul agreed to nominate a foreign instructor who
would come to Hubei on contract to train troops for a monthly salary of
three hundred taels. The consul recommended a certain Wilkes,[3] now living
in Nanjing, who had served as an army commander in a Western country.

A fortnight passed. This Wilkes came to Wuchang and had his interview with the governor-general. He then went to Chief Commander Li's
residence to discuss with him details of the drill program, boasting all the
while of how important his previous rank had been and how special his expertise was. Since Wilkes had lived in China for many years and managed to
speak Mandarin,[4] there was no need for an interpreter. After meeting with
Chief Commander Li, he asked to be introduced to the army secretary. Chief
Commander Li told Yuan Bozhen to come over to meet Wilkes.

Yuan Bozhen had expanded his outlook during his sojourn in Shanghai and understood the social etiquette of greeting foreigners. As soon as

he saw Wilkes, he rushed forward with his outstretched hand to shake Wilkes's hand.

"So, Elder Brother is the army secretary," said Wilkes. Yuan Bozhen did not wait for him to finish before interrupting with several yeses.

"We might as well stick to Chinese," Wilkes interjected. "To be honest with Elder Brother, I've met several of your country's officials who spoke a little foreign language. At first, I could still barely make out what they were trying to say. Soon they could not understand a word of mine, nor could I understand a word of theirs. I didn't know what to do. I kept shaking my head, but they just kept rattling away. I suspected the way they talked was somehow derived from Latin, not something that the average, nonacademic person would bother to learn. So I told them, 'When I was in South Africa, I could understand the monkey's speech. But with you honorable gentlemen, I don't know what to say.' Now, I beg Elder Brother to be considerate and simply speak Chinese."

At Wilkes's sarcastic remarks, Yuan Bozhen's face turned completely red. He managed to say with a grin, "I didn't know Elder Brother could speak Chinese, or I would have spoken it in the first place." Wilkes thereupon chatted with Chief Commander Li some more before he left.

From that day on, Yuan Bozhen met with Wilkes often and got to know him better. He would sometimes give several silver dollars to the cook at the Foreign Matters Bureau to roast some beef and bake some bread as treats for Wilkes. But Wilkes would say, "These are simple fare to us foreigners. We eat them at every meal. Elder Brother, please don't waste that kind of money again. A glass of foreign wine for guests would be special enough."

Yuan Bozhen thought to himself, "There's no way that one could entertain guests with nothing but wine. He is poking fun at me again. Let me ask around tomorrow at the Foreign Matters Bureau to find out how it should be done." It goes without saying that Yuan Bozhen was paying close attention to good manners when it came to dealing with foreigners.

After Wilkes became the foreign drillmaster, he asked the governor-general for funds to outfit the troops of the Valiant Defense Army with new rifles and uniforms, giving them a completely fresh look. Yuan Bozhen saw the change and bought, at his own expense, a drill shirt and a pair of leather boots so he could blend in on the sideline during troop inspection. Wilkes waited until all the troops were issued new uniforms before summoning them to the drill ground every day. He taught them verbal commands and different formations and marches. After seven or eight weeks, the troops looked exceptionally neat and tidy, a far cry from how they used to look.

Wilkes told Chief Commander Li and Yuan Bozhen, "In a few months, these troops will be ready for action. But I must warn you: It's known that

Chinese soldiers tend to disperse or defect in times of danger. If this happens, it'll have nothing to do with me as drillmaster. It's up to you to prevent that from happening."

"As long as they're good at ceremonial maneuvers," remarked Yuan Bozhen, "that should be good enough. In the future, when high-ranking Chinese or foreign officials pass through here, we can have the troops stand in formation to welcome them and send them off. As long as they know how to follow foreign practices such as holding up their rifles properly and firing cannons in salutation, we should get by."

Wilkes laughed, with a touch of scorn, "I see. So that's why China drills its troops! That should be easy. No worries. You can leave that to me."

Yuan Bozhen then realized that he had again said the wrong thing and felt ashamed all over. Fortunately, Chief Commander Li was standing beside them and saved the day by changing the subject.

Another month or so went by. Ever since his wife died, Yuan Bozhen had been busy with official duties and had no chance to return to his native district. Now he wanted to find some way to take a trip back to Jiangxi province.

One day, Yuan Bozhen heard that Intendant Huang had returned from his mining mission to Yunyang. He quickly went to pay him a visit, taking with him the gramophone and gas lamp that he had brought back from Shanghai. They met. Intendant Huang spoke of his mission to Yunyang and then asked Yuan Bozhen what post he was serving. Yuan Bozhen gave a rundown of his own affairs and added a request for Intendant Huang's help with his wish to go back to Jiangxi for a visit.

Huang listened. Then he burst into laughter and delivered a grand speech of deep truth that shook Yuan Bozhen out of his sweet "slumber." And so it goes:

> What's left of the feelings between spouses is fleeting like a dream;
> Ambitious men set their sights only on future goals of career glory.

It is not clear what Intendant Huang had to say. Read on to find out in the next chapter.

NOTES

1. According to ancient legend, this bird of flight transported fairies from place to place. The most famous landmark erected to commemorate the legend was the Yellow Crane Tower built in Wuchang, Hubei province, in the early third century. More

than 1,700 years later, in the mid-1950s, its site gave way to the construction of the approach bridge to the main bridge across the Yangzi River at Wuchang and Hanyang. The landmark was rebuilt in the mid-1980s at a location close to the original site.

2. Formally launched in 1873 in Shanghai, the China Merchants Steam Navigation Company was one of the industrial projects initiated by Li Hongzhang (1823–1901), a leading official in Qing diplomacy and programs of modernization. For his life and career, see the essays in Samuel Chu and Kwang-ching Liu, eds., *Li Hung-chang and China's Early Modernization* (Armonk, NY: M. E. Sharpe, 1994); also Albert Feuerwerker, *China's Early Industrialization: Sheng Hsuan-huai (1844–1916) and Mandarin Enterprise* (Cambridge, MA: Harvard University Press, 1958).

3. It is Wu-ke-si in romanization.

4. In the original, the term *Jinghua* (Beijing dialect) is used. It is translated here as Mandarin to suggest a more or less standard form of spoken Chinese.

• 5 •

The hunt for the Wealth Voucher
rebels leads to a good friend's death;

The investigation into local mining
rights gives rise to covetous thought.

As soon as Intendant Huang heard Yuan Bozhen express his desire to go back to visit his native district, he could not help but laugh out loud: "If Venerable Uncle wants to go back, how difficult can it be? But there's this saying handed down to us from the ancients: 'Public service before private affairs; country before family.' Just think. First, your late wife has passed away for some time now. There's no point to go back for more grief. Even if she were alive, it'd still be hard to make the call. We live in topsy-turvy times, and the imperial throne's concerns are the responsibility for capable men to devote themselves to. So, it'd be hard to say. Besides, the empress-dowager and emperor have returned to the capital. Once it's decided that a comprehensive effort is to be made to adopt new policies, let's say, just in the few areas of military training, education, and fiscal management, who knows how many people will be promoted and get rich along the way?

"We look around in official circles now and find that there're more jobs for expectant intendants than anything else. It seems that the status of expectant intendant would qualify one for any job, whether in administration, diplomacy, agriculture, industry, commerce, or mining. If you don't have the title, you'll never rise to be a bureau chief, no matter how talented or senior you might be. It looks like Venerable Uncle doesn't care about promotions or fame. But you should know that your current post carries the prospect of excellent commendations. After a couple of rounds, you could move up to the rank of expectant intendant. I've been there, done that. I'm not bluffing you."

Yuan Bozhen found Intendant Huang's words totally convincing and appreciated them greatly. There and then, he cast aside all thought of going home. We will leave this for now.

Ever since the Wealth Voucher rebellion in Xinti took place,[1] high officials in Hubei province had been scared stiff. They tried to hunt all of the rebels down so that, so to speak, still ashes would not ignite again. One day, a member of the governor-general's private staff identified a certain returned student from Japan, who went by the name Tianlei, to have been a Wealth Voucher leader; so he must not be allowed to roam free and must be brought to justice if the region was to be safe. The governor-general summoned Chief Commander Li that evening, told him what he had learned, and ordered him to pay off informers both inside and outside the provincial capital in order to capture this man.

On returning to his office, Chief Commander Li confided the governor-general's instruction to Yuan Bozhen and asked him to come up with a plan. It turned out that this Tianlei had been close friends with Yuan Bozhen for more than a month before he ran off to Yichang to avoid being recognized.[2] Now, if Yuan Bozhen would only send him a secret message to warn him to flee, he would have been a true friend indeed. But, desperate for his own merit commendation, Yuan Bozhen turned this into an opportunity for himself.

To Chief Commander Li he replied, "Let Your Student look into this tomorrow morning. There ought to be leads we could follow."

The next day, on the pretext of visiting with Zeng Songsheng at the Translation Bureau, Yuan Bozhen found out all there was to know about Tianlei's whereabouts. He conveyed the information to Chief Commander Li, who then relayed it confidentially to the governor-general, who then ordered a battalion commander named Zhou to go with a few soldiers in a small boat to Yichang, where they would join forces with the district commander for the arrest.

Meanwhile, Tianlei had been talking to several friends about raising money to start a newspaper in Shanghai. These friends came from the two provinces of Sichuan and Hunan and found lodging on a busy street in the city. Tianlei stayed with a relative outside the city. His relative was called Chen Boxing, an old prefectural degree-holder from Yichang.

Around midnight one night, Chen Boxing was fast asleep. Without warning, the Grand Venerable Magistrate showed up with all his rural braves and soldiers of the city garrison, who were carrying a countless number of lit lanterns and torches.[3] Brandishing swords and spears, they had Chen Boxing's house thickly surrounded. When Chen Boxing was awakened by the commotion, several tens of the soldiers had already broken down the front door and burst in. As soon as they saw Chen Boxing, they dragged him out from bed and handcuffed him.

Chen Boxing's wife, Woman Duan, who was more than six months pregnant, saw her husband being restrained by the soldiers. She was terrified.

She brushed aside all sense of shame and lunged forward with all her might to grab a soldier's arm with her bare hands.[4] The soldier gave her lower abdomen a hard kick. Woman Duan let out a shrill cry and fell flat on her back to the floor. That was the end of her.

Some of the soldiers dragged Chen Boxing out the front door while others kept searching the house. Moments later, they found Tianlei and had him handcuffed as well. They also ransacked the place and made off with anything of value that they could find. There were two small children in the house. They just left them crying and wailing on the floor. Pushing and shoving, they brought Tianlei and Chen Boxing before the Grand Venerable Magistrate and Commander Zhou. After identifying the two men by name, they escorted them back to the district seat, shouting and yelling along the way.

Once they were inside the Grand Venerable Magistrate's office, they lost no time in extracting confessions from them. The magistrate reckoned that Chen Boxing was not named in his superior's arrest warrant and decided to lock him up for now until further instructions came. The next day, he handed Tianlei over to Commander Zhou and sent twenty garrison soldiers to escort them back to the provincial capital. The news spread. Several of Tianlei's comrades feared implication and fled that very night to Guangxi province, where they sought refuge among the outlaws of secret societies.

Meanwhile, Tianlei had to endure untold suffering on the way to the provincial capital. Convinced that he would not be able to save his own life, he refused to eat and drink. By the time they reached the harbor of Wuchang, he was barely breathing and could hardly talk. Alarmed by his condition, Commander Zhou hurried to see Chief Commander Li with details of what had happened. When Chief Commander Li boarded the boat to see for himself, Tianlei was already dead. Chief Commander Li also panicked and went immediately to report to the governor-general.

"If he's dead, then that's the end of it," said the governor-general. He gave instructions for the magistrate to examine and dispose of the body according to regulations and concluded his investigation into this case of anti-government activity. The governor-general gave Yuan Bozhen sole credit for catching Tianlei and complimented him lavishly to Chief Commander Li.

Yuan Bozhen had heard about Tianlei's plan to start a newspaper with his friends. He was worried that these friends would still publish the newspaper in the treaty port Hankou across the river and make his past connections with Tianlei known to the public. To forestall this, he sent a memorandum to the governor-general. In it, he argued that foreign governments all had laws to regulate newspaper publication by private individuals and companies. China had no such laws. All the newspapers now being published by private individuals did nothing but vilify government officials. While it was true that newspapers had the responsibility of monitoring the government and that freedom of speech should be respected, they tended to publish devious ideas like equal rights and revolution to promote heterodoxy. All this went against the teachings of the sages and the legal institutions of the dynasty, with detrimental effects on people's loyalty. The governor-general would do well, therefore, to ban the private publication of newspapers. As to the periodicals published by returned students from abroad, they should not be allowed to go on sale in the provincial capital. To a similar end and to get at the heart of the problem, all organizations set up to discuss current affairs should be banned.

The governor-general read the memorandum and found himself in agreement with both its arguments and proposed measures. He instructed the prefect of Wuchang to take action accordingly.

Zeng Songsheng only knew that it was the governor-general who ordered Tianlei's arrest but not that Yuan Bozhen had a hand in it. He even suggested organizing a memorial service for Tianlei to Yuan Bozhen and gave up the idea only after Yuan Bozhen warned him about certain government reprisal.

Since Yuan Bozhen had rendered services to the governor-general's satisfaction, the governor-general was prepared to take special care of him.

Time went by quickly. Before long, Wilkes completed his yearlong contract of troop training in foreign military drills. It was not known what commendation the governor-general requested for him, but Yuan Bozhen was allowed to move up from his current status as expectant subprefect to that of prefect to await job assignment in Hubei. As soon as he heard the news, Yuan Bozhen lost no time in expressing gratitude to the governor-general. Colleagues and fellow provincials with expectant statuses came to his residence to congratulate him. He kept busy over this for half a month.

Meanwhile, Yuan Bozhen got a letter from Yangchai, saying that he had obtained, through the patronage of a certain Manchu prince, a department directorship within the Ministry of Foreign Affairs. Yuan Bozhen felt happy for him.

A few days later, an urgent report came to the governor-general from the magistrate of Zhushan district. It read: "There are several antimony mines in the western section of the district. Three years ago, Wang, a local elite, found the ore deposits to be abundant. He petitioned and obtained the mining rights for them. But he has since run into a shortage of funds and has now, unexpectedly, come up with a foreign partner, who is in charge of the operation. From all indications, it seems clear that he intends to sell the mines to foreigners. Your Lowly Subordinate has tried several times to intervene, but Wang, emboldened by foreign backing, has refused to cooperate. I beg Your Highness for instructions at your earliest convenience as to how this may be resolved."

The governor-general went over the report and knew that he could not dictate a judgment from afar; someone had to be delegated to go there to conduct an on-site investigation. He thought immediately of Yuan Bozhen, who in his opinion was attentive to matters related to foreigners. Thereupon, he issued a letter of instruction for Yuan Bozhen to go to Zhushan district to deal with the situation.

On receiving the letter, Yuan Bozhen did not drag his feet. He went the next day to see the governor-general, who verbally instructed him to avoid rash action and use discretion in his investigation. To this, Yuan Bozhen quickly answered in repeated affirmatives. He then took leave to go to see Chief Commander Li to apprise him of the assignment and of the need for someone to fill in for him in his secretarial post while he was away. Next, he visited close friends to say good-bye. With a servant as a companion, he went on his way. They took a boat to Xiangyang district where they switched to the land route to continue their journey.

It took them over ten days to travel on land to Zhushan district. Yuan Bozhen met with the magistrate and learned the details of the case. The magistrate reiterated what he had stated earlier in his report, adding, "Just last month, Your Lowly Subordinate again sent someone to investigate. We didn't expect Elite Wang to be so fearless because of his foreign connection. He ordered the miners to beat our man up. Your Lowly Subordinate was at a loss to know what to do and could only report it to the governor-general." Yuan Bozhen believed every word he heard. The magistrate had a residence prepared for him.

The next day, without warning, the elite Wang Defu, who owned the mines, came to request an interview. He heard that a special investigator had arrived from the provincial capital and quickly showed up in formal attire. Yuan Bozhen invited him in and asked him for his side of the story.

Wang Defu began, "Junior Me wouldn't dare lie to Grand Venerable Elder. It has been three years since Junior Me started working the mines, which have yielded a modest profit. Unfortunately, our district magistrate didn't keep a tight rein on his subordinates and allowed them to extort bribes. Junior Me had to spend one hundred to two hundred taels every year just to make sure they wouldn't cause trouble.

"Last month, one of our mines hit underground water and caused a flooding. I was thinking of draining it with a water pump. It so happened that a missionary by the name Plassen was passing through the area.[5] He heard that Junior Me was working the mines and came to take a look around. He told Junior Me that a water pump could be ordered from a certain foreign firm in Shanghai. He also explained how to use it.

"There were several underlings of the magistrate's office who were upset because Junior Me didn't give them enough bribes. When they saw the foreign missionary walking alongside Junior Me, they incited the village lowlifes to spread rumors that Junior Me had brought a foreign missionary there to scoop out their eyes.[6] They had Junior Me and the missionary heavily surrounded. Asking no questions, they were about to inflict harm. Junior Me was desperate and could only call out my miners to drive them away and do my best to get the missionary to safety.

"The underlings knew their plan didn't work and accused Junior Me instead of beating them up. Grand Venerable Elder must have come here on account of this. This is why Junior Me hastened to come forward with the details and pray that Grand Venerable Elder would not simply take the magistrate's word for it and have Junior Me wrongfully accused."

Yuan Bozhen listened intently to the very end and said to Wang Defu, "I understand what happened. You can go now. I'll have an inspection of the mines soon and then deliberate." Wang Defu answered in several quick affirmatives before leaving.

Two days passed. Yuan Bozhen told the magistrate to get an escort of attendants and a horse ready for his inspection tour to the western section of the district. With Wang Defu leading the way, Yuan Bozhen examined the mines, which certainly looked well endowed with mineral veins. Yuan Bozhen also summoned the headman of neighborhood security to inquire into Wang Defu's clashes with the underlings of the magistrate's office. The headman's reply was close to what Wang Defu had described. Yuan Bozhen had a good grasp of the basic facts. Wang Defu also asked the locals to plead with Yuan Bozhen to put in a good word for him when Yuan Bozhen went back to the provincial capital to report to the governor-general. Wang Defu later sent over a gift of two hundred taels.

As soon as Yuan Bozhen returned from his inspection tour, the magistrate came over and asked, "Has the investigation today confirmed what Your Lowly Subordinate reported earlier?"

"There's some discrepancy," said Yuan Bozhen.

"When will Your Excellency be returning to the provincial capital?"[7] The magistrate inquired again.

"It's going to be tomorrow," said Yuan Bozhen. Soon after the magistrate left, his servant came by with a parting gift of one hundred taels.

Yuan Bozhen had noticed the mineral veins to be quite abundant. He was envious. After receiving the two cash gifts, he contemplated, "This mining business is really where the profit lies. I can make great gains from it." He thought hard for a plan so the antimony mines would come under his control. And so it goes:

The Qin court covets the rare, exquisite jade of Zhao;
Bian He loses his prize possession as a consequence.[8]

It is not clear how Yuan Bozhen would handle the matter. Read on to find out in the next chapter.

NOTES

1. See chapter 2, note 4.
2. He was Xiang Guomin in chapter 4.
3. For "rural braves," see chapter 1, note 16.
4. Physical contact of a woman with a man from outside the family or household was deemed inappropriate, even morally debasing.
5. Plassen is Bo-la-sen in romanization.
6. This was one of the widespread rumors that aroused fear and anger among the Chinese toward Westerners during the late Qing. Some Chinese believed that Westerners extracted minerals from human eyeballs for export back to their countries for industrial use.
7. Your Excellency was usually reserved for the governor-general but is here applied to Yuan Bozhen, who was the governor-general's emissary. The magistrate certainly wanted to please Yuan Bozhen so that when Yuan Bozhen reported to the governor-general, he would speak in his favor.
8. These two verses are based on a series of famous legends and events in ancient history and suggest a direct connection between the Qin state's desire for the precious jade and Bian He's lost possession. But there is an anachronism. Bian He had lived over five hundred years before the Qin state finally gained possession of the jade in the third century BC. The two lines here simply make the point that the difference in power allowed the strong (Yuan Bozhen) to take advantage of the weak (the mine owner).

· *6* ·

Mining shares are peddled on
Fuzhou Road to attract investors;

A company is set up in Guangxin
prefecture to produce camphor.

As we were saying, Yuan Bozhen found Wang Defu's mines to be rich in mineral veins and potentially very profitable. He wanted to seize the rights to the mines for himself. After going back and forth over this in his mind, it became clear that he could get those rights by taking certain steps without giving his real intent away.

He told his servant to pack up. The next day, he bade farewell to the Zhushan magistrate and went back to the provincial capital by the same route as he had come through Xiangyang prefecture. On arrival at the Wuchang pier, he had his luggage sent home before going to see the governor-general. He gave an account of what he had found out during his trip to Zhushan, adding, "While there's no hard evidence that this Wang Defu has sold his mines to foreigners, it's obvious that he had foreign backing in beating up government agents. He also showed the foreign missionary around to look for mineral veins in the mines. There's no guarantee that he won't, at a later date, enter into a collusive partnership with foreigners. The best thing to do now in order to forestall future foreign involvement would be to revert all the mines to government ownership and management. I wonder what Great Grand Teacher would think about this?"

"Government management means government investment," said the governor-general. "Given the shortage of funds at this time, where are we going to find the money for it?"

"The money doesn't have to come from government coffers," explained Yuan Bozhen. "It could be raised by selling shares."

The governor-general nodded. As he was about to say something, other callers had arrived to see him. Yuan Bozhen had to leave.

61

He went immediately to see Chief Commander Li and told him about his interview with the governor-general regarding his Zhushan mission. He followed up with a glowing description of the abundance of antimony veins at Wang Defu's mines and a projection of the great profits that could be derived from them. He also proposed that if the mines could switch to merchant management under government supervision,[1] he and Chief Commander Li should come up with the money, take over the mines, and turn this into a lucrative venture. He got really excited as he spoke.

Chief Commander Li listened and was tempted right away. He told Yuan Bozhen, "You go home now to wait for news. Let me take this up with Teacher. We'll see what happens." Yuan Bozhen felt jubilant as he went back to his residence. We'll leave this for now.

Indeed, Chief Commander Li paid a visit to the governor-general the next day and expressed interest in developing the Zhushan antimony mines and selling shares to raise the money. The governor-general had always known Chief Commander Li to be a very wealthy man, with tens of thousands of taels to his name, but asked anyway how he would go about finding enough capital.

"We could send Yuan Bozhen to Shanghai to raise twenty thousand to thirty thousand taels," Chief Commander Li replied. "This shouldn't be hard. As for a start-up fund, Your Subordinate could find some way to arrange an advance on it." The governor-general grinned and gave his approval.

The next day, the governor-general sent an order to the Zhushan magistrate, saying, in a nutshell: "The local elite Wang was working the mines in the interior but got involved all of a sudden with foreigners. In trying to obstruct the investigation by local government agents, he clearly had something to hide. The magistrate was thereby instructed to pay Wang some compensation and revert the mines back to government operation. All this was to prevent valuable resources from falling into foreign hands."

On receiving his order, the magistrate dispatched officials to the western section of the district to reclaim Wang Defu's mines in the name of the government, paying him a compensation of only several tens of taels for the land. Wang Defu realized that the decision had come from the governor-general. There was nothing he could do except heave a deep sigh of grief. His earlier investment had all come to naught, and he still had to pay off every one of his miners. Wang ended up going bankrupt, with nowhere to air his grievances.

As soon as Chief Commander Li heard that the governor-general had sent out his order, he invited Yuan Bozhen over for a discussion. Chief Commander Li was willing to put up twenty thousand taels toward the project and asked Yuan Bozhen to go to Shanghai to raise another twenty thousand, making a grand total of forty thousand taels. While there, Yuan Bozhen would purchase two mining machines for the project. In the event that the money to be raised fell short of twenty thousand, Chief Commander Li was prepared to come up with the full amount himself. All future profits from the mines would be divided into ten parts: two would go to the government, as a contribution, and one to Yuan Bozhen for his trouble.

Immediately after Chief Commander Li worked out this plan, he reported it to the governor-general. He proposed to have Yuan Bozhen replaced by someone else as secretary of the Valiant Defense Army so Yuan Bozhen could look after the Zhushan mining operation. The governor-general's letter of appointment came a few days later. Once Yuan Bozhen had it in hand, he went to see the governor-general to thank him. For the next three to four days, he conferred with Chief Commander Li before setting out with his luggage to Shanghai.

Yuan Bozhen had some experience in what he was going to do, unlike the fresh hand that he was on the earlier occasion. Before he left, he wrote to an old acquaintance in Shanghai to ask him to rent a house for him in the British Concession. On arrival there, he moved straight into it and posted a plaque on the front door, "Authorized Zhushan Mining Administration, Hubei Province, by Order of His Highness the Governor-General."

On the following day, he paid a visit to the intendant and the magistrate of Shanghai, which was, as to be expected, reported in the newspapers. Next, he called on a few friends, and the old gang from his previous visit came gathering again. Off he went to the theater by invitation from one, and to the restaurant from another. There was much more action for him this time than during his last visit.

Amid all the fun-filled activities, Yuan Bozhen got carried away and ensnared himself, once again, in the trap of seduction. Nine days out of ten he slept at a brothel with a prostitute by the name of Precious Jade Flower. Some seventy or eighty nights went by like this. His friends teased him by announcing it like a news headline: "He drills flesh mines hard on Fuzhou Road every night. Concern is, he might wreck his machine before he stops." Yuan Bozhen heard it and felt a tad embarrassed. But as soon as he broached the subject of mining shares, nine people out of ten shook their heads. For more than three months after he arrived in Shanghai, he accomplished nothing.

One day, the comprador of the foreign firm who had previously sold him the copper coin machine invited him to a dinner party at the Hongyu Brothel on No. 3 Road.[2] There were enough guests to fill two tables. In the course of the dinner, Yuan Bozhen mentioned the difficulty of selling shares for the mining project. Someone by the name of Shi Daoren among the guests said, "It may be a good idea to try advertising it. Officials now all rely on newspaper advertisements to get things done, whether setting up schools or soliciting relief donations. People will then show up with offers to help. Otherwise, they'd only have the chills of the northwesterly wind to count on." Yuan Bozhen heard these words and fully concurred.

On returning to his house after dinner, Yuan Bozhen drafted an advertisement by the light of the table lamp. He told his servant the next day to take it to several newspapers for a quote before choosing one to publish his advertisement. Indeed, ever since that day, many who were interested in buying shares came to ask about the mining project's stipulations. Over a dozen of them agreed to buy, but all insisted that they would put up the money only after operation started. As the Mid-Autumn Festival was fast approaching,[3] Yuan Bozhen felt a little desperate because no money had yet been raised.

One day, he ran into Shi Daoren again and asked him for suggestions. Shi Daoren smiled and replied, "Elder Brother can wait until the Festival is over. Then, spare no expense on dinner parties at Western-style restaurants, horse-drawn carriage rides, and visits to theaters and brothels. Put on a grand show. Talk big until heaven tumbles. People will then start piling in with their money to buy your shares."

Yuan Bozhen found this amusing at first but saw the truth in it after thinking about it. When the festivities were over, he indeed became a big spender in social circles to create top-notch appearances in whatever he did. In less than a month, he had more than six thousand taels in hand, all from several wealthy investors.

As he was planning to carry on in this manner, a telegram came unexpectedly from Chief Commander Li in Hubei, telling him to stop selling shares at once and hurry back to the provincial capital. Yuan Bozhen was stunned and puzzled over the reason. He had no choice but to pack up right away, and, without telling anyone, he boarded a westbound steamer up the Yangzi River.

On arriving in Wuchang, he found out that Chief Commander Li had come under impeachment in Beijing for his abuse of authority, taking bribes, and so on. This was why he decided so suddenly to lie low for a while and put the mining project on hold. This turn of events left Yuan Bozhen in a quandary. The thought of returning the shareholders' money was unrealistic. Not only was something like this never heard of before, but besides, he no longer had the full amount for reimbursement. If he did not pay the shareholders back, they were sure to come demanding their money. What should he do?

Two days passed, and there came the surprising news that the governor-general of Liangjiang in Nanjing had resigned because of illness; the imperial government had instructed the governor-general of Hubei and Hunan to transfer there temporarily to fill the vacated post in an acting capacity. Yuan

Bozhen figured that the acting assignment would not last long. He came up with a plan. As soon as the governor-general left for Nanjing, he went to see the governor who was now the acting governor-general to request a leave of absence on account of his fund-raising project. He then sneaked back to his native Xinyu district with the shareholders' money.

It had been three years since Yuan Bozhen left home. After his wife died, Yangchai's family had been looking after his household affairs for him and was keeping them in good order. Even the community had become more enlightened than before. Everything from English-language school to mining company to criminal correctional center was being proposed or sponsored by the locals.

On arriving home, Yuan Bozhen spent a few days meeting with relatives and friends. In the course of these visits, he heard someone mention that the wood of camphor trees in places like Guangfeng and Yushan in Guangxin prefecture was a major local product. Foreigners were recently known to be taking stealthy steps with the intention of setting up a camphor production company there. If this resource should fall into foreign hands, it would be the locals' tough luck. Yuan Bozhen kept these words close to heart.

Several days later, he ran into a friend who had just returned from Nanchang.[4] His friend told him that a foreigner had indeed arrived in the provincial capital with an application to the governor for the rights to produce camphor. The governor and the director of the Foreign Matters Bureau were trying desperately to come up with an excuse to turn it down. This instantly gave Yuan Bozhen an idea. He told his servants to rent a fast boat and hurried to Nanchang that night. Once there, he submitted a petition to the governor for permission to establish a company for camphor production in all areas of Guangxin prefecture.

The governor had been hard-pressed for a formal reason to deliberate against the foreign application. He was only too glad to receive Yuan Bozhen's submission, which he could use in rejecting the foreign application. He summoned Yuan Bozhen for an interview to make general inquiries and granted approval the next day.

With the governor's written authorization in hand, Yuan Bozhen raised two thousand taels' worth of shares in Nanchang. At the same time, he wrote to the investors in Shanghai to explain that the hills in Zhushan district had shifted position, making it hard to get at the antimony veins. He now proposed to divert their funds to camphor production in Guangxin prefecture in Jiangxi province to make their investment profitable. He asked if they would agree. On receiving this letter, the shareholders in Shanghai knew well that they would probably never see their money again. They might as well go along with it. Every one of them gave consent.

Yuan Bozhen waited until the two thousand taels were in hand before requesting the provincial treasurer for an official seal. With several close friends, he went upstream on a boat to Guangxin via Guixi and Geyang. He rented a large house outside the city for his camphor company. At first, he hoped to proceed according to Western practice and hire a foreign engineer as supervisor. The shortage of funds, however, made this infeasible. He had to fall back on the traditional method of production. A couple of warning signs were put up on both sides of the front door: "Restricted Area of the Company" and "Authorized Personnel Only." It was with the two thousand taels raised in Jiangxi that he started the operation. As to the funds of the Shanghai investors, he swallowed them whole.

Reader, you will note that all the camphor trees in the villages of Guangxin prefecture were the private property of the locals. No one could take possession of a tree without paying a fair price for it. Besides, the locals were extremely superstitious. They insisted that once trees had been around for many years, they were inhabited by tree spirits and must not be wantonly chopped down. Now, even with the offer of a fair price, it was not easy to buy one tree.

In the month after his arrival in Guangxin, Yuan Bozhen sent his men into the villages to make purchases but managed to buy not even ten trees. Some owners heard that the trees would be used to produce camphor and doubled the price right away. Yuan Bozhen was annoyed by the villagers' refusal to budge and their stubborn hold on the trees as if they were treasures. He had no recourse but to ask the Shangyao magistrate for a few orderlies. He told them to go with company workers to the villages to tag the bigger trees, regardless of ownership, with a claim written on paper strips, "Reserved for Company Use." When the time came, they sent loggers to fell the trees without paying for them. Owners were given a promissory note of reimbursement at twice the current price once camphor was produced. Furious but fearful of officials, the villagers did not openly voice their anger.

One day, company workers chopped down a very big tree. After the branches and leaves were removed, it still took twenty to thirty workers to haul it back to the factory. Along the way, they trod through a field grown with green vegetables and trashed it like a water buffalo had just gone over it. The owner of the field saw it and felt a stabbing pain in his heart. With all his strength, he rushed forward to stop them. The workers did not even bother to argue. They punched and kicked the owner until he was badly wounded, lying on the ground, about to report to the King of Hell. The other villagers saw what happened and were outraged. Some three or four hundred of them rushed to avenge the landowner. And so it goes:

Oppression is enforced through the application of arbitrary power;
The whole community is aroused in agitation as a consequence.

It is not clear how the workers who were hauling the tree back would react. Read on to find out in next chapter.

NOTES

1. The government-supervised, merchant-managed partnership (*guandu shangban*) was a common arrangement for industrial projects during the late Qing. See Albert Feuerwerker, *China's Early Industrialization: Sheng Hsuan-huai (1844–1916) and Mandarin Enterprise* (Cambridge, MA: Harvard University Press, 1958).

2. Also called Hankow Road in the British Concession, where many of the early Chinese newspapers were published.

3. It falls on the fifteenth day of the lunar eighth month, also known as the Moon Festival, when family members get together to celebrate the fullest moon of the year as a symbol of their bond and happiness. Lit lanterns, moon cakes (typically made of mashed lotus seeds and other sweet ingredients), and seasonal fruits are featured on this occasion.

4. Capital of Jiangxi province.

• 7 •

New rules are drafted to forestall
school education's harmful effects;

Preemptive action is the key to
success in handling foreign relations.

$\mathcal{A}$s we were saying, the villagers saw the workers beat up the landowner as they were hauling the camphor tree away and were upset over their bullying behavior. Like a swarm of bees, some three or four hundred of them came rushing to avenge the landowner. Taking notice from a distance, the workers knew they were outnumbered. They decided to drop the camphor tree, and they ran all the way back to the factory. Yuan Bozhen was resting on the opium couch-bed. They gave him a full account of what just happened. Before they could finish, the loud noises of an angry mob were heard at the front door. The villagers were breaking into the building.

Opium pipe in hand, Yuan Bozhen quickly got up from the couch-bed. He opened the back door and made a run for his life. He ran over one *li* without stopping.[1] The dozen or so workers at the factory did not dare confront the intruders and fled in all directions. Finding no one inside, the villagers trashed the place and stripped it of all articles of value. They did not find any money because all the company's cash was deposited in the money shop. Knowing that the building was rental property belonging to a local, they stopped short of demolishing it. After they smashed the furnishings inside, some of the villagers were sent back to their village to carry the injured landowner to town on a door board. All of them then marched into the office of the Shangyao magistrate to ask him to examine the landowner's injuries and demanded compensation.

The Shangyao magistrate sensed the crowd's agitation and did not want it to get further out of hand. He complied with their request to examine the landowner's injuries and, expressing sympathy and support, persuaded them to go back to their village.

Meanwhile, from a good distance away, Yuan Bozhen found out what happened and hurried back to town to see the magistrate. He gave an account of how the village mob pillaged and destroyed his factory and asked the magistrate to inspect the damages and punish the ringleaders. The Shangyao magistrate knew very well that the trouble had started when company employees attacked the landowner. It would be awkward for him to side with Yuan Bozhen. He verbally agreed to do what Yuan Bozhen requested but privately sent someone over to ask him to leave Guangxin prefecture as soon as possible to avert further mishaps.

Yuan Bozhen reckoned that he had suffered losses because of the villagers' actions. However, he could use their actions as a perfect excuse to write off all the investments of the Jiangxi and Shanghai shareholders. He decided to follow the Shangyao magistrate's suggestion. He took all the company's cash out from the money shop and, with it as travel expenses, left with his employees by boat that night to return to the provincial capital.

On arriving in Nanchang, he reported to the governor on how the villagers, on their strength of superior numbers, trashed and looted the factory, took away the company seal, and so on. He asked that an order be sent through the Guangxin prefect to the Shangyao magistrate for the arrest and punishment of the offenders. He also wrote to all the shareholders to inform them of what had happened and explain how their investments had totally evaporated as a result.

In point of fact, however, Yuan Bozhen still had some four thousand to five thousand taels of leftover money in hand. Mindful of what Intendant Huang had said about career prospects for expectant intendants as bureau chiefs, he wanted to use the money to purchase an expectant intendant status for himself. Unfortunately, the government had recently terminated all categories of credential sales. Even if he wanted to buy one now, he would have no way of doing so. He decided, for the time being, to return to Xinyu for the New Year to take care of his affairs back home.

It was after the Lantern Festival that he went on the road again.[2] He passed through Jiujiang to Shanghai where he met with the shareholders and told them what he had wanted to say. He then went from Shanghai to Tianjin and took the train into Beijing. He was going to find Yangchai and ask him to show him a shortcut to an official career and riches.

Yangchai had been corresponding with Yuan Bozhen and knew what he had been doing since they last met. But he did not expect Yuan Bozhen to show up in Beijing without prior notice. On seeing him, he inquired about the purpose of his trip to the imperial capital. Yuan Bozhen told him the truth. Yangchai said, "Brother, officially, your earlier commendation in Hubei was in recognition of your services in the Valiant Defense Army whereas, in fact, it was because you helped to catch the rebel leader and ban newspaper publication. Both suited the governor-general's purposes very well. That's why he included you in the commendation. The grandees now in power at the imperial court are like that, too. They talk about reform all day, but reform is no more than window dressing for them. Deep down, they're concerned with nothing but their own careers and wealth. If you play your hand right, it won't be hard to get yourself the expectant intendant status.

"The Manchu prince in charge of the Ministry of Foreign Affairs is the most powerful man right now.[3] He's related to the governor of Jiangsu by marriage. Let me figure out some way for you to come under his patronage. Then, run a few errands for him. Alternatively, make an application to the Board of Appointments for a transfer of your official status to Jiangsu province and ask the prince for a letter of reference to the Jiangsu governor. It'll take no time at all for you to get recommended for an expectant intendant status. But to get all this started, it'll cost you about two thousand taels."

"With that kind of money," asked Yuan Bozhen, "wouldn't it be easier to make a direct purchase of the expectant intendant title instead of going through the motions just to get a commendation?"[4]

"Brother, you mustn't think of it that way," said Yangchai. "Besides, such purchases have been abolished. Even if they weren't, how could a purchased expectant intendant title compare to one gained through commendation? Once you come under the prince's patronage, his influence can easily get you a commendation for it or even an actual job. My only worry is that you don't have the money. If you do, you should really be seeking additional help from other patrons."

"Like who, besides the prince?" asked Yuan Bozhen. Yangchai walked over to Yuan Bozhen and whispered something in his ear. Yuan Bozhen quickly nodded, "I see, elder brother. Please, do think of a way for me."

Yuan Bozhen stayed at Yangchai's home from that time on. Several days went by. One day, Yangchai came home from work and said, "What we talked about the other day is off to a good start. Here in Beijing we use money drafts issued by the Four Heng shops.[5] Go get them ready. We've got something planned for tomorrow." Yuan Bozhen did not waste any time. He went right away to get two money drafts ready, one for two thousand taels and the other for two hundred.

The next day, Yangchai told Yuan Bozhen to change into formal attire and prepare a student's calling card. The two brothers then set out together on a mule-drawn carriage. They first stopped by the customs station at the Front Gate to see a certain Esteemed Elder Bai.[6] Yangchai handed both money drafts over to him; the one for two hundred taels was a present for him. Having done his part, Yangchai waited at the customs station.

Esteemed Elder Bai rode with Yuan Bozhen on the mule-drawn carriage northward on Chungwen Gate Street. They got off outside the entrance of the prince's residence. Esteemed Elder Bai went in first and came out after a while to accompany Yuan Bozhen to go inside to an exquisitely appointed study. Before long, the prince came out. Yuan Bozhen rushed forward to perform salutation and offer greetings. The prince smiled and told both of them to sit down. He asked Yuan Bozhen where he had served as an expectant official and what assignments he had undertaken so far. Yuan Bozhen answered every one of his questions.

The prince then pointed to Esteemed Elder Bai, "I'm quite busy and often don't have time for guests. You can talk to him if you have anything in mind." As he was speaking, he stood up. Those attending him on both sides announced, "Our guests are leaving." Yuan Bozhen replied with several affirmatives and left with Esteemed Elder Bai. They took the same mule-drawn carriage back to the customs station.

Yangchai saw them and quickly came up to greet them. He saluted and thanked Esteemed Elder Bai. Esteemed Elder Bai said, "We're friends. There's no need for such formalities." Yangchai saw that many people were waiting to speak with Esteemed Elder Bai and knew he was busy. Together with Yuan Bozhen, he bade farewell to Esteemed Elder Bai and hopped on the carriage to go home.

A few days later, there was news that the governor-general of Hubei had arrived in Beijing for an audience with the empress-dowager and emperor and had taken up residence on Xiaxie Street. Yuan Bozhen heard the news and prepared a calling card to go to see him. As soon as the governor-general saw the calling card, he invited him in. On meeting Yuan Bozhen, he asked when he had come to the capital and whether he had any free time. Yuan Bozhen replied, "If Great Grand Teacher has errands to run, please give the word."

The governor-general said, "I'm currently drafting the bylaws for the Imperial University.[7] If you have nothing else to do, give us a hand." Yuan Bozhen quickly responded twice in the affirmative.

"The goal of the university is to promote science, not philosophy," continued the governor-general. "The philosophy that comes from abroad tends to spawn devious ideas like revolution and equal rights and must not be incorporated into the curriculum. Instead of having our students study foreign philosophy, we might as well emphasize the study of Chinese classical works and assign these a heavier weight in the program. This is a way of preserving our national essence and abiding by what Mencius once said about proper learning as a defense against the teachings of Yang Zhu and Mozi.[8] Of all the principles that currently guide our efforts to draft the regulations and bylaws for the new educational system for the whole country, this is the most important."

As Yuan Bozhen was listening, he recalled what Yangchai had said.[9] Every one of his words turned out to be true. After the governor-general finished on the subject, he talked briefly about other matters. Yuan Bozhen then took leave to go back to Yangchai's house.

From that day on, Yuan Bozhen went every day to Xiaxie Street to take part in the drafting of educational regulations and bylaws. There was, in fact, already an ample supply of able hands at the governor-general's place and hardly need for extra help. But since the governor-general had suggested it, Yuan Bozhen could not very well have stayed away. Besides, when the regulations and bylaws were completed, it would be a great reward if his name could be included in the report to the throne, along with a request for some kind of commendation for him. He kept busy at Xiaxie Street for over a month.

The next upcoming event was the birthday of the prince, whose patronage Yuan Bozhen had recently sought. Yangchai was a subordinate of the prince's. As a rule, he had to prepare a birthday present. Together with Yuan Bozhen, he put up one hundred taels. A department director in the Ministry of Foreign Affairs ("Puppet Mo") and a department director in the Ministry of Commerce ("Muddle-headed Wu") also chipped in, fifty taels apiece. With a grand total of two hundred taels, they prepared a fairly decent birthday present for delivery to the prince.

On the day of the birthday, they were all elegantly dressed to go to the celebration at the prince's residence. The prince did not care too much about the value of the presents, but on reading the well-wishing messages inscribed on folded ceremonial paper sheets, he caught the name Yuan Bozhen and recognized it as someone who had recently asked favors of him but had not been given any yet. Because it was only a minor-year birthday celebration,[10] there were not as many guests. He decided to meet with Yuan Bozhen.

After Yuan Bozhen performed salutation, the prince asked him to be seated. "You still haven't left the capital after all this time?" To this, Yuan Bozhen replied, matter-of-factly, that he had been helping with the drafting of educational regulations and bylaws on Xiaxie Street. The prince then inquired about the guiding principles of the regulations and bylaws. Yuan Bozhen replied, "Frankly, education is not like military training or fiscal management. Military training has the goal of putting down internal unrest, and fiscal management has the goal of enriching the country. Education may be said to aim at the promotion of human talent. Faulty regulations will only encourage students to go astray and produce the criminal kind that agitates for revolution and equal rights. This is why the regulations being drafted all emphasize the importance of classical studies. In short, our goal is to establish proper learning and eliminate treacherous teachings."

Yuan Bozhen's words carried a distinct ring of reason and truth and sounded convincing to the prince, who thereupon lavished praise on him. He then let Yuan Bozhen go back to join the other guests.

Another two months passed, and the drafting of educational regulations and bylaws was completed. Since the governor-general had so many people that he wanted to mention, he did not include Yuan Bozhen on his list of commendations. Word of the neglect gradually reached the prince's ear. He felt sorry for Yuan Bozhen and decided to find a way to help him get ahead.

It so happened that one of the prince's in-laws had just been appointed director-general of tribute grain transport.[11] The prince sent him a note recommending Yuan Bozhen. It was a wish that the director-general could not afford to ignore. He therefore requested in his memorial to the throne Yuan Bozhen's appointment to his personal staff. Esteemed Elder Bai conveyed the news to Yuan Bozhen, who went immediately to the prince's residence to thank the prince for the great favor. He next visited the director-general of tribute grain transport and expressed gratitude for the opportunity to serve under him.

After he went home that day, he had a discussion with Yangchai. He observed that the director-general was a high official overseeing tribute matters and that this assignment to the Lianghuai region probably involved mostly fiscal affairs.[12]

"No, not so," Yangchai said. "Now that the sea route is available, tribute grain transport continues only in name, not in reality. The power and authority of the director-general are similar to those of a governor-general or governor and are not limited to fiscal administration. When you go this time, never mind what jobs you'll be given. You just go with the flow and put up the appearances that you are in favor of reform. You should be raking in enough riches to enjoy."

Yuan Bozhen asked, "Lianghuai is a key entry point into our country. There must be many foreigners and missionaries passing through. If I'm assigned to the Foreign Matters Bureau, what should I do?"

Yangchai listened, let out a snort, and said, "It's easy to deal with matters relating to foreign contact. If there's anything that requires serious negotiation, you simply send a telegram to ask for advice from the minister in charge of the Region of the Southern Seas in Nanjing and from the ministers in charge of foreign affairs in Beijing.[13] Accountability will then be off your shoulders. It's the same with us in the Ministry of Foreign Affairs. When we run into something messy, we either refer it to the governors-general and governors in the provinces for suggestion or, to get it over with, basically go along with the foreign demand with whatever input from whomever, wherever. If this still doesn't do the trick, there's always the last resort of seeking the throne's deliberation. There's nothing we can't get away with."

Yuan Bozhen was about to go on asking questions when his servant came in to announce that someone saying he was sent by the prince was here to see Venerable Master Yuan. And so it goes:

By chance comes an encounter with an accomplished individual;
Persistence leads to making friends with a bully of a man.

It is not clear who had arrived from the prince's household. Read on to find out in the next chapter.

NOTES

1. One *li* is about one-third of a mile.
2. The Lantern Festival is on the fifteenth day of the Chinese New Year. Lanterns were traditionally believed to have the function of repelling bad fortune, evil spirits, and crop-harming insects.
3. The Ministry of Foreign Affairs was established in 1901, as required in the Boxer Protocol signed earlier that year with foreign nations to end the Boxer conflict. Prior to that, there had been the Zongli Yamen (Office for the general management of trade affairs with various countries), established in Beijing in 1861, to manage relations with Western countries.
4. Here the author seemed to contradict himself. Only a few paragraphs earlier, Yuan Bozhen was supposed to be aware of the end of the credential sale.
5. The name refers to Hengli, Henghe, Hengxing, and Hengyuan, the four largest and most reputable money shops in Beijing during the late nineteenth century. They suffered crippling losses after their vaults were looted during the Allied occupation of Beijing in 1900.
6. The Front Gate was the arrow tower in front of the center gate into Beijing's Inner City.
7. This episode refers to the post-Boxer reform that created a countrywide educational system from preschool through primary school, middle school, high school, and university, with rules and regulations approved by the throne. Yuan Bozhen was supposed to be involved in drafting those for university education.
8. According to Mencius (c. 371–289 BC), Yang Zhu preached a self-centered if not selfish view of life, and Mozi went to the other extreme to propose altruism and universal love. Mencius's criticisms of the two, though polemical and simplistic, were upheld through the centuries in the Confucian tradition.
9. Earlier in the chapter, Yangchai described high officials' support for reform as lip service rather than wholehearted commitment. In this instance, the point is that

the educational reforms being proposed were of a restrictive kind rather than an open accommodation of Western ideas and practices.

10. The birthday of every tenth year (decennial) was called a "major birthday" (*da shengri*), and of other years, a "minor birthday" (*xiao shengri*).

11. It was a long-established practice of the Qing dynasty for the finest produce and products from the Yangzi delta, such as rice, teas, and silks, to be sent via the Grand Canal to Beijing for imperial use. The director-general of tribute grain transport was responsible for the smooth operation of this stupendous undertaking. As steam navigation became a more efficient mode of transportation from the mid-nineteenth century on, tribute grains and other goods often took to the sea route along the China coast, leaving the Grand Canal more and more in a state of disuse except for local and regional traffic. Chinese competitors gradually moved into steam navigation against foreign companies. See Kwang-ching Liu, *Anglo-American Steamship Rivalry in China, 1862–74* (Cambridge, MA: Harvard University Press, 1962) and Stephen Halsey, "Sovereignty, Self-Strengthening, and Steamships in Late Imperial China," *Journal of Asian History* 48, no. 1 (2014): 81–111. In 2014, China's Grand Canal was approved and inscribed by UNESCO as a World Heritage Site. See "The Grand Canal," UNESCO, http://whc.unesco.org/en/list/1443.

12. The Lianghuai region was named after the Huai River that runs through Eastern China out to the sea, and it includes the economically vital province of Jiangsu.

13. The minister in charge of the Region of the Southern Seas in Nanjing was a post created in the early 1860s as one of the Qing measures to deal with Westerners in China. A parallel position was established in Tianjin with responsibility for the Region of the Northern Seas. The governors-general in Nanjing and in Tianjin held the positions, respectively, as concurrent appointments.

• 8 •

An old friend's cooperation helps
resolve a Sino-foreign dispute;

A police surcharge is enforced
in the name of policy innovation.

As we were saying, Yuan Bozhen heard that someone had come from the prince's household to see him. He went hurriedly out to the living room. It turned out to be none other than Esteemed Elder Bai.

Esteemed Elder Bai explained that he dropped by to say good-bye because he knew Yuan Bozhen would be leaving Beijing soon. Yuan Bozhen kept saying he did not deserve the courtesy as he let Esteemed Elder Bai take the seat of honor. They chatted on sundry matters: what the director-general of tribute grain transport was like as a person and why Yuan Bozhen's appointment this time came as a special favor. Quite some time had gone by before Esteemed Elder Bai took out a list he had on him and handed it to Yuan Bozhen, saying, "Here are a few things I beg to impose on you to look for when you pass through Shanghai. Send them when you get them. Please pay for them first. I'll reimburse you later in full."

Yuan Bozhen took the list and looked it over. It consisted of silks, imported goods, and other items. They would cost over one hundred taels in total. He understood the meaning of this at once and said to Esteemed Elder Bai, "These are things I should get as a token of my respect for you. They shouldn't be of any cost to Elder Brother."

Hearing this, Esteemed Elder Bai steadfastly declined. Only after Yuan Bozhen insisted again and again did he get on his feet to thank him: "How could I possibly feel easy about this great favor you'll do me?" He then added, "It's the time of day when the prince might want me there for some errand." He said good-bye and went to the prince's residence.

Meanwhile, Yuan Bozhen started packing and got his luggage ready. He bought souvenirs, like dried mushrooms and embroidered handicraft articles, as gifts for others. Next, he went to the prince's residence, the Xiaxie Street office, and the homes of fellow Jiangxi provincials to say good-bye. On the day divined to be a day of good fortune, he left Beijing as a member of the tribute grain transport director-general's entourage. From the port of Tianjin, they boarded the Xinji steamship for Shanghai, where they found transit lodging at the Sea Goddess Temple. Since the director-general had to see friends, they stayed there for three days. Yuan Bozhen availed himself of the free time to buy all the items on Esteemed Elder Bai's list, and he entrusted them to a comprador of the Xinji steamship for delivery to Beijing.

After the director-general completed his social calls, they left the Sea Goddess Temple on the fourth day on a steamship that plied the Yangzi River. They went up to Zhenjiang where they switched to a smaller steamship to go to Qingjiangpu. When they docked, the magistrate of Shanyang district arranged for the director-general and his close aides to move into a spacious house he had prepared for them. Yuan Bozhen was new to the area and did not know anyone. He found temporary lodging at a big inn near the tribute grain transport office.

A few days later, the director-general took up his post and moved into the official residence adjacent to his office. Yuan Bozhen went with others to celebrate the occasion. From that day on, he hoped from day to day that he would soon be assigned a lucrative job to make it worth his while. Nothing, however, came from above for over a month. Yuan Bozhen was running out of patience.

Then one day, he heard a colleague mention that a certain foreign instructor had traveled here from Wuhu. While on the steamer, a few pieces of his luggage had been stolen, and he was demanding a compensation of three thousand taels from local officials. Members of the Foreign Matters Bureau did not know what to do. Yuan Bozhen inquired where this foreigner had worked and what his name was. His colleague replied, "It's not known where he has worked before as instructor. It's only known that he's called Wilkes."

Yuan Bozhen did not expect to hear the name Wilkes. An idea came to him instantly. He changed into formal attire and went to the tribute grain transport office to ask to see the director-general on urgent business. The guard at the gate went inside with his request. Indeed, the director-general summoned him at once and asked what the urgency was about.

Yuan Bozhen replied, "Humble Prefect just heard that a traveling foreigner called Wilkes has lost his luggage and is demanding a compensation of three thousand taels from the Foreign Matters Bureau. Is this true? If it is, Humble Prefect knows Wilkes and is at your service if there's anything that Humble Prefect could do."

"Oh my!" exclaimed the director-general. "So Wilkes is a friend of yours! He's making a big fuss at the Foreign Matters Bureau and asking for three thousand taels for his stolen luggage and not a scrap less. It's just marvelous that you know him. Please go talk to him to see what can be done." Yuan Bozhen saw that this assignment was in hand and felt pleased. He immediately responded several times in the affirmative before leaving.

The next day, he found out from others where Wilkes was staying. He put on the foreign outfit that he had bought while working in the Valiant Defense Army and set out to see Wilkes on his own. Wilkes recognized Yuan Bozhen as someone from his past but had no idea that he came on account of his affair. After they greeted one another, Wilkes asked what Yuan Bozhen had been doing since they last saw each other. Yuan Bozhen sensed his sincerity and gave an overblown account of his recent work under the prince and his role in drafting the educational regulations by order of the governor-general of Hubei.

Wilkes said, "I heard this prince is in charge of the Department of Army Training that the Chinese government has recently set up.[1] I want to get a job with it as instructor. Do you think it may be feasible?"

"It shouldn't be too hard," replied Yuan Bozhen. "The director-general of tribute grain transport posted here is an in-law of the prince's. If he's willing to write a letter of recommendation for you, it'll almost be as good as done."

Wilkes looked dumbfounded on hearing this. After a pause, he said, "I'm afraid I've ruined my own chances. The director-general will probably refuse to write anything for me now. What should I do?"

Yuan Bozhen quickly inquired about the reason. Wilkes recounted in detail how he had lost his luggage and how he was demanding compensation from the Foreign Matters Bureau.

"How much is your luggage worth?" Yuan Bozhen asked.

"Not much in money terms," replied Wilkes, "but all my important letters were gone."

"If it's not about the money," continued Yuan Bozhen, "why don't you just drop the whole thing and stop asking for compensation?"

"But I've already made my demand known," said Wilkes.

"I do have a solution if you are interested," Yuan Bozhen went on.

"Tell me what it is," Wilkes pleaded.

Yuan Bozhen said, "I'll speak on your behalf to the director-general tomorrow and ask that he instruct local officials to catch the thieves to get your luggage back. I'll also request that he write a letter of recommendation for you. Once you get the job as instructor of the Department of Army Training, you'll quit making the big fuss about lost belongings."

"It's a very smart plan," said Wilkes. "Still, as a matter of saving face, they should pay me a nominal sum, say, a few hundred taels. Otherwise, it'd look like I was extorting all along."

"That shouldn't be a problem," replied Yuan Bozhen. "Let me follow up on it. We'll see what happens." They chatted some more before Yuan Bozhen took leave.

Next morning, as agreed, Yuan Bozhen went to see the director-general. He relayed Wilkes's request for a letter of recommendation for an instructorship. The director-general thought for a while before saying, "This I can do, but I wonder what he now wants for compensation for his luggage."

Yuan Bozhen replied, "Humble Prefect surmises that the case could be closed if Your Esteemed Person would agree to catch the thieves, offer him a compensation of three hundred taels, and write a letter of recommendation for him."

"I know what to do," said the director-general. He then told Yuan Bozhen to go.

In anticipation that the director-general would handle the matter the way he suggested, Yuan Bozhen wanted to give Wilkes a heads-up. After he got back to the inn, he changed into casual clothing. Because it was raining, he put on a foreign-style cape. Wearing his pair of gold-rimmed sunglasses and puffing on a full-size cigar, he made his way to see Wilkes. As soon as Wilkes's pet dog saw Yuan Bozhen approach in that outfit, it started barking at the top of its lungs. Wilkes came out and had to look closely before recognizing Yuan Bozhen. He could not help but break into a hearty laugh: "My friend, you could have fooled me with that appearance. Even my dog didn't recognize you. I heard someone say this some time ago. There was this place near a mountain in China where a tiger came out to attack people in broad daylight. The locals tried all methods to get rid of it but failed. Then, one day, there was this man passing through. Like you, my friend, he had a cape on, wore a pair of dark glasses, and puffed on a cigar, making thick smokes. The tiger saw from a distance this black beast coming toward him, eyes flashing with a hostile stare and mouth emitting smoke, and couldn't make out what kind of a monster it was. Horrified, it ran away, never to be seen again in the area."

Before Wilkes could finish, Yuan Bozhen took his cape and sunglasses off and said with a grin, "Don't just make fun of me. Let's get down to business." At this, Wilkes stopped saying anything more. He invited Yuan Bozhen to sit down and asked if he had seen the tribute grain transport director-general.

"I did," Yuan Bozhen replied. "The director-general adamantly refused at first to write a reference letter for you. Then I sang the praise of your ability as best I could, adding that if His Esteemed Person would not write it, someone else most definitely would. He then showed some willingness to change his mind. It looks like the matter will be resolved in two to three days. That's why I came to let you know."

As Wilkes was about to ask for details, his friend, a foreigner, walked in. Wilkes left Yuan Bozhen aside to chat with his friend. Since their conversation had been interrupted and he felt out of place, Yuan Bozhen decided to go home and went out in the rain. We will leave this for now.

Meanwhile, the director-general followed up on Yuan Bozhen's proposal. After discussing it with his private secretary, he had the letter of recommendation drawn up. Giving it to the director of the Foreign Matters Bureau, he instructed him to take three hundred taels out from the Relief and Redress Bureau and deliver the money and the letter to Wilkes to end the dispute. The director did not dare waste any time. In not quite a week, he took care of everything related to Wilkes. Wilkes saw that his wish had been met and decided not to press for anything more. After visiting Yuan Bozhen to thank him, he packed up and moved on to his new destination.

The director-general wanted to assign Yuan Bozhen to the Foreign Matters Bureau after he had helped settle the dispute with a foreigner. However, on further inquiry, he found out that Yuan Bozhen did not know any foreign language, and he changed his mind. Since the imperial government had announced the plan to establish a police system, he decided to delegate the task of creating one in his jurisdiction to Yuan Bozhen. Aside from operating costs, Yuan Bozhen was allowed to draw a monthly salary of 120 taels with an additional 50 taels for sundry expenses.

On receiving his letter of appointment, Yuan Bozhen went to the director-general's office to express gratitude and to seek detailed instructions. After speaking with the director-general, he then realized that he would only have one thousand silver dollars for operating costs each month, to be allocated from the building surcharges. With this budget, he could only afford to set up the semblance of a police structure, say, with a few sculptured clay constables to stand guard in the streets.

Yuan Bozhen thought of the idea of setting up a police academy first and using it as a pretext to skim something off for his own pockets. But there were no resources at his disposal other than the allocated building surcharges. To profit under these circumstances, he had to devise a way to increase his revenue, which, once approved by his superiors, could satisfy his desire for personal gain. He worked hard for three to four days and came up with a plan.

Reader, what plan do you think he had in mind? The truth is that Yuan Bozhen at this time was no longer the same man he used to be. He had heard from someone that the Japanese government had instituted a levy on prostitutes, called "discreet surcharge." Divided into three categories, prostitutes were required to pay a monthly fee for their licenses in order to make a living with their bodies. The revenues from this levy were used toward the hiring of police detectives.

Qingjiangpu was a commercial hub. There were easily several hundred prostitutes of any and all descriptions. If every one of them was required, as in Japan, to pay a fee of two to three taels every month, the small sums would add up to a substantial total of one thousand taels. Besides, the levy could be officially declared a deterrent against whoring in an effort to strengthen community morals—a just cause that even his superiors would be hard-pressed not to endorse.

Our good fellow Yuan Bozhen had his mind made up and drafted a proposal accordingly. The core of it argued that prostitutes had earnings every month, over one hundred taels for the successful ones and several tens of taels for the lesser ones. The monthly payment of a fee of two to three taels would not affect them too much. Revenues from the levy would be used to hire policemen, who could in turn protect them from gangsters and thugs. Prostitutes would stand to benefit from this, too.

He made all this sound very sensitive, reasonable, and persuasive. After he finished the draft, he copied it out in the proper official format. On the day of his duty at the tribute grain transport office, he brought it with him and handed it to the director-general. The director-general was appalled at first by the idea of a levy on prostitutes. On reading the proposal closely, however, he found it very well argued. Thereupon, he discussed it with his private secretary and decided to allow Yuan Bozhen to give it a try.

Yuan Bozhen was delighted by the director-general's approval. That same evening, he hired, through a colleague, a secretary called Wu Guixiang from Shaoxing, who had worked as a judicial assistant before,[2] and told him to draw up a proclamation. He then employed a copyist to make over ten copies of it for posting on the walls of thoroughfares and alleyways. He also sent two of his servants to the brothels. The names and birthplaces of prostitutes were compiled into a registry to prevent irregularities like fraud and evasion when the time came to enforce the levy. This gave rise to endless rumors among residents of Qingjiangpu that scared prostitutes and kept them away from their usual business. And so it goes:

> A government proclamation spawns rumors of a disturbing kind;
> The protection of flowers comes not from any love of floral life.

It is not clear what rumors the locals thought up and circulated. Read on to find out in the next chapter.

NOTES

1. The Qing government did establish the Department of Army Training in 1903 with Prince Qing (Yikuang) in charge. It was replaced by the Ministry of War in 1906.

2. Shaoxing of Zhejiang province was famous for its judicial experts, who were well versed in legal stipulations and precedents. Many joined the private staff of officials as tent friends. For "tent friends," see chapter 1, note 12.

The following illustrations are taken from the famous *Dianshizhai huabao* (Dianshizhai pictorial), bound edition (Shanghai: Dianshizhai, 1884–1898). They depict similar situations to those that Yuan Bozhen experienced during his trips to Shanghai and elsewhere in his official postings. (The annotations are the translator's.)

For a complete online edition of this work, see "Dian shi zhai hua bao," http://daten.digitale-sammlungen.de/~db/0007/bsb00075644/images/. For a study of this important source of late Qing urban culture, see Ye Xiaoqing, *The Dianshizhai Pictorial: Shanghai Urban Life, 1884–1898* (Ann Arbor: Center for Chinese Studies, University of Michigan, 2003).

Foreign army drills and troop inspection in Shanghai left a deep impression on Yuan Bozhen; hence, his suggestion to Chief Commander Li, who relayed it to the governor-general of Hubei and Hunan, to adopt foreign drills for the Valiant Defense Army. Seen here is possibly a scene of the Shanghai Volunteer Corps parade at the racecourse. The Volunteers consisted of different nationalities under the command of British officers.

會操存真
西商經起數萬里
外恐受土、
著歎誠國家蒙遺
兵輪往來
作經商各埠以為保
護而兵輪
不能常駐也應有不
測各商自
湧費斧即推知兵之商
人以為說
率以昨教導安常則商也
而遇變即
兵衛身家保貨財計無有
便作此者

Lawlessness sometimes breaks out in a brothel, as seen here when more than ten men are trashing the place because of a feud with its owner or over a prostitute.

大鬧妓院
申江妓院之盛甲於天下嘗見
紈袴少年偕花天
酒地之場作喝雉呼盧之舉
維揚州三月煙花白
下之朝金粉方之茂如矣乃
前夜有博徒十數
周權

The young man has mortgaged family properties for foreign silver dollars, which he has been spending on a prostitute. He is seen being dragged by his mother by his braid off the horse-drawn carriage.

A man and a woman carry on their illicit affair openly in an opium den. While they are chatting cozily and puffing opium, someone plays a practical joke on them by stealing their shoes.

An imposter claiming to be a government agent came to Orchid Fragrance Lane to arrest a prostitute but was bribed off with several tens of silver dollars. When the real agent shows up the next day, a heated dispute ensues. The brothel's pimp wounds the agent with a knife and is arrested by the police. The commotion is depicted in the center left of the drawing. Prostitutes' rooms are seen on the second floor.

提人釀禍
李煥堯

The famous Western-style restaurant Yipingxiang on No. 4 Road (now Fuzhou Road) has an animal exhibition at the front door as an attraction. Before the leopard that is now on display, there were snakes.

全豹

本埠四馬路一品香番菜館前有巴蛇數條供人觀玩近又以巨金購一豹卷養其中有人往視據云豹生不過十閱月而大巳如獅犬哮聲如丞伏籠中喰以生牛肉頃

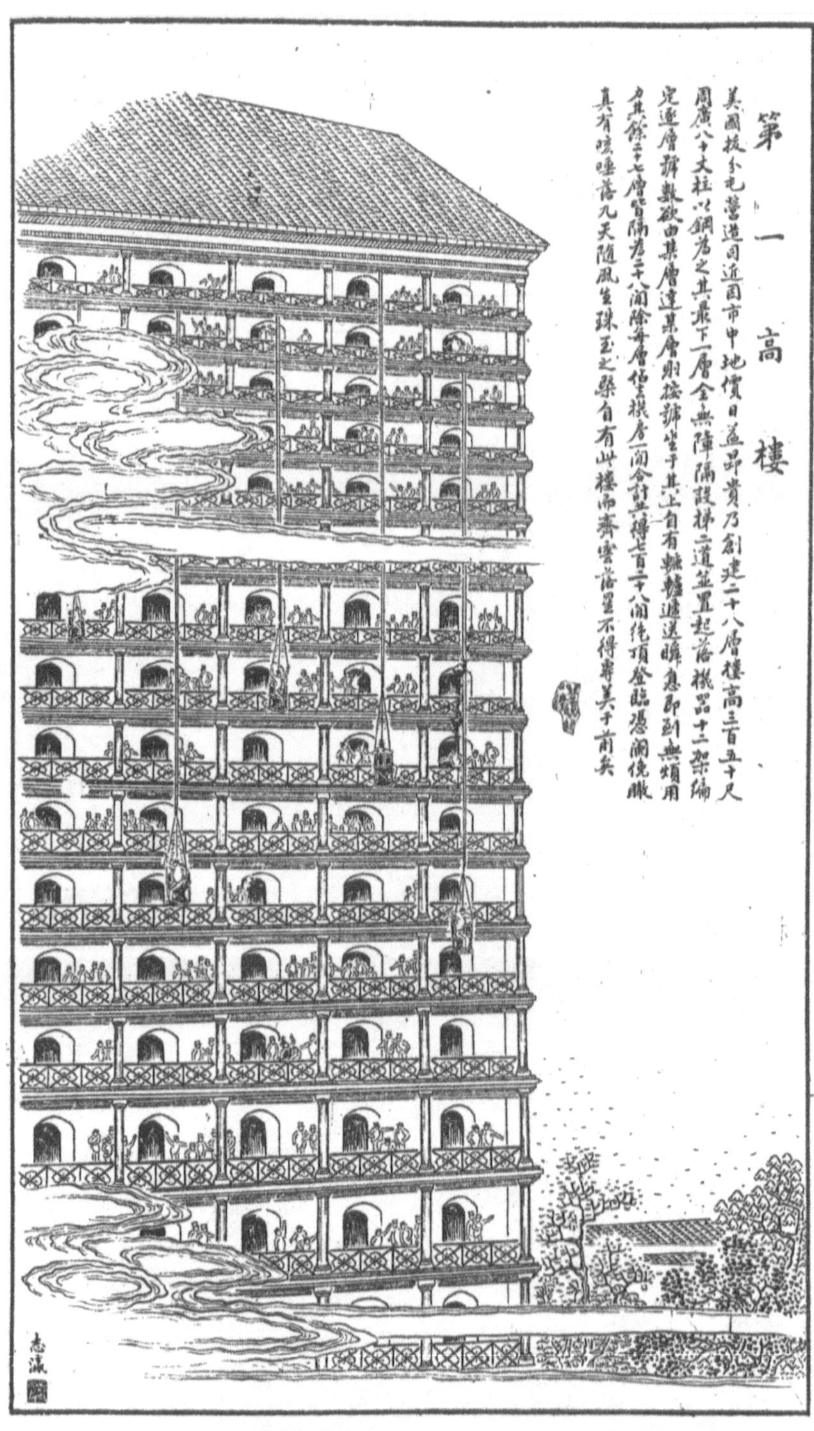

Chinese imagination not only idealized Western government and culture (chap. 1) but also came up with a view of a skyscraper in the United States that was as high as the clouds, with 28 floors, "steel pillars," and elevators operating on the outside.

• *9* •

An old flame cannot reignite
as the nestled bird is scared away;

The heartache lingers as the
male fox sets out to look for a mate.

As we were saying, the people of Qingjiangpu spread all kinds of rumors among themselves as soon as they read the proclamation about the levy on prostitutes to support the police. Some said that the police force should have a budget of its own and questioned the rationale for the levy. It must be, they concluded, for the police officers to fatten their money pouches. Prostitutes were only the start. Soon, all thirty-six trades would be taxed one after another until the whole area was squeezed dry.

Others opined that the levy targeted prostitutes for now but might well be the first step in doing what they did in the foreign concessions in Shanghai. Accordingly, the government would soon hire two surgeons specializing in infectious diseases. They would give prostitutes a physical checkup every week. If their genitalia were found to have contracted diseases, they would be prohibited from receiving customers. Such prevention might well be justified as a police responsibility—nothing to marvel at.

The levy, still others claimed, was a forewarning that prostitution would be banned altogether. Additional heavy dues would keep coming until prostitutes could no longer earn enough to make ends meet.

Finally, there were those who argued that prostitution was not, properly speaking, a business, because it required no capital outlay. If prostitutes were required to pay a surcharge because of the need to establish the police, how could this be considered decent government policy? Besides, since the police would keep a detailed logbook of the prostitutes' facial features and native origins, the police chief would no longer be the chief of police but, patently, the head pimp. His subordinates were likely to get freebies whenever they showed up at brothels.

All this chatter among the locals frightened the prostitutes, who were unsure of what the future might hold. Meanwhile, Yuan Bozhen pretended to hear nothing. While issuing the proclamation for the levy, he obtained the tribute grain transport director-general's permission to hire a former detective of the Shanghai Municipal Council to be the police instructor.[1] With the recruitment of several tens of good-for-nothing young men, he started the academy. After three months or so at his job, the instructor managed to familiarize his students with the basics of policing. They even looked manly when they carried their rifles at right shoulder to march a few steps or stand guard.

Yuan Bozhen saw these results and reported them to the director-general. With the director-general's approval and in accordance with police regulations, he provided each of the academy students with a uniform and a baton and sent them to walk beats in shifts on busy streets.

The local people did not have much to say at first. A half month later, however, two policemen were accused of molesting women in public, and a few others became the butts of jokes, either for gambling or for relieving themselves in the streets. To save face, Yuan Bozhen had every one of these offenders kicked off the force. At the same time, he recruited several tens of the wretched poor and trained them at the police academy for filling future vacant positions.

Ever since his wife had died three or four years earlier, Yuan Bozhen had lived alone. Previously, in Hubei and in Beijing, on festive occasions he had sought pleasure with friends at brothels. Soon after he came to Qingjiangpu, he met a prostitute called Little Jade Phoenix. They became very close. Later, because of the police project, he felt obliged to avoid scandal and distance himself from her. Only when it became too hard to bear would he try to dodge attention and sneak back to Little Jade Phoenix's place for their liaison. Consequently, after the levy was enforced, other prostitutes had to pay several taels every month and put up with the policemen who came to their doorsteps with payment notices. Only Little Jade Phoenix's brothel was spared all this. With its special connection to the police, even gangsters and thugs, with their threats and extortion, stayed away.

Yuan Bozhen assumed that his ties with Little Jade Phoenix were unknown to others. But as the saying goes, "Don't do anything you don't want others to know." The affair between Police Chief Yuan and Little Jade Phoenix was, in fact, common knowledge to every gangster and thug in town. Since Yuan Bozhen did not have too many enemies yet, he was able to get by without incident. But then, in the span of a few days, Yuan Bozhen had dealt harshly with some thugs and fired several of his patrolmen who had been thugs before and who now bore their former chief a huge grudge. They colluded with thugs to look for a chance for revenge.

One night, Yuan Bozhen came home from a party at a colleague's house. Half-drunk, he was reminded of the body's carnal desire next to its craving for alcohol. He changed into flashy clothes. Without telling anyone, he took to the deserted streets and alleyways that led to Little Jade Phoenix's establishment. Along the way, he saw several of his patrolmen loitering here and there in front of houses, either dozing off or smoking. He was glad that none of them noticed him. Only once did he bump into someone who looked like the patrolman Chen the Tiger, whom he had just fired, but he did not make much of it.

When he got to Little Jade Phoenix's brothel, he went straight in. It was close to midnight. There were still banquet guests playing the drinking game of guessing hidden objects in closed fists at the top of their lungs. Seeing it was the police VIP who just walked through the doors, Little Jade Phoenix left her guests right away to go back to her chamber. Sitting cozily by him and putting her arm around his shoulders, she poured out the sweet talk of how much she had missed him. Yuan Bozhen was swept off his feet and could not wait to swallow Little Jade Phoenix whole. He wished so desperately for the loathsome drinkers to leave, so he could get started with her.

After cuddling for a while, they heard, unexpectedly, someone asking on the outside, "Is the Honorable Master Yuan here?" Before Yuan Bozhen could send Little Jade Phoenix to find out who it was and what he wanted, the man was barging into the room. As soon as he saw Yuan Bozhen, he let out a derisive laugh, "My, my! The police chief himself! Is this the kind of place you should come to fool around in?"

As he was speaking, he raised his hand and slapped Yuan Bozhen in the face. He then grabbed Yuan Bozhen's braid and gave it a hard yank. Yuan Bozhen landed instantaneously on the floor. Several more slaps and a kick in the groin followed. Dazed from the beating, Yuan Bozhen could only cry out, "Help!" from the floor, defenseless like a pig under the butcher's knife.

Several more men came in. Little Jade Phoenix witnessed all this and was scared out of her wits. She slipped out through a back door of her chamber into another prostitute's room. These men were about to beat Yuan Bozhen half to death, but Yuan Bozhen's luck did not run out. Some of these men wanted to loot the place. While ransacking the room, they accidentally tipped over an imported kerosene lamp with a glass shade that was sitting on the table. The kerosene spilled and burned, and flames engulfed the whole table. These men saw the serious trouble they started. "Damn!" they cussed as they got out of the room, leaving Yuan Bozhen behind, and scrambled for the way to the front door. Once outside the building, they quickly dispersed.

Left alone in the room, Yuan Bozhen still hurt from the beating. As soon as he saw the flames on the table reaching three to four feet high, he panicked. Despite the aches all over his body, he struggled to get to his feet and shouted for help. He also grabbed the bright-red, satiny cotton quilt from Little Jade Phoenix's bed and threw it over the table. The fire was put out instantly.

At this point, the madam and the pimp-owner of the brothel rushed in. There was the odor of burnt kerosene, but the room was otherwise intact. They saw bruises and bumps on Yuan Bozhen's face, his clothes dirty with dust and ashes, and guessed that he was probably hurt. They called Little Jade Phoenix back into the room to examine his injuries and gave Yuan Bozhen all kinds of pain-killing medicine.

The pimp-owner knelt before Yuan Bozhen on both knees. He explained that he had never expected the thugs to make trouble inside his establishment; when he and others went to look for the police, no policeman was there to be found. As he talked, he knocked his forehead on the floor to apologize. Yuan Bozhen noticed that all those around him were also nervous. He, too, was too frustrated for words and could only gnash his teeth and shake his head.

Little Jade Phoenix told the others to leave the room. She went over to Yuan Bozhen and loosened his clothes to examine his wounds. Fortunately, none of his vital body parts had sustained serious injuries. In a soft voice, she asked Yuan Bozhen if he had ever offended those thugs that they dared act so viciously.

Yuan Bozhen sighed and told her how he had recently punished the thugs and fired some of his patrolmen. He also mentioned bumping into Chen the Tiger on his way over. As he was recounting all this, he came to the conclusion that these men were responsible for the humiliating incident. Little Jade Phoenix nodded. She took out a piece of rough, black cloth from the chest under her bed and used it to massage Yuan Bozhen's bruises for a long time. She then asked Yuan Bozhen to rest and get some sleep.

Yuan Bozhen wondered what happened to the drinking guests from earlier in the courtyard. Little Jade Phoenix replied, "They were long gone, terrified by those men."

Yuan Bozhen decided not to stay until morning. He did not want those at the police station to know what had happened and make a joke of it. He asked Little Jade Phoenix to tell the madam and the pimp to hire a sedan chair for him to go home right away. Little Jade Phoenix could not persuade Yuan Bozhen to stay, and she did what she was told. She saw Yuan Bozhen off in the sedan chair.

Yuan Bozhen notified the police station that he was injured from a stumble and fall after having too much to drink. He lay in bed, too weak even to light his opium pipe; his servant lit it for him. The next day, he sent for a reputable doctor specializing in injuries to treat him and had someone request a ten-day sick leave for him at the director-general's office.

He became enraged whenever he recalled what happened that night. He wanted to make a big fuss about it, but it would be indiscreet for him to do so. He wanted revenge but knew not how to get it. All he could do was order his men in private to find the flimsiest excuse to arrest Chen the Tiger and bring him to the magistrate's office. He was willing to let the whole thing drop after teaching Chen the Tiger a really good lesson.

In the course of the next several days, his injuries healed. He was convinced that it would not be safe to visit Little Jade Phoenix anymore. But life as a widower was lonely and could not go on forever. From that time on, whenever in conversation with colleagues, he expressed his desire for a new wife.

One day, a Manchu Bannerman colleague by the name Fuzhongding mentioned the daughter of a certain Master Kuan.[2] Miss Kuan had studied foreign languages from a tender age. When she was fifteen or sixteen, she accompanied the wife and children of an imperial commissioner who was sent on a diplomatic mission to Britain, France, Italy, and Belgium. She had since returned home. Not only was she fluent in Western languages but she also paid close attention to the politics and social customs of foreign countries. Master Kuan himself had served as a deputy commander-in-chief of a Banner. He was very pleased with the way his daughter turned out and treasured her like a piece of precious jewelry. Although she had reached the age of marriage, she embraced Western principles and insisted that marriage was something for life and must never be dictated by parents. Every man and woman should be able to exercise his and her natural right to choose a spouse.

Yuan Bozhen asked intently, "Is she married now?"

"No, not yet," replied Fuzhongding.

"What a pity!" sighed Yuan Bozhen. "A progressive young lady like that isn't meant for someone like me."

Smiling, Fuzhongding disagreed, "How could Elder Brother say that? An imperial decree has already declared the legality of marriage between Manchu and Han.[3] With Elder Brother's good looks and ability, you can send her your resumé and your photograph with the express intent for marriage. Ask her for a date. I am sure a happy union would result from just a brief encounter."

Reader, Yuan Bozhen was already in his thirties and looking for a second wife. How could he possibly obtain Miss Kuan's consent to marry him?

Clearly, Fuzhongding was teasing him. Yet the toad that fancied the taste of the swan's delicate flesh failed to take notice.

After Fuzhongding left, Yuan Bozhen thought, "This Miss Kuan, with her extraordinary background and remarkable talent, is pretty unique. If I could marry her, I'd gain myself a good wife and use her father's connections when I look for a job or want to fill a post in the future. My only worry is that she won't marry me. What should I do?"

It took only an instant before another thought came to him, "I'm, after all, a provincial degree-holder with the status of an expectant prefect and above all, a protégé of the prince. It's true I'm over thirty but I can still pass muster as someone in his twenties. No one could tell. Besides, there's no need for a matchmaker. It'll all be done through private correspondence. Even if it didn't work out, no one would know. It shouldn't make me look like a fool."

With this conclusion, he decided to act on Fuzhongding's suggestion. First he went to a photographer's studio to have a 7.5-inch photograph taken. Then he wrote his marriage proposal out on a new-style Japanese letter sheet with a golden border. He listed his titles and provided his resumé, along with a statement of his affection for Miss Kuan. After some tacky words as a preamble, he asked for a meeting with Miss Kuan.

With both the photograph and letter ready, he found out Master Kuan's home address. As he was about to send the packet off through the post office,[4] a guard came unexpectedly to the police station to say that the director-general wanted to see him right away. Taken aback by the tone of urgency, Yuan Bozhen had to put his personal affairs aside for now. And so it goes: [original missing].[5]

NOTES

1. The Shanghai Municipal Council began in 1854 as an organization of foreign merchants and later became the virtual governing body of the foreign concessions, with the support of the foreign consuls in the area.

2. The Manchus had organized themselves since the late sixteenth century into units called Banners, eight in all and each with combined social, economic, and military functions. See Mark Elliott, *The Manchu Way: The Eight Banners and Ethnic Identity in Late Imperial China* (Stanford, CA: Stanford University Press, 2002). For historical and other reasons, some Han Chinese were included in the Banner registries.

3. The Qing court officially declared the legality of mixed marriages between Manchus and Han Chinese in 1902.

4. China's modern postal service was in its infancy, with heavy foreign (primarily British) input in terms of organization and personnel. The author specified the role of the post office in Yuan Bozhen's approach to Miss Kuan to highlight the novel aspect

of his courtship. The traditional arranged marriage would have required negotiations between a matchmaker and the parents or elders of both sides.

5. The closing verses of this chapter are missing from all the editions consulted. But the reason does not seem to have been the physical incompleteness or corruption of the original page. In the 1906 edition (2nd printing) of the novel used for this translation, at the end of most chapters, where space is available, there is a decorative artwork. This chapter also has it, so the lack of space would not have been the reason for the missing verses. The omission was very likely an oversight in page layout. The last paragraph reached the end of the line, and the concluding verses would have appeared on a fresh line but were overlooked. Instead, a pictorial design took up the space.

• 10 •

A superior's favor incurs add-on
duties at the correctional center;

In search of marital bliss, a letter
is sent with a marriage proposal.

It so happened, only a few days before, the imperial commissioner sent by Beijing to scrape and skim the wealth off the Jiangnan region had passed through Qingjiangpu.[1] Yuan Bozhen led all his patrolmen to form a line of welcome on his arrival. When he left, Yuan Bozhen again brought all his men out in formation to bid him farewell. All this produced a sycophantic effect that impressed the imperial commissioner not a little.

Before boarding his ship at departure, the commissioner said to the tribute grain transport director-general, "Prefect Yuan is a very capable man. Now, this stretch of the Grand Canal's north bank is infested with thugs, riff-raff, salt smugglers, kidnappers, and other undesirables. Local officials can't keep all of them under control. It may be useful to set up a correctional facility to rehabilitate offenders so as to help them become law-abiding subjects."

The director-general inferred from these remarks something of a special connection, either of blood or social ties, that prompted the imperial commissioner to compliment Yuan Bozhen so openly. Little did he know that the commissioner did not have Yuan Bozhen in mind when he broached the subject of a correctional center. However, acting on the assumption that the commissioner did, the director-general later sent a guard to summon Yuan Bozhen to his office to discuss the matter of setting up a correctional center.

On finding out the reason for the meeting after he saw the director-general, Yuan Bozhen said, "A correctional center goes hand in glove with the police system. We should indeed have one. But the source and amount of its budget will have to be officially allocated and made known to the public by Your Esteemed Person."

93

The director-general thought for a while before saying, "Go ahead and draft the regulations. I'll figure out the funding for it in due course." Yuan Bozhen answered several times in the affirmative before leaving.

Once back at the police station, Yuan Bozhen started drawing up the regulations. Suddenly, he broke out laughing. "Smart as I am, why am I so dumb this time? This thing called correctional center has already been set up in several provinces. Wouldn't it save me a lot of headache if I just wrote to a friend in Hubei province for a copy of the existing regulations and gave them to the director-general as my own handiwork?" His mind made up, he wrote a letter to Intendant Huang in Hubei for a copy of the regulations of the Hubei Correctional Center. He would use them when he received them. We'll leave this for now.

There was an old Buddhist establishment in Qingjiangpu called the Amitabha Monastery. Some twenty to thirty monks lived there. All its land and building assets had come from the donations of members of the Boat Transport Association.[2] Many people also visited there year-round to burn incense and make wishes. Their gifts and donations also added up to quite a tidy sum. Consequently, the monks enjoyed an abundant supply of daily necessities. The life of plenty led all of them, from the abbot to the lowly monk, to break every one of the monastic rules: They smoked, they drank, they frequented brothels, they gambled.

When the Boat Transport Association was still a powerful organization, the monks were under its protection. No one dared lift a finger against them. Ever since the transport of tribute grain and other goods shifted to the sea route, association members had lost their hold on permanent employment and their share of local prominence. The monks, however, showed no sign of recoiling from their extravagant, promiscuous lifestyle. They even colluded with smugglers and bandits and let them use the monastery for their hideouts. Local officials and community leaders were well aware of this but chose to act deaf and dumb. Their reluctance to confront only encouraged the monks to behave more brazenly.

Two months before, a salt smuggler by the name of Li Guobin, while resisting arrest, had injured some guards of the salt control unit in the Jiangyin area. The governor of Jiangsu province issued a warrant to all prefectures and districts in his jurisdiction for Li Guobin's arrest. On receiving it, Yuan Bozhen followed procedure and instructed his subordinates at the police station to keep an eye out for the wanted man.

It so happened that Li Guobin was hiding in the Amitabha Monastery at the time. Yuan Bozhen's men got wind of this. Yuan Bozhen knew that Li Guobin had many followers and did not want to risk danger by capturing him on his own. Aside from relaying the information to the tribute grain transport director-general, he teamed up with the area's battalion officers in a joint operation. They waited until midnight one night to launch a surprise raid on the monastery. They grabbed everyone in sight, monk or no monk, and arrested a total of thirty to forty people. Little did Yuan Bozhen know that one of his men with ties to the salt smugglers had tipped off Li Guobin, who got away.

Yuan Bozhen had the monastery searched thoroughly. Though Li Guobin had escaped, they found massive quantities of foreign rifles, bullets, and contraband goods. Yuan Bozhen left a few of his men to guard the entrance to the monastery and returned to the police station with the rest.

He interrogated the abbot Huixiu about Li Guobin's whereabouts. Huixiu insisted that he did not even know Li Guobin. Yuan Bozhen was furious and ordered his men to give Huixiu two hundred lashes with a rattan stick. Never before in his life had Huixiu suffered such a heavy beating. He subsequently confessed and revealed that Li Guobin was hiding in a small opium den about one-third of a mile away and that the patrolman Zhou Chunrong was the one who had tipped Li Guobin off about the raid.

Yuan Bozhen had Zhou Chunrong brought before him at once. "You cocky son of a bitch!" he cursed. "How dare you let the criminal escape!" He told his men to give Zhou Chunrong four hundred rattan lashes before announcing his decision to send him to Suzhou for the governor to deal with him. On hearing this, Zhou Chunrong fell to his knees, knocking his forehead on the floor, pleading, "Have mercy, Chief! Please, please allow me to capture Li Guobin instead and bring him back. I promise."

"Go then. Make sure you catch him!" ordered Yuan Bozhen. Yuan Bozhen sent thirty patrolmen to go with Zhou Chunrong for the arrest while he asked the battalion soldiers to take the monastery culprits to the district government office for temporary detention. As for the confiscated rifles and ammunition, he had them stored at the police station until the tribute grain transport director-general decided what to do with them.

After taking care of business, Yuan Bozhen smoked opium for a while. Before long, the patrolmen returned, indeed, with Li Guobin in custody. Yuan Bozhen was very pleased. He had Li Guobin brought before him. Once Li's identity was verified as the wanted man, he had shackles put on him as a matter of procedure and told his men to take him to the district government office for incarceration. The whole police station kept busy through the night until daybreak.

The following morning, Yuan Bozhen paid a special visit to the director-general to give a detailed report on Li Guobin's capture and the monks' violation of the law. "In the opinion of Humble Prefect," he added, "the Amitabha Monastery has rich assets. Since the monks have broken the law, it's an opportune time to confiscate their assets and use them for the correctional center. I wonder what Your Esteemed Person would think of this."

Before Yuan Bozhen could finish, the director-general came out with high praise: "Elder Brother, you really are capable and have a sharp mind! We'll handle it the way Elder Brother suggests."

Yuan Bozhen went on, "If so, when will Li Guobin be transferred to the provincial capital? How are the Amitabha Monastery monks going to be dealt with? All of this will have to await Your Esteemed Person's instructions, so the magistrate can take appropriate actions."

"Of course," said the director-general. "There's one problem, though. Since the monastery's assets have now been confiscated, where are the monks going to go?"

Yuan Bozhen replied, "Please allow Humble Prefect to look into this. We could let those monks who so choose return to secular life and take up a different line of work. For those who are unwilling, we could leave twenty to thirty percent of the monastery's assets as the source of their livelihood. The point is to save them from total displacement."

The director-general nodded, "That sounds even better."

On returning to the police station, Yuan Bozhen again set out with several tens of his patrolmen to the Amitabha Monastery to search the abbot's office. They found deeds of the monastery's lands and buildings, made a list of the articles confiscated on-site, and posted a closure notice on the monastery's front gate, where several patrolmen took turns to stand guard at all times.

The community leaders of Qingjiangpu were taken by surprise at the government's sudden action to shut down the Amitabha Monastery. Some of the busybodies inquired discreetly at the magistrate's office and found out the monks' involvement in serious crimes. They decided not to intervene. Several days later, the monks who had been tried and convicted of collusion with the smuggling gang were taken to Suzhou for further interrogation. Those who had simply violated monastic rules were ordered to return to secular life. The rest were granted clemency and set free.

The freed monks returned to the monastery and found the government had shut it down. They were truly reduced to the proverbial state of Absolute Void. Their shock then turned to grief. They stood there facing the entrance and sobbing bitterly for a while. Two of the more intelligent monks said, "It's all our fault. There's no use to cry now. Before it's too late, we can go to our chief patrons to beg them to intercede on our behalf. There may still be a chance to save the situation."

Wiping tears, the other monks agreed. "It makes good sense. Besides, we have no place to go anyway. Let's try to work out our own future."

We will leave the monks to their plans. Meanwhile, after seizing the monastery's deeds, Yuan Bozhen tried for a few days to figure out the actual value of its total assets but got nowhere. As he was about to write to the magistrate with the request to order Huixiu to report all of it, the prominent community leader Zhao Yesheng came to the police station. Yuan Bozhen invited him in. After some small talk, Yuan Bozhen realized that Zhao Yesheng had come to speak on the monks' behalf. An idea came to Yuan Bozhen. He said purposefully, "I'm afraid it's the director-general's decision to confiscate the monastery's property. He even plans to report the case to the throne so it'll go on permanent record. There's nothing I could do or say."

"All very true, of course," replied Zhao Yesheng. "But Grand Venerable Elder certainly has full power in processing the case. Besides, the higher-ups will have no way of finding out the overall value of the monastery's assets. If only Grand Venerable Elder would show the monks a little mercy outside the law, they would be forever so grateful that they would repay you somehow."

Yuan Bozhen said, "If there's anything I could do for them, I would. It wouldn't be for getting anything in return."

Sensing flexibility in Yuan Bozhen's tone, Zhao Yesheng turned bold. "The monks just discussed it among themselves and planned to offer Grand Venerable Elder one thousand taels for making it possible for them to keep half the monastery's assets. Junior Me countered that one thousand taels would be too small an amount. Besides, Grand Venerable Elder is a man of such high principles that he would not accept anything from them. As an alternative, Junior Me suggested, they could make a donation of two thousand taels to the police fund. Then, Grand Venerable Elder might be persuaded to think of something for them—"

Yuan Bozhen did not wait for him to finish before interjecting, "There's no way that they could keep half the monastery's assets. They should consider themselves lucky if they could keep what's not shown in the confiscated books and records."

Zhao Yesheng heard these words and hurried to respond several times in the affirmative. "Please settle it the way Grand Venerable Elder just suggested without going after the other assets. I'll tell them to contribute two thousand taels to the police budget."

Zhao Yesheng was looking earnestly at Yuan Bozhen for a sign of assurance. Yuan Bozhen felt a little uneasy and added, "This can't be decided right away. We'll discuss it further tomorrow." Zhao Yesheng saw that Yuan Bozhen did not want to be rushed. He stood up to leave. Yuan Bozhen let him go without saying anything more.

The next day, Zhao Yesheng, wary of appearing pushy, decided not to go to see Yuan Bozhen himself. Instead, he asked Yuan Bozhen's closest friend,

Yan Zihou, to go on his behalf. Yan Zihou came from the same province as Yuan Bozhen and passed the provincial examination the same year as he did. As soon as Yuan Bozhen saw him, there was no need to beat around the bush. He insisted that the monks pay three thousand taels and he would agree not to go after the monastery's assets that had not been seized or disclosed. Yan Zihou heard the condition and assented to it in full.

Two days passed, and, indeed, the draft for the agreed-upon amount came from the money shop. Yuan Bozhen had assumed that there was not much left of the monastery's assets after the confiscation. Little did he know that most of the monastery's deeds had been mortgaged elsewhere. The nearly ten thousand taels worth of assets that he had uncovered on-site totaled only one-third of the monastery's entire wealth. Yuan Bozhen had gotten the short end of the stick, whereas Yan Zihou and Zhao Yesheng each pocketed far more behind the scene.

After Yuan Bozhen double-checked the list of the monastery's confiscated assets, he entered them in a logbook for presenting to the director-general. His plan was that once the copy of the regulations of the Hubei Correctional Center was in hand, he would set up a local facility accordingly.

Due to the correctional center project and the Li Guobin incident, Yuan Bozhen had delayed sending out his letter and photograph to Miss Kuan. Now that both matters had been settled, he tended to his personal affairs again.

This day, he took out the letter and the photograph and looked closely at them again. Then he placed them into a foreign-style, double-layered pink envelope, made a couple of impressions with his seal on the flap corners, and had a servant take it to the post office. It was sent by registered mail to the Kuan residence.

Reader, one must not assume that Yuan Bozhen had nothing but wealth rolling in by itself or that he was set for good fortune for life. This time around, not only would he run into the misfortune of losing money but he would also meet up with his unlucky star. And so it goes:

> To make a choice on the ballot is supposed to be a civilized act;
> Let's hear the freedom bell toll from the realm of womenfolk.

It is not clear how Miss Kuan would react once she received Yuan Bozhen's letter and photograph. Read on to find out in the next chapter.

NOTES

1. This probably refers to the southern tour of the imperial commissioner Tieliang (1863–1938) in 1904–1905 to investigate and reform the fiscal practices of the provinces in central China. Jiangnan literally means "south of the Yangzi River" but refers to one of the most economically vibrant regions in China, including areas in Jiangsu and Zhejiang provinces, as well as cities like Shanghai and Nanjing.

2. Powerful local and regional organizations had developed along the Grand Canal in connection with the tribute goods transport from the Yangzi delta to Beijing (see chapter 7, note 11). However, as steam navigation came into play in the mid-nineteenth century, these organizations declined in function and prominence, along with the displacement of many whose livelihood had depended on water transport on the Grand Canal.

The dress-up embrace of
Great Universality dazzles every eye;

Vengeance over a private feud
goes public in the newspapers.

As we were saying, this Miss Kuan of the Kuan household was indeed a one-of-a-kind progressive person in all of China. Not only was she proficient in Western languages and conversant with Western customs but she had also traveled to a good number of Western countries. She made many Western friends and had no qualms about mingling with men. It was not out of the ordinary for her to shake hands or exchange kisses with them. As she often declared, "When education for women is promoted, there's no question that women's power will surge. A woman is free to get intimate with any man she desires. This is called a heaven-given human right. Not even her parents and husband are supposed to interfere with it."

For this reason, she was still not married, though she had reached the age of marriage. At the same time, she had been involved in short-lived affairs with more than one of her men friends. Those who knew her past would say that her civilized behavior was far too advanced for them and resisted the thought of marrying her. She had, therefore, waited in vain for her opportunity until now.

One day, Miss Kuan received a letter from a newly founded medical college for women in Shanghai. It was an invitation to her to become an honorary member on the advisory board. As she was packing her bags to go to Shanghai, she got a surprise letter from Yuan Bozhen with the proposal of marriage. Reading it, she thought, "This man understands the courtesy of writing such a letter and is a degree-holder occupying a cushy position. He must be a member of the reform faction."

On examining the photograph, she mused, "He's got passable facial features. But I can't tell anything about his personality from this. Let me write a reply to ask him to meet face to face. If he turns out to be a mild, gentle sort,

I'll settle down for good and become wife and husband with him." She put the letter and photograph away before she wrote a reply, which was mailed from the post office.

No sooner had Yuan Bozhen sent out his letter and photograph than Intendant Huang's reply came from Hubei, along with a copy of the regulations of the correctional center there. Yuan Bozhen had his private secretary Wu make a few changes and copy them out in the format of a formal memorandum. He went to see the director-general of tribute grain transport and presented it to him. As much as the director-general was keen on new policies, he was not completely familiar with the language used in the regulations.[1] After browsing through several lines, he told his servant standing behind him to take the memorandum to his private secretary for official affairs to read and decide. This was why Yuan Bozhen's original submission was not returned until the next day, along with the permission to proceed as proposed.

Once he obtained the authorization, Yuan Bozhen hired a group of masons and carpenters to demolish the Buddhist statues in the Amitabha Monastery and convert the buildings into several tens of workshops and areas for classes and meetings. He also wrote to his old friends in Shanghai, like Shi Daoren and Guan Xiangbin, to ask them to recommend several master artisans who knew how to weave towels and make foreign soaps. Together with the locally hired carpenters, blacksmiths, engravers, and tailors, they would serve as the center's instructors.

Yuan Bozhen was keeping busy with all this when a surprise reply came from Miss Kuan. Inside the envelope was a foreign-made letter sheet on which it was inscribed, "Your proposal was well taken. Please come to our humble home at seven o'clock tomorrow evening so I may properly welcome you.[2] Be sure to come." Yuan Bozhen was beside himself with joy and quickly put the letter away for safekeeping.

The next day, he had a proper shave of his head by a barber. All articles of clothing he was going to wear, from undergarment to gown, were new, as if he was gearing up for an intimate encounter. As the sun was about to set behind the hills, he fetched several of his diamond rings and pieces of jade jewelry and left for the Kuan residence by himself. To the doorman, he stated his request to see Miss Kuan. The doorman was used to seeing the young miss's interactions with men and did not find it odd. He showed Yuan Bozhen to a chair in the reception room and announced Yuan Bozhen's arrival over the partition to the inner chamber.

Shortly afterward, the clacking sound of leather shoes came from behind the partition. Yuan Bozhen quickly lifted his head and saw Miss Kuan coming into the reception room. She was in full Western attire, showing her slim waist and thrusting bosom. Yuan Bozhen lunged forward to shake her hand.

Miss Kuan held his hand and would not let it go, her dark eyes giving Yuan Bozhen's face a searching look.

She asked, with a smile, "Are you the one who sent the letter and photograph the other day?"

"Yes, I am," replied Yuan Bozhen.

"Have you ever traveled abroad, studied Western languages?" asked Miss Kuan.

"I've not been abroad," answered Yuan Bozhen. "I did study English for a while." On hearing this, Miss Kuan sat down with Yuan Bozhen. She started telling him about all her overseas travels and the places she had visited and how useful and indispensable Western languages were. She went on and on and on, adding, "I swear I'll do my best to promote education for Chinese women and propagate women's rights. Will you be willing to support me financially to the best of your ability?"

"It's a tough one," Yuan Bozhen thought to himself. "If I don't agree to support her, this meeting will be the end of my earlier effort. Why don't I just say 'yes' for now and deal with it later?"

"It's a very worthy cause," he replied. "I'll do my best to assist you financially."

"Good, good!" exclaimed Miss Kuan. "Since you are willing to help, will you get two hundred silver dollars ready for me by tomorrow? I have good use for them."

"She said it with a tease," Yuan Bozhen decided. "I mustn't refuse her. Let me settle this right now with my emerald thumb ring."

He stood up, took his emerald thumb ring off, and handed it to Miss Kuan with both hands. Before he could say anything, Miss Kuan was already thanking him, "This is a token of your affection for me. I can only accept it with gratitude. About the two hundred silver dollars we just talked about, I must trouble you to get them ready by tomorrow. Let there be no mistake."

Yuan Bozhen was a little taken aback by Miss Kuan's shrewdness and could only mumble, "Yes, yes. There won't be any mistake." Seeing that Yuan Bozhen had agreed, Miss Kuan told a maid to ask Master Kuan to come out to meet Yuan Bozhen. Yuan Bozhen had no choice but to perform a full salutation on greeting Master Kuan. Master Kuan spoke with an accent of the Beijing dialect.[3] Babbling away, he asked Yuan Bozhen many questions. Although Miss Kuan was sitting beside them, Yuan Bozhen could not very well turn to speak to her. On the pretext of some official business that required attention at the police station, he stood up to take leave of both Master and Miss Kuan.

He went home, in a subdued mood. Through the night, he went back and forth in his mind over the encounter. Being a manly man and a respectable official, he promised Miss Kuan at once the amount of two hundred silver dollars and could not now go back on his words. He still had the monks' money gift. As long as this relationship with Miss Kuan would work out, it should be fine to spend whatever was necessary.

Never mind Yuan Bozhen's own calculations. Let us switch focus. After Yuan Bozhen left, Miss Kuan said to her father, "As your daughter sees it, this man must be a shady character. He is obviously over thirty years old but pretends to be twenty-something. He obviously had a wife before but pretends not to have been married. So your daughter simply played along. It serves him right for me to swindle several hundred taels from him to spend."

Master Kuan disagreed and tried to persuade his daughter, "As I see it, this man may be older than he admits. As an official, he would not dare dump one wife to marry another or have a secret mistress behind his wife's back. Besides, his credentials are solid, not fabricated. I mean, we are a household of noble lineage. If he keeps his promise and sends two hundred silver dollars over tomorrow, we shouldn't toy with him anymore. You have already squandered the years of your youth. If you keep saying who's too good or no good for you, fewer men will come to propose marriage as you get older. Regrets then won't do you any good."

Miss Kuan heard her father's words and saw the truth in them. Without saying anything more, she went back to her room to sleep.

She got up the next morning and had lunch after freshening up. A servant came into her room with a letter, saying that it was from Master Yuan of the police and required an immediate reply. She opened the envelope and found a money draft for two hundred silver dollars, along with a note asking for acknowledgement of its receipt. The note was written in very courteous language. She went over it twice before writing a reply in accord with what her father had said the night before.

She first acknowledged having received the money draft and then invited Yuan Bozhen to another meeting in three days to discuss marriage and related matters. Finally, she enclosed a gem-inlaid gold ring, partly to express her gratitude for the emerald thumb ring that Yuan Bozhen gave her and partly as a token of her consent to marry him. After sealing the envelope, she handed it to her servant to give to the messenger.

Yuan Bozhen had never expected that marriage could be so swiftly arranged. He could barely contain his excitement as he was reading the letter and wasted no time in putting the ring on his finger.

Three days passed. He went to see Miss Kuan, as he was instructed. It turned out to be a far cozier meeting this time than the first. Miss Kuan explained to Yuan Bozhen why she was willing to marry him and told him to arrange all wedding-related matters according to the customs and etiquettes of civilized countries: There would be officiating parents or elders, witnesses, nuptial vows, and signatures on a marriage certificate. Westerners mostly held weddings in a church or a government office. Since there was no such precedent in China, they should find a garden, a fellow provincials' club, or a temple as the venue for the ceremony.

"After the recent makeover," Yuan Bozhen suggested, "the Amitabha Monastery has been refurbished into a school complex, spacious and tasteful. We can have our wedding there. As to the date, we can leave it to the person officiating the ceremony to decide."

"There's no need," interjected Miss Kuan. "I've already told father that the twenty-eighth day of the coming eleventh month on the lunar calendar is going to be New Year's Day according to the Western calendar. We'll get married on that day."

"Very good, very good," Yuan Bozhen agreed.

Yuan Bozhen chatted with Miss Kuan for a long time that day. As he was about to leave, they exchanged a couple of kisses and held hands. Yuan Bozhen then went back to the police station.

Time flew. In the twinkling of an eye, it was the middle of the eleventh month. Yuan Bozhen already had everything meticulously planned, from household furnishings to the wedding banquet. He also rented a new house as their future home. Since there was no family member or relative on his side among the invited guests, he asked an expectant intendant with the same surname but not from his clan to be his officiating elder and Fu-zhongding, his witness.

The renovations at the Amitabha Monastery had been completed, but the hired trade instructors had not yet arrived. Yuan Bozhen went to see the director-general of tribute grain transport to report on the work's completion. At the same time, he requested a leave of absence for five days on account of his marriage with Miss Kuan. The director-general readily gave his approval. After Yuan Bozhen left, the director-general told the accounts department to send a wedding gift to the police station. Yuan Bozhen's colleagues learned the news and sent gifts as well. Those who understood Western ceremonials offered nothing but floral wreaths.[4]

On the morning of the wedding, the Amitabha Monastery was lavishly decorated. After the officiating elders and guests on both sides arrived, Yuan Bozhen, clad in his embroidered robe, set out in a large sedan chair to the Kuan residence to perform the ritual of picking up the bride. A full band of musicians accompanied him, playing drums and trumpets along the way.

Meanwhile, the guests at the Amitabha Monastery did not wait long before seeing Yuan Bozhen and Miss Kuan arrive together as a couple. Miss Kuan did not wear any phoenix headgear or ceremonial cape. To everyone's astonishment, she was dressed instead in an all-white Western dress as if she were mourning a death in the family.[5] Then they saw the couple each take a certificate out from their sleeves and put it on the table. Facing the assembly, they recited their nuptial vows and affixed their signatures to the certificates. Then the officiating elders and witnesses signed the certificates. Finally, husband and wife bowed to each other to conclude the ceremony.

The more informed guests understood that the ceremony was over and went up to the couple to offer good wishes. They thanked them in return. There were only two or three women among the guests, all Miss Kuan's friends. None of them went up to congratulate the couple. There was some disorder among the guests when they were asked to sit down at the banquet tables. It was already two o'clock in the afternoon when the guests finished the feast and left.

According to Western practice, the newlyweds were supposed to go on a trip after the ceremony. Yuan Bozhen had booked a government boat for the purpose. He now went with Miss Kuan in sedan chairs to the pier and boarded the boat. He told the skipper to take it up the canal. They toured some four to five miles before disembarking to return to their residence. From that day forward, when Yuan Bozhen was not at work, he stayed home to enjoy his family bliss.

Several days later, the contracted master artisans arrived from Shanghai. A date was chosen for the inauguration of the correctional center. A good number of instruments and machines had also been purchased for the purpose of teaching inmates a trade.

When Yuan Bozhen came home from the correctional center one day, he picked up one of the Shanghai newspapers that he read every day and started reading it. Before he could finish, he let out a loud cry and pounded his fist on the table. And so it goes:

> Shameful deeds and devious schemes are hard to hide;
> New feuds and old grievances come a-haunting together.

It is not clear why Yuan Bozhen made such an outburst. Read on to find out in the next chapter.

NOTES

1. The original could even be read to suggest that he was not fully literate.

2. Notice the Western clock time used here. It was meant to indicate Miss Kuan's "progressive" lifestyle.

3. The Chinese original is *Jinghua*, better translated in this context as the "Beijing dialect" with its accent. Compare chapter 4, note 4.

4. This is satire. According to Chinese custom, floral wreaths were appropriate for funerals.

5. As befits a Chinese bride in traditional practice, red would be the primary color of her clothing to symbolize good fortune and happiness. Even now, if the ceremony is held in a Christian church where white is the preferred color, the bride will change into predominantly red or colorful garments at some point in the festivities that follow.

$$\bullet \; \textit{12} \; \bullet$$

Harsh words in heated argument
cause affection and fortune to vanish;

Endurance through hardship yields
fruits of fame and riches in the end.

As we were saying, Yuan Bozhen was reading the newspaper, but why did he pound his fist on the table and let out a loud cry? The reason was this. Before Miss Kuan was married, she had a bosom friend named Guo Zizhi from Zhenjiang, a returned student from Japan. They would ride cozily together in a carriage; they even shared the same bed. At the time of the Kuan-Yuan wedding, Guo Zizhi was away on a visit back to Zhenjiang and knew nothing about it. After he came back to Qingjiangpu, he called on Miss Kuan. Only then did he find out that Miss Kuan had gone for another man. Guo Zizhi was furious.

After looking into it, he determined that Yuan Bozhen was the one who initiated the courtship and lured her away. He spent all his time, therefore, digging up dirt in Yuan Bozhen's past to look for a chance for revenge. Before long, he came by information about Yuan Bozhen's embezzlement of funds from the prostitute surcharges and the bribes that he had pocketed in the Amitabha Monastery affair. He wrote to a friend who was working for a newspaper in Shanghai to ask him to publish the information as verified facts. It so happened that this friend was a fellow student of Tianlei's and hated Yuan Bozhen with all his heart for having a hand in Tianlei's death. He had the letter published, along with an editorial postscript in which he wondered aloud if Police Chief Yuan Bozhen's superiors knew anything about his corruption. As Yuan Bozhen was reading the newspaper, he found all that jabbing him where he really hurt. That was why he burst out in a loud cry.

Yuan Bozhen only blamed the newspaper for it but had no idea that Guo Zizhi was behind it. In vehement language, he condemned the newspaper staff. When Miss Kuan heard him, she tried to calm him down, "There's no use cussing now. Maybe you should send Elder Brother Square Hole to

Shanghai to make them happy.[1] Otherwise, the newspaper will keep cranking out stories like that."

Head lowered, Yuan Bozhen thought for a long time but could not come up with a plan. He had no choice but to ask Miss Kuan to write to her friend working for another Shanghai newspaper to think of a way to intercede.

A week later, her friend wrote back. He explained that the editor-in-chief of the newspaper had been a good friend of Tianlei's and was determined to make trouble for Yuan Bozhen. For six hundred taels, however, he would stop writing about Yuan Bozhen in the newspaper. For an additional four hundred taels, making a total of one thousand taels, he would be persuaded to print a retraction to explain that the earlier story about Yuan Bozhen was merely hearsay, not fact. He would not budge for anything less.

Yuan Bozhen read the letter and stamped his feet in remorse, "We shouldn't have asked an intermediary to talk to him. This only encouraged him to jack up his price."

Miss Kuan replied, "It's called 'a water bucket fallen down the well' and makes one liable to extortion. But, wait, I am going to Shanghai because of the women's school of medicine. I'll take this opportunity to level with them. Who knows? Maybe it wouldn't cost us as much as one thousand taels." Yuan Bozhen was unwilling to let Miss Kuan leave home to travel. Miss Kuan, however, just kept insisting, "I have my right to freedom. No one, no matter who, can interfere with it!"

Yuan Bozhen had no choice. He took out one thousand silver dollars and several tens more for travel expenses and gave them to Miss Kuan. He let her pick the date to get on a ship for Shanghai with her maid.

Meanwhile, the director-general of tribute grain transport had read the newspaper account and became suspicious. He confidentially instructed an expectant intendant with the surname Qin to investigate Yuan Bozhen. Qin, a man of the world, was a friend indeed. As soon as he was given the assignment, he let Yuan Bozhen know about it through private channels. Yuan Bozhen was scared and had to ask close friends and colleagues to plead with Qin for a cover-up. After negotiating back and forth several times, Intendant Qin finally showed some willingness to help if Yuan Bozhen would offer him one thousand silver dollars. Yuan Bozhen had no recourse but to agree. Intendant Qin then reported to the director-general that the charges against Yuan Bozhen were all false, fabricated by the newspaper reporter on account of some old grudge. The investigation ended in a complete whitewash.

In a matter of days, Yuan Bozhen reckoned he had squandered some two thousand silver dollars. Together with the wedding costs, he had used up the entire money gift from the Amitabha Monastery monks. Very distraught, he moaned and groaned all day. In addition, there were frequent charges of extortion and abusive behavior against his men at the police station. Moreover, due to slackened security at the correctional center, two inmates had escaped.

Yuan Bozhen grew more and more ill at ease. He came to this conclusion: "If I don't resign my two posts now to get a fresh start, there'll surely be trouble in the offing." He pondered over this for a couple more days. Then, he wrote two letters to Beijing, one for Yangchai and the other for Esteemed Elder Bai, asking them to put in a good word for him to the prince for another cushy job. After the letters were sent, he paid a special visit to the director-general. He explained that the allegations against him in the newspaper, though unfounded, had led him to consider the need to resign his posts in the interest of discretion and avoidance. He asked that someone else be appointed to replace him at the police station and the correctional center.

The director-general knew that Yuan Bozhen was connected to the prince and did not want to treat him lightly. He tried to calm him down, saying, "These jobs pay little and are no doubt demanding. But, please, do stay a couple more months. When the time comes, you'll be duly rewarded with better career opportunities."

Having tried to resign but to no avail, Yuan Bozhen withdrew himself. He was hoping to discuss this with Miss Kuan when she came home. Who would have thought that Miss Kuan was just like the yellow crane that had flown away?[2] Letters to urge her to hasten back only solicited replies about how busy she was in Shanghai: She could barely keep up with all her commitments, like the recent ones at the Women's Center for Vocational Training and the Foreign Women's Dance Club. She would have to wait until the end of the year for a break to come home. Subsequent letters to beckon her back got very much the same responses. There was nothing Yuan Bozhen could do except wait.

He waited until the year-end conclusion of office business, but Miss Kuan was still not home. Only the maid who had accompanied her came back on her own. Yuan Bozhen lost no time in questioning her about madam's activities in Shanghai.

"I'm not sure," the maid replied. "I only saw her go out every day for horse-drawn carriage ride and Western-style dinner. Men and women friends came and went in an endless stream of traffic. She slept out nine nights out of ten."

Yuan Bozhen asked if there were male friends who were particularly close.

"I don't know them all," said the maid, "but there is this man Guo with the nickname 'Mr. Horn' who was the closest." Yuan Bozhen felt dejected after hearing what the maid said.

Several days later, a reply came from Esteemed Elder Bai in Beijing. When Yuan Bozhen opened the envelope, he found a letter of recommendation written by the prince to the director-general. Reader, you should know that of late, the several grandees of the Grand Council were not supposed to write private letters regarding anyone's career prospects.[3] Happily, the prince and the director-general were in-laws and could still write to one another. With the prince's letter in hand, Yuan Bozhen was assured that the gifts he had earlier sent to Esteemed Elder Bai had not been in vain.

He waited until the Chinese New Year before taking the letter with him on his well-wishing visit to the director-general. The director-general read it and found himself in a dilemma. By established practice, provincial appointments in the region were made by the governor-general of Liangjiang. Within his tribute grain transport administration, there was no easy, lucrative job that he could think of. He went back and forth over this in his mind, only to recognize his awkward position. Then he recalled the recent Board of Revenue decision to require all plots of land previously allotted to military households to be converted to regular, taxable farmland.[4] He could use the collection of outstanding dues owed by military households as an opportunity for Yuan Bozhen to make some money.

As soon as government offices resumed work in the new year, he issued an official order for Yuan Bozhen to collect such outstanding land dues, starting in the Liangjiang area. On receiving the assignment, Yuan Bozhen knew that his work would involve a tour of various prefectures and districts. He went to the director-general's office to express gratitude for the appointment. As soon as his duties at the police station and correctional center were taken over by successors, he packed his bags and went on his way.

Yuan Bozhen could not rest easy, however, knowing that Miss Kuan was still in Shanghai. So he started his assessment and collection of land dues owed by military households in Zhenjiang and Changzhou and moved gradually on to Suzhou and Shanghai. Once in Shanghai, he found an inn to settle in. He wasted no time in making his way to the women's school to look for Miss Kuan.

He never expected to have to wait till nightfall before Miss Kuan came back. When husband and wife saw each other, Miss Kuan did not wait for Yuan Bozhen to speak. Instead, she volunteered a full account of how busy she had been over the past several months with invitations to assist in all kinds of women's projects.

"With all that you just talked about," asked Yuan Bozhen, "when do you think you can come home?"

Miss Kuan replied, "What I do here is for advancing the welfare and happiness of our two hundred million women compatriots.[5] As long as I can reach this goal, it doesn't matter even if I have to offer up myself. As for the time to go home, I can't say for sure."

"You must have a little spare time at this hour," said Yuan Bozhen. "Let's go to my inn to talk about something important."

Miss Kuan shook her head. "There's still a banquet I have to go to. I don't have time."

"Who invited you to the banquet?" asked Yuan Bozhen. "Take me along."

"It'd be fine to go with you," replied Miss Kuan, "except that once you get there, you'll have to smoke opium. This habit is not considered civilized. If other people see it, it will make me look bad. So, it's not all right to go with you."

Deep down, Yuan Bozhen was hurt to hear these words. But he sounded nonchalant in his reply: "If you say so; you are free to do whatever you please."

He stood up as he was speaking and left in a fit of anger. Miss Kuan saw Yuan Bozhen's reaction but did not really care. She went to the banquet on her own. There is nothing more to be said about this.

For days after this, Yuan Bozhen closely watched Miss Kuan's activities. After three or four days, he found what the maid had said before to be completely true. He himself even saw the man nicknamed Mr. Horn twice. Miss Kuan did come to the inn several more times, but they were all routine visits. What she did behind his back was really too embarrassing to tell.

One day, Miss Kuan and Mr. Horn were again seen riding in a horse-drawn carriage, her hand holding a large plum flower. They paraded themselves shamelessly together in public. Yuan Bozhen could no longer contain the rage that had filled his chest. When she came to the inn that evening, Yuan Bozhen had a grave look on his face and asked, "Are you having an affair with that Guo character? If not, why did you have time to go carriage-riding with him and none for me?"

"This is exactly my right to freedom," retorted Miss Kuan. "It's a sacred and inviolable right. How dare you interfere with it!"

Yuan Bozhen let out a derisive laugh. "No wonder the government doesn't like reform, and all the reformers had their heads chopped off. It's really true that when one goes to the extremes of reform, one is no different from a beast."

Miss Kuan was furious to hear him compare her to a beast. "I'm no beast!" she blasted back. "You dog-shit officials put up the fierce appearances of tigers and wolves when you deal with the common people. When it comes to foreigners, you show your faces as groveling minions. It's people like you who are beasts!"

"Never mind, never mind!" replied Yuan. "Our life joined together by fate has perhaps come to the end."

"Who cares if it's the end?" Miss Kuan shot back. "Revolution within a family happens all the time.[6] But our marriage was what you first came begging of me, not I of you. Now, after you've wasted the prime years of my life and ruined my maidenhood, you want a revolution. You must compensate me with two thousand taels for the shame you've brought on me. I'll then agree to tear up our marriage certificates and terminate our relationship. If not, I'll find an arbitrator to deal with you and write in the newspapers to make you look bad. Let's see if you could still keep your dog-shit government job!"

Before she could finish, Yuan Bozhen was already trembling with rage and could hardly utter a word. Miss Kuan had said what she had wanted to say. She stormed out of the inn, body erect, bosom thrusting.

Yuan Bozhen had never expected Miss Kuan to be so insensitive, so lacking in fairness. Regretting that he had ever married this wretch of a woman, he sulked through the night. The next day, he came up with an idea. "I'd be ruined if Miss Kuan was serious about money compensation for our separation and would write in the newspapers if I refused to go along. Why don't I stall? I'll leave Shanghai first and write to tell her father about it. I'll then figure out a solution."

His mind made up, he settled his bills at the inn right away. He bought a ticket for an inbound ship up the Yangzi River and left that very day. He stopped at Nanjing to resume his assignment to assess and collect outstanding dues on military plots in the area.

Poor Yuan Bozhen! On his trip to Shanghai this time, he did not have a chance, not even once, to visit a brothel or go for a horse-drawn carriage ride. All he got was a bellyful of frustration. The only upside was that his collection assignment turned out to be a lucrative one. In prefectures and districts with military plots, the supervising lieutenants and captains recognized him to be an agent sent by a superior. So they threw him a welcoming banquet on his arrival and, when he left, presented him with a parting cash gift, ranging from twenty or thirty taels to forty or fifty. Even in areas with no outstanding dues, the officers did the same. The reason was that they realized their military stations would soon be abolished, along with their posts.[7] They therefore availed themselves of every opportunity to ingratiate themselves with people close to the higher-ups so that it might be easier for them when the time came to look for work.

After making his rounds through various prefectures and districts over a period of three months, Yuan Bozhen came home, his money pouch fully loaded. Once back in Qingjiangpu, he went to report to the director-general to conclude his mission.

Yuan Bozhen had worried that once this assignment came to an end, there would be nothing profitable lined up for him. But within a few days, the director-general again summoned him for a meeting. And so it goes:

> There's no need to wait 'til the job is done before reward comes;
> A lucky streak with money is what helps one move up the ranks.

It is not clear for what official business Yuan Bozhen was summoned. Read on to find out in the next chapter.

NOTES

1. The expression refers to money. The Chinese copper cash (coin) had a square hole in the middle. Miss Kuan used "Elder Brother" in this context in part to tease and in part to state the obvious that money could be used to solve Yuan Bozhen's problem.

2. For the reference to the yellow crane, see chapter 4, note 1.

3. The Grand Council was the Qing emperor's advisory and secretarial group. It consisted of a handful (no fixed number) of Manchu nobles and Han Chinese ministers who, as council members, served him on a regular, if not daily, basis.

4. Military households were a feature of the system of military stations or "colonies" (*weisuo*) that the Ming dynasty had established throughout the empire, alongside the system of civil administration. The coexistence of the two systems had been a source of confusion to contemporaries and historians alike. In times of peace, the soldiers were supposed to cultivate the land ("military plots") to achieve some degree of self-sufficiency. After conquest, the Qing government had tried to dissolve these military stations, retaining only those in proximity to the Grand Canal for security. In 1902, as one of the ongoing reforms, the Qing court took the final step to get rid of this Ming relic, along with its structural remains, in its administrative reorganization.

5. Chinese writers during the late Qing routinely estimated their country's population to be four hundred million. The number for women was a simple derivative from that total.

6. For "revolution" (*geming*) as used here, see "Translator's Introduction," note 21.

7. See note 4 above.

• *13* •

Commendation for the intendant status
fulfills a long-standing career desire;

Supervision of school affairs calls for
implementation of authoritarian rules.

As we were saying, Yuan Bozhen went in to see the director-general of
tribute grain transport to find out what instructions he had for him. The
director-general began, "The Board of Revenue has made the decision that
the post of director-general of tribute grain transport will be abolished soon.
But I received a letter yesterday from the prince, saying that it'll be the Old
Buddha's seventieth birthday this fall;[1] all officials should contribute money
toward the celebrations, each according to his rank and post. I think it's still
necessary for me to make such a contribution. But all my immediate subordinates are relatively junior. I don't want to force them to pay. If I donate
several thousand taels on my own, the amount will still be too small. That's
why I want to have a discussion with you and others about this."

On hearing these words, Yuan Bozhen realized that the director-general
probably assumed he had money and expected him to pay a share. A thought
came quickly to him: "I've of late relied on this man for my jobs. Whether his
post is going to be abolished or not, I'll still be seeking his favors later on. I
mustn't turn him down at this point."

So decided, he struck a respectful pose and replied, "What Your Esteemed Person just said is very true. Humble Prefect would be glad to make
a contribution. Your Esteemed Person has so kindly looked after Humble
Prefect all this time. So, for his small part, Humble Prefect wouldn't think of
asking his name to be included on the list of contributors."

"How much, Elder Brother, can you give?" asked the director-general.

Reader, the director-general had expected Yuan Bozhen to be willing to
contribute, at most, one hundred to two hundred taels. To his great surprise,
Yuan Bozhen calmly replied, "Humble Prefect would beg Your Esteemed

117

Person's forgiveness for not being able to do more. He can only offer one thousand taels."

The director-general was ecstatic to hear that Yuan Bozhen was willing to contribute such a large sum. He lavished praise on him. After Yuan Bozhen left, the director-general sent for other officials and hoped that they would do the same. To his dismay, of the seven or eight officials that he summoned, none agreed to give more than two hundred taels, and then only reluctantly. Knowing that Yuan Bozhen was the prince's protégé and seeing how willing he was to help out with a large contribution, the director-general felt beholden and somewhat uneasy. Since his own post would soon come to an end, he was prepared to do Yuan Bozhen a good turn before that happened.

With this in mind, in his official assessment of Yuan Bozhen's work in the collection of outstanding dues on military plots, he rated Yuan Bozhen's performance as exceptional. In a supplementary memorial attached to his report to the throne,[2] he requested that Yuan Bozhen be allowed to skip the step of substantiation in his status as expectant prefect to be elevated to expectant intendant. He informed Yuan Bozhen of this after he had sent out his main and supplementary memorials. Yuan Bozhen had not expected the director-general to favor him with such preferential treatment. Pleasantly surprised, he hurried to perform the kowtow to express his gratitude.[3] We will leave this for now.

As for Miss Kuan, after Yuan Bozhen left Shanghai, she was thinking of asking several people to act as her negotiators. Then, one day, out of the blue, she received her father's letter, asking her not to do anything rash. If Yuan Bozhen, he wrote, should feel that his reputation as husband had been blemished, both sides might end up in litigation. In the end, everyone and everything would be judged according to the *Legal Code of the Great Qing Empire: Statutes and Precedents*.[4] There was no room in it for anyone to justify any behavior in the name of freedom and revolution.

After reading the letter, Miss Kuan wrote her reply: "That being the case, I still want him to pay for my living expenses from now on."

When Yuan Bozhen returned to Qingjiangpu this last time, he met with his father-in-law. Master Kuan first told him about his effort to reason with his daughter. Then he suggested that Yuan Bozhen pay Miss Kuan thirty silver dollars every month as living expenses: "Husband and wife fight all the time. Once my daughter calms down, she'll make up with you." Yuan Bozhen had no choice but to agree. From that day on, he played the part of the knowing husband whose wife was openly cheating on him.

Days passed, and a Board of Appointments document came from Beijing with the throne's approval of the director-general's recommendation. Officials both high and low came to congratulate Yuan Bozhen. It goes without saying that quite a lot of festivities went on at Yuan Bozhen's house.

Reader, ever since Yuan Bozhen heard Intendant Huang's words in Hubei about expectant intendants, he had hoped day and night to get a commendation to become one. Intendant Huang said that of all the current official assignments, the majority went to expectant intendants. Once an expectant intendant, it would be easy for one to land a job as director of some new project, whether in administration, foreign affairs, agriculture, industry, commerce, or mining. Now, with this title finally in hand, Yuan Bozhen felt an indescribable joy, like a scholar who had been personally picked by the emperor to study in the Imperial Academy, or a Buddhist devotee who had attained spiritual enlightenment.

But it was joy mixed with worry in Yuan Bozhen's current state of mind. The joy was that he could now use reform, in his capacity as expectant intendant, as a pretext for raking in enormous amounts of personal wealth. The worry was that once the post of tribute grain transport director-general was abolished, he had no clue as to whom he might turn in the future for patronage.

While Yuan Bozhen was mulling over all this, a foreigner who had travelled from Beijing via the inland canals to Qingjiangpu came to see him. Yuan Bozhen asked him for his name and the purpose of his visit. He replied that his name was Stanley,[5] a good friend of Wilkes's. He had been recruited by the governor-general in Hubei to become instructor at the Normal School and was on his way over there. Wilkes himself had been hired by the prince for a position in the Department of Army Training and had asked him to deliver a letter to thank Master Yuan for arranging the earlier recommendation. Yuan Bozhen took the letter. The two chatted for a long time before Stanley took leave.

After Stanley left, Yuan Bozhen recalled how he had been remiss in communication with the governor-general in Hubei ever since the governor-general went to Beijing for an imperial audience and then returned to his post. It would seem opportune now for him to send the governor-general a letter to convey his fond memories of previously working under him and to get a sense if he would be willing to be his patron again. He thereupon wrote to Chief Commander Li with his letter to the governor-general attached and asked him to forward it on his behalf. He also treated Stanley to a Western-style dinner and asked Stanley to put in a good word for him when he met the governor-general. Stanley readily agreed. The next day, Stanley boarded a ship bound for Hubei.

We need to say no more about Yuan Bozhen's calculations at this time. On the other hand, the governor-general was one who valued his former protégés. When he was in Beijing and took up the task of drafting the regulations and bylaws for the Imperial University, he had Yuan Bozhen busily involved for several months. Whenever he thought of this, he felt a little uneasy. His current efforts to promote education in Hubei needed staff. After receiving Yuan Bozhen's letter and listening to what Stanley had to say, he felt the tug of old ties in his heart even more. He knew Yuan Bozhen could not stay in Qingjiangpu for long, so he sent an official request to the director-general of tribute grain transport for Yuan Bozhen's transfer back to Hubei to help out with the educational projects.

As it happened, the director-general had been hard-pressed to find Yuan Bozhen a good job after successfully recommending him for promotion to expectant intendant. Then the request came for Yuan Bozhen's transfer from the governor-general of a neighboring province. He was only too happy to accommodate and let Yuan Bozhen go. Since Yuan Bozhen did not have any unfinished or pending assignments, the director-general urged him to accept the transfer. Yuan Bozhen did. He visited colleagues and fellow provincials to say good-bye. He also told Master Kuan the news and asked him to relay it to Miss Kuan. On the day of departure, he boarded a vessel to go up the Yangzi River.

Arriving in Hubei, he made his rounds of visits to Intendant Huang, Chief Commander Li, and several other old friends. He next went to see the governor-general and thanked him profusely for his patronage. The governor-general said, "Now that your official status has been elevated, anything not commensurate with it would be inappropriate. For now, you'll take up the job as superintendent of the Normal School. We'll leave the rest to future discussion."

On hearing this, Yuan Bozhen did not think twice before getting on his feet to show his gratitude. They next talked quite a bit about what had happened since they last met. Yuan Bozhen then left.

It is true that Yuan Bozhen had by now made the rank of expectant intendant and enjoyed a grander lifestyle. However, apart from the two servants, he still lived alone, without a wife. He found temporary lodging in an inn and held off making permanent plans until his appointment became official. He stayed there for ten days, but no news came. As he began having doubts, the governor-general's letter finally came to appoint him superintendent of the provincial Middle School. What happened was that the governor-general had forgotten what he told Yuan Bozhen the other day. He did mention the Normal School, but it turned out to be the Middle School instead.

With the letter in hand, Yuan Bozhen went to thank the governor-general for the appointment. He then reported to the school. Knowing that the new school superintendent was coming, the entire student body was on hand to greet him. Yuan Bozhen reviewed the curriculum. There were subjects like military science and law as well as mandatory physical training every Saturday. He did not like it at all. After he returned to the inn that night, he worked out a new curriculum by the lamplight.

There were to be three areas of concentration: moral education, academic education, and physical education. In moral education, only the *Four Books* and *Five Classics* were to be studied.[6] No theories from abroad, such as those about the struggle for survival, natural selection and evolution, equal rights, freedom, and race, were allowed. Academic education consisted only of science, mathematics, geography, and history. Subjects like politics, law, and naval and army studies were excluded. In physical education, strolling and ball games were permitted, but sports days and events such as track meets and race walking were eliminated.

The reason for this design was that foreign philosophies could easily corrupt students' minds. Subjects like politics, law, and military science were not what students should know or learn. Sports days were akin to the promotion of the martial spirit and should be banned as unnecessary.

He also prescribed various forms of greetings. When students met with their superintendent and instructors, they would perform the kowtow to pay their respects and must not display any air of self-importance or arrogance. They were expected to abide by the regulations in their daily speech and behavior. Excessive freedom was shunned. Serious breach of the rules was punishable by expulsion; minor offense would result in a permanent demerit on record.

After he finished drafting the new regulations, he submitted them to the governor-general for his approval the next day. Then he posted them in the classrooms for all to read. The students had by now studied in the school for about two years. After looking over the new regulations, they all denounced Superintendent Yuan in bitter language and called him pigheaded. The smart ones came up with excuses to apply for a leave of absence and gradually dropped out. Only several tens of them who were doggedly bound by their slave mentality stayed on for a few more months before they would graduate. Noticing that many senior students had withdrawn from the school, Yuan Bozhen promoted students from the junior class to fill their vacancies. The upheaval at the school slowly died down.

But the salary for the Middle School superintendent was only five hundred taels a month. During the days when Yuan Bozhen lived with Miss Kuan as husband and wife, he had taken a liking to foreign things. Every aspect of his daily life from home furnishings to meals had been reoriented accordingly. With his current job at the school, it was inconvenient for him to live at the inn for long. So he got himself a house where the furniture and utensils were all of Western style. His salary was simply not enough to cover these expenses. It was his heart's earnest desire that he could stumble on some fortune to support his lavish taste and spending.

Yuan Bozhen's old friends in Hubei were still there, except for Zeng Songsheng, who had gone to Beijing on someone's recommendation to work as an instructor at the Academy of Five City Gates. Yuan Bozhen interacted with them just like in old times. The foreigner Wilkes was gone, but Stanley took his place. Yuan Bozhen met with him often and came to know him quite well.

Stanley received his original training as a mining engineer. He was a very close friend of the managers of the German and French banks. They would do things together whenever they had a chance. Previously, Yuan Bozhen had to give up the mines in Zhushan district halfway through the project. Whenever he looked back, he always thought it a great pity. One day, in casual conversation, he mentioned the mines to Stanley and suggested that Stanley come up with the capital so the mines could become a joint Chinese-foreign venture.

"I'm tied down by my job right now," said Stanley. "Besides, I'm not an explorer, nor am I licensed to prospect mines. Even if the Zhushan mines are exceedingly profitable, I haven't been there to assay them myself. It's impossible for me to find the money for a joint venture based on what you say. If money is the main obstacle that prevents you from working the mines, I could go to the foreign banks to get a loan for you, as long as the governor-general is willing to be the guarantor. Any amount is feasible. There's no need for a joint venture."

On hearing this, Yuan Bozhen instantly recalled that the governor-general had been looking for funds to finance his new projects and had said he might get foreign loans for them. So he followed up: "Would you be able to borrow large sums of foreign money for projects other than mining if the governor-general would be the guarantor?"

"There's no reason that it couldn't be done," replied Stanley. "But in addition to the governor-general's guarantee, there'd have to be assets for collateral." Yuan Bozhen asked for details and kept them in mind.

Two days passed. Yuan Bozhen went to see Chief Commander Li to get a better sense of the governor-general's likelihood to borrow foreign loans and the amounts needed. "The goal at present is to borrow four hundred thousand to five hundred thousand dollars," explained Chief Commander Li. "There have already been over ten offers from lenders. They all fell through because those who handled the negotiation wanted high commissions for themselves. If one could exercise self-restraint and limit the commission to three-hundredths to four-hundredths percent of the amount, the loan should go through without a hitch."

Yuan Bozhen then repeated what Stanley had said about foreign loans. Chief Commander Li remarked, "As I just said, as long as the commission is kept at a reasonable rate, you can go ahead to start the negotiation. I'll bring your proposal to the governor-general's attention." Yuan Bozhen inquired further about assets for collateral. Chief Commander Li replied, "There are the copper coin and steel factories. Any one of these two would do."

Reader, the common saying certainly holds true: "Men would die for wealth; birds would die for feed." From this conversation, Yuan Bozhen came up with the idea to profit himself by arranging foreign loans. He bade goodbye to Chief Commander Li immediately and hastened back to find Stanley at the Normal School. And so it goes:

Apathy is the reaction to the seizure of resources by another race;
National debt is the legacy to be bequeathed to fellow countrymen.

It is not clear what Yuan Bozhen wanted to say to Stanley on meeting him. Read on to find out in the next chapter.

NOTES

1. The Old Buddha was a reference to the empress-dowager Cixi (1835–1908), whose devotion to Buddhism earned her that nickname. She has often been characterized, simplistically, as the de facto ruler of late Qing China for more than forty years, until her death. For a clarification of her role in the tripartite or composite "throne" (as institution) since the early 1860s, see Luke Kwong, *A Mosaic of the Hundred Days: Personalities, Politics, and Ideas of 1898* (Cambridge, MA: Council on East Asian Studies, Harvard University, 1984), chapter 2.

2. A supplementary memorial (*pian*) was like an enclosure in the main memorial (*zou*) but could dwell on a totally unrelated subject.

3. Kowtow is the highest form of respect or obeisance performed to a deity or an authority figure. It involves the prostrate posture and knocking of the forehead on the floor.

4. The compilation of this work began shortly after the Manchu conquest in 1644 with the Ming legal code as the primary reference. Major revisions took place intermittently until the mid-eighteenth century when it achieved its definitive framework, subject to later revisions based on recent precedents. For a partial translation of it, see *The Great Qing Code*, trans. William Jones (Oxford: Clarendon Press, 1994). Also, see Derk Bodde and Clarence Morris, *Law in Imperial China: Exemplified by 190 Ch'ing Dynasty Cases* (Cambridge, MA: Harvard University Press, 1967). Divorce was permissible, often with the husband and his elders as the active party seeking to "eject" (*chu*) the wife from the household (say, if she was childless or failed to show filial piety toward her parents-in-law).

5. It is Xian-de-li in romanization.

6. These were staple readings in the Confucian tradition for China's educated elite.

$$\bullet \quad 14 \quad \bullet$$

Deft skills in making money are
applied to maximize mining profits;

Army duties become a concurrent
job when no other deputy is found.

As we were saying, Yuan Bozhen was overjoyed to hear that Chief Commander Li was willing to speak to the governor-general on his behalf. He went to the Normal School to look for Stanley. As soon as he saw Stanley, he took him into an empty room and asked, "You said the other day that you could arrange foreign loans if the governor-general was the guarantor and there were assets for collateral. Is that really true?"

"Of course it is," answered Stanley.

"If someone wanted a loan now," Yuan Bozhen went on, "what would be the actual amount he'd get for every hundred taels borrowed, minus the commission?"

Stanley replied, "Your country has gone by the standard rate of ninety-five percent in contracting foreign loans."

"Is it possible to get like ninety-seven or ninety-eight percent?" asked Yuan Bozhen.

"Sure, sure. With a higher interest rate, lenders would make such a loan. It's the broker who wouldn't have as much to gain."

Yuan Bozhen continued, "Our government has always borrowed at the annual interest rate of six percent, and occasionally, higher at six and a half percent. If it's seven percent, how much would the broker get for commission?"

"It's hard to speculate," said Stanley. "It all depends on how the loan will be used, the total amount borrowed, and whether the bankers of the lending country will impose additional conditions on top of the interest."

At this point, Yuan Bozhen told Stanley about his conversation with Chief Commander Li. "I see," said Stanley. "There's no need to rush. Let me write to the banks in Shanghai to make inquiries first. I'll let you know."

"Very good, very good," Yuan Bozhen replied. After Yuan Bozhen left, our good man Stanley did write to Shanghai to inquire.

Meanwhile, Yuan Bozhen noticed the need for someone to look after his household affairs during his second sojourn in Hubei. He thought of his late wife Woman Wu's brother, a poor scholar back home without a teaching job in recent years. Yuan Bozhen wrote to him in Xinyu district, asking him to come to Wuchang, where he might find him work. Woman Wu's brother was called Wu Zhishi (literary name Yidong), a mediocre, pedantic type from a small village. On reading Yuan Bozhen's message of affection and concern, there was no reason he would not want to go. He left right away.

One day, Yuan Bozhen came home from the Normal School,[1] and there Wu Yidong was, arriving with tied-up bundles of personal effects on his back. It had been a long time since the in-laws last met. After a few greeting pleasantries, they spent the whole evening chatting.

Next day, Yuan Bozhen went back to the Middle School and picked an argument with the man in charge of the accounting department. He fired him on the spot and replaced him with Wu Yidong the same day. This would save him the cost of caring for Wu Yidong and would furnish, at the same time, an eye and ear personally loyal to him at the school.

Wu Yidong turned out to be an extremely rigid-minded, tightfisted sort. Once he took up the job, he imposed cutbacks on all items of regular expenditure. Even the cooking ingredients for students' meals and the oil they used for their night lamps were not allowed a bit of waste. He bought only the cheapest ingredients and gave not a hoot when students found their food unpalatable. Cutbacks were his only concern. Students were upset and wanted to confront him. They stopped short, however, of a direct showdown out of respect for Superintendent Yuan. Later, after Yuan Bozhen left the Middle School for reassignment to the Provincial Mining Bureau, they could no longer hold back. As a result, they withdrew *en masse* from the school. This happened later, and there is no need to dwell on it now.

Two weeks after their conversation, a messenger came from Stanley to invite Yuan Bozhen over for a meeting. Stanley explained, "The bank's reply has come from Shanghai. The issue price of the loan will be seventy percent of its book value, with seven percent annual interest and one and a half percent commission for those brokering it. The lender will send a representative to oversee the collateral assets before the loan is fully paid off. For a railroad, for example, the supervisor will have complete control over its management; for mines, the supervisor will have complete control over production and marketing of the products. What you need to do now is to confirm what assets the other side is willing to put up for collateral and whether the stipulated arrangement of supervision is acceptable. Their reply will then decide whether it's a go or no go."

Yuan Bozhen lowered his head to think for a while before saying, "You got in touch with the bank, Chief Commander Li introduced the borrower, and I have been the intermediary between you and Chief Commander Li. It's too much of a roundabout way of doing things. Why don't I take you to see Chief Commander Li? The two of you can talk face to face, so I don't have to go back and forth."

"That makes sense," replied Stanley. "Please go with me tomorrow."

"Very good," said Yuan Bozhen.

The next day, Yuan Bozhen indeed took Stanley to see Chief Commander Li. They spoke off and on for seven or eight days. Settlement was in sight. Stanley enclosed details of the arrangement in a letter to the bank in Shanghai and asked for a prompt reply. Another week went by when the bank cabled its agreement to proceed as proposed. A date would have to be set for both sides to sign the contract. The funds could then be transferred.

At this news, Yuan Bozhen crunched the numbers. When the loan went through, minus the share for Chief Commander Li, he would get over six thousand taels for his part. He went to see Chief Commander Li and suggested that they each add several thousand taels to his commission to make a grand total of fifteen thousand taels. With that amount, they could start working the antimony mines in Zhushan district again. Chief Commander Li listened and said it was a very good arrangement.

Another month or so passed quickly by. The loan money had been issued and transferred, and various payoffs distributed. Chief Commander Li went to see the governor-general. Rumor had it, he claimed, that foreigners had recently expressed a desire to take over the antimony mines in Zhushan district. He and Yuan Bozhen planned to prevent the mining rights from falling into foreign hands. They were prepared to raise Chinese capital to work the mines.

In response, the governor-general asked, "Yuan Bozhen already has responsibilities at the school. Can he divert attention to mining, too?"

Chief Commander Li thought for a while before answering, "For three years now, Intendant Huang has been the superintendent of the Provincial Mining Bureau of Hubei. By regulation, it's time to replace him. Wouldn't it be expedient to appoint Yuan Bozhen to succeed him? His duties at the school could be assigned to someone else. It's one solution to two problems. Yuan Bozhen wouldn't have to take on both at the same time."

The governor-general had always listened to Chief Commander Li. After hearing what Chief Commander Li had just said, he nodded in approval.

A day later, without fail, Yuan Bozhen was appointed superintendent of the Provincial Mining Bureau, and his administrative job at the school was given to someone else. Yuan Bozhen submitted a memorandum to thank the governor-general. He kept rather busy for a while because he had to turn over his school duties, on the one hand, and get ready for his new job, on the other.

Unlike the post of Middle School superintendent that came with a fixed salary, the superintendent of the Provincial Mining Bureau was a position capable of generating extra sources of income. As soon as Yuan Bozhen obtained this job, visitors showed up in throng. He became the star among expectant intendants. Moreover, he moved in wider social circles now, with an expanded network of eyes and ears, and came to know all there was to know about the intricacies of making money. When foreign merchants demanded to work the mines at a specific location in a district, he would stall and let the Foreign Matters Bureau handle the troublesome negotiations. If it was Chinese merchants who applied for mining rights, he would make known, through a go-between, the amount of grease money required, based on projected production, for the application to go through. Anything short of the stipulated amount would result in instantaneous rejection on some excuse that it did not meet the Ministry of Commerce regulations, that it ran counter to local interest, and so on. There was no end to this kind of nit-picking. In the event that the mineral ores turned out to be abundant, he would come up with some excuse to reclassify the mines as government-owned and, by hook or by crook, take them over for his own gain.

As to the antimony mines he had once developed in Zhushan district, he sent agents who were familiar with mining to go there with a drilling machine and a water pump and hire workers to set up a processing plant. The operation was in full force in public view again. Those mines were actually very rich in high-grade ores. Now, with plenty of funding and the dedicated effort of local officials to protect them, they yielded huge profits. The one person who was jealous and heartbroken was the former mine owner, Wang Defu. He was filled with so much rage that he wanted to tear Yuan Bozhen in half to vent his ire.

Let's say no more for now about Yuan Bozhen's luster as a star official and his smoothened path to riches, and switch attention to Guangxi province. For ten years now, all of its leading officials like the governor and the military commander-in-chief had been a corrupt, sex-crazed lot. They showed no concern for the country's conditions or the people's well-being; they only cared about scraping wealth off common folks for their own gain. These folks, having been scraped clean, had lost their means of livelihood. They could only join ex–garrison soldiers who had been decommissioned over the years to become bandits. The soldiers who continued to serve in the garrison were supposed to get a monthly stipend. Instead, they received not even half of it because of the graft of their brigade and battalion commanders. In some instances, they were not paid anything at all for more than six months, even up to a year. These were desperate individuals. Driven by poverty, they could only collude with bandits for a share of the loot. Some simply took their uniforms off and left their bases to go about like bandits. They burglarized homes and robbed houses in this expense-free venture.

Consequently, the region of Liuzhou and Qingyuan was infested with bandits. Local officials feared reprimand from the imperial government and kept quiet about it. Later, because of the repeated efforts by "speaking officials" to impeach them,[2] the dire state of affairs was exposed. The imperial court issued a stern warning to the province's leading officials with a deadline for them to stop the proliferation of bandits and exterminate them. Who would have thought that the more attempts were made to get rid of bandits, the more bandits surfaced? Within a year, there was hardly a stretch of land with peace and quiet in the province's jurisdiction of several thousand square *li*. Occasionally, small groups of marauders crossed the provincial border from Hunan to raid the areas of Suining and Chengbu. Fear and anxiety were widespread. Martial law was enforced everywhere.

The governor-general of Hubei had earlier stationed an army near Wugang prefecture to stop outside bandits from infiltrating his jurisdiction. By this time, the larger bandit groups in Guangxi had been eradicated by government troops, but remnants of their forces had dispersed in all directions and spilled into adjoining provinces. Consequently, an emergency had arisen in Hunan, which was the other province under the governor-general's administration.

One day, an urgent telegram came to Hubei from Hunan. The governor-general summoned Chief Commander Li to discuss the need of sending another army to suppress the bandits in Hunan. Reader, the governor-general knew well that Chief Commander Li was nothing but an empty shell of an army man, good in appearance but useless in action. If he were to lead troops to the front, his whole being—heart and soul—would immediately fall apart. Yet it would not be right not to consult with him. After all, he was the director of the province's Bureau of Defense and Garrison Affairs.

Listening to the governor-general, Chief Commander Li thought to himself, "The Guangxi bandits are now like a shot arrow at the end of its flight, a spent force. Even if I personally took charge of the mission, there shouldn't be any danger or harm. But the governor-general definitely would not let me go. After the trouble is quelled, the person who led the field campaign will receive commendation and promotion. The deputy director of the Bureau of Defense and Garrison Affairs is a loyal protégé of mine.

Why not send him to tough it out for a few months so he'll get the commendation and promotion afterward?"

To the governor-general, he replied, "It would be hard to reassign any of the commanders already at their military stations and posts. Only the deputy director of the Bureau of Defense and Garrison Affairs is available. He's familiar with the conditions in Guangxi after spending years there as an expectant official. We could authorize him to get recruits for an army to go to Hunan to bolster defense. He should be able to do the job."

"This sounds good," replied the governor-general. "But then someone else would have to be found to replace him as deputy director."

Chief Commander Li was startled to hear that. Another quick thought flashed through his mind. "There have been all kinds of mismanagement since I became head of the Bureau. If the deputy director is not someone I can trust, he may very well try to score points for himself by exposing my past tracks like a map. What should I do?" Yuan Bozhen came immediately to mind as the only person he could count on when his future career was on the line. It should be all right to give Yuan Bozhen the job.

"The deputy director would have to be an old hand, with relevant experience," he said. "Yuan Bozhen worked under me before as a secretary in the Valiant Defense Army. He's familiar with military affairs. Please, give this man the job."

The governor-general asked, "He has responsibilities at the Mining Bureau already. How could he divide his attention for something else?"

"This shouldn't be a problem," replied Chief Commander Li. "His job at the Mining Bureau is not a demanding one, without much urgent business to preoccupy him. If we concurrently appoint him deputy director of the Bureau of Defense and Garrison Affairs, he's more than capable of handling both."

"In that case," said the governor-general, "we'll settle it the way you suggested." Seeing that the governor-general was willing to go down the path he wanted, Chief Commander Li felt relieved. After he left the governor-general's office, Chief Commander Li told Yuan Bozhen everything that he and the governor-general had discussed. Never even in his dreams had Yuan Bozhen expected to land another lucrative job so easily. He was exceedingly grateful.

A day later, to be sure, the letter of appointment came from the governor-general. On returning home after thanking the governor-general in person, Yuan Bozhen found a houseful of guests who came to congratulate him. On this occasion, even all the brigade and battalion officers showed up. Finally, Intendant Huang arrived in formal attire, complete with cap and gown. As soon as he saw Yuan Bozhen, he clasped his hands in salutation. With a hearty laugh, he said, "Elder Brother, I recall telling you this several years ago: 'Once you get the status of expectant intendant, you'll be made director of some bureau or other.' My words have now come true. You should thank me!"

Yuan Bozhen was about to respond when he saw a man walking hurriedly in, with the look of a weary wayfarer on his face. And so it goes:

Sycophants have maneuvers like monkeys have climbing skills;
Power and profit attract them like mutton's scent attracts ants.

It is not clear who was walking in. Read on to find out in the next chapter.

NOTES

1. This is possibly a mistaken reference for the Middle School where Yuan Bozhen was the superintendent. The context does not suggest that Yuan Bozhen went home after a visit with Stanley at the Normal School.

2. In Chinese dynastic history, there had always been some kind of a built-in mechanism at the imperial court to serve the watchdog function over government policy, officials' conduct and performances, and other issues in the central, provincial, and local administrations. During the Qing dynasty, it was the Censorate with its censors ("speaking officials") that had the responsibility to report and criticize administrative abuses and to impeach officials for misconduct, even on the basis of hearsay (*fengwen*).

$$\cdot\ 15\ \cdot$$

Grandees play favorites with those
who beseech their patronage;

Colleagues throw a banquet to
celebrate his transfer and promotion.

As we were saying, Yuan Bozhen lifted his head to see who was coming in. It turned out to be none other than Zeng Songsheng. What happened was that Yangchai wanted a transfer out of Beijing after serving as an official in the Ministry of Foreign Affairs for two years. But he was not senior enough to get his turn. Details were unclear, but he managed this year to ingratiate himself with Chief Eunuch Cui, who had been a protégé of Rawhide-tanning Li and who could now, for a fee, fix officials up with coveted posts and jobs.[1] Just the month before, several customs superintendents had served their full terms in office and would be replaced. Chief Eunuch Cui did Yangchai a favor by giving him a heads-up that, except for the post at Jiujiang, the other two vacancies at Tianjin and Denglai could each be fetched for thirty thousand to fifty thousand taels.

After Yangchai heard the news, he was determined to get the post at Denglai. He did not expect the negotiation to drag out, only to deadlock at fifty thousand taels, with half, at twenty-five thousand taels, to be paid up-front as down payment. Yangchai tried all he could to raise the money in Beijing but could only come up with seventeen thousand to eighteen thousand taels. He wanted to write to Yuan Bozhen for help, but it would be indiscreet to put something like this down in black and white. Zeng Songsheng, a mutual friend, was in Beijing. It was summer vacation at the Academy of Five City Gates, so Yangchai asked Zeng Songsheng to take the trip for him to discuss the matter with Yuan Bozhen in person.

Zeng Songsheng saw the many guests at the house and did not find it convenient to say what he had come to say. When Yuan Bozhen asked him, he merely explained he was going home on a leave of absence and dropped by

133

for a visit while passing through. He waited until all the guests had left before relaying the message with which Yangchai had entrusted him.

As he was listening, Yuan Bozhen had a thought going through his mind: "The position I just obtained came as a result of Yangchai's long-time help and support. Now Yangchai is asking me for help with his own career. There's no reason I shouldn't give him a hand." Without hesitation, he agreed to offer five thousand taels. He told Zeng Songsheng to first send a coded telegram to Beijing and then remit the money.

Zeng Songsheng stayed at Yuan Bozhen's house for a few days before heading back to Beijing. Yuan Bozhen took the opportunity to buy three hundred to four hundred taels worth of silks, imported goods, and sundry items for Zeng Songsheng to bring back. He also wrote a letter for Zeng Songsheng to take to Yangchai for forwarding, along with the presents, to Esteemed Elder Bai. The letter contained nothing but his plea with Esteemed Elder Bai to put in a good word for him to the prince whenever he got a chance.

After Zeng Songsheng left, Yuan Bozhen mused, "The sudden loss of more than five thousand taels this time couldn't have been helped. I must find a quick way to make up for it." From that time on, he came up with a hundred excuses to squeeze and extract every bit of cash from the Mining Bureau. Likewise, whenever the Bureau of Defense and Garrison Affairs ordered supplies, transferred funds, paid salaries, and did whatnot, he would think of a way to skim something off: whether to inflate the expense claims with false markups or create wholly fictitious quotas. His methods were extremely clever. Not even Chief Commander Li knew anything about it; it was as if he had been fully insulated from all this inside an iron barrel.

We will leave Yuan Bozhen's exploits in Hubei for now and turn our attention to the superintendent of the Department of Educational Affairs in Beijing.[2] After the governor-general had returned to his post in Hubei, the superintendent of educational affairs in Beijing implemented the school regulations and bylaws that the emperor had approved for the whole country. From that time on, all projects to promote education in the provinces would come under his purview. At first, he had much idle time on his hands, and his subordinates, whether transferred from the provinces or specially recruited, were mostly there for window-dressing purposes. What no one had foreseen was that after two years, the provinces really started setting up schools, and the traffic of official correspondence increased in volume to the point of becoming burdensome. Though more staff was hired, they were still shorthanded. It was all due to the fact that school education in China was in its infancy. Among those who were there supposedly to take care of business, few had the experience.

One day, the superintendent of educational affairs noticed that of all the provinces that had established government and private schools, Hubei had the largest number of these and demonstrated the most orderly administration with distinct results. He therefore sent an official communication to the governor-general in Hubei, requesting him to recommend a few of his subordinates who were familiar with educational issues to help out in Beijing.

By this time, the bandits in Guangxi had been suppressed, and the Hubei army deployed earlier to Hunan had been disbanded. With its commander returning to his original post at the Bureau of Defense and Garrison Affairs, Yuan Bozhen's acting stint as deputy director came to an end.

When the governor-general received the education superintendent's official request, he did not want his close aides who were running the schools in the provincial capital to leave his side. He thought of Yuan Bozhen. Yuan Bozhen had helped draft the regulations of the Imperial University, supervised the Middle School after his transfer, and contributed funds to the Japanese language school. Besides, he had just finished his acting appointment at the Bureau of Defense and Garrison Affairs. After discussing it with his private secretaries, he decided to nominate Yuan Bozhen for reassignment to Beijing. We will leave this for now.

Back to Zeng Songsheng. After he left Hubei with Yuan Bozhen's letter and presents, he hurried back to Beijing. He was on the road for half a month before reaching the capital. He went to see Yangchai right away and reported his conversation with Yuan Bozhen in Hubei. Yangchai said, "The money got here from Hubei a few days ago, but it was too late. Someone jumped ahead of me and took the dandy away."

Zeng Songsheng was shocked. "What are you going to do?"

Yangchai replied, "It's a good thing that I only put five hundred taels down for deposit, nothing more, and the rest of the money is in the money shop. The 'other side' felt that they owed me a lot and has been looking hard everywhere for something else for me.[3] They came up with a post in the Department of Finance.[4] But I figured that the Ministry of Foreign Affairs has really good promotion prospects, and I've already gained two to three years of seniority there, with the chance of promotion to an Assistant Secretary.[5] I didn't want to give that up so easily. I talked this over with the 'other side' and pleaded with them to let my brother Yuan Bozhen get the Finance job instead. This is how I'd like to repay my brother for his generosity. They've not yet agreed. When they do, I'll send my brother a telegram to let him know, so he can quit his mining assignment to make haste to Beijing."

"Oh, I see!" said Zeng Songsheng. "But are you going to take the letter and presents your brother asked me to bring back to Esteemed Elder Bai?"

"Why not, since they are already here?" replied Yangchai. "In the event that my brother came to Beijing and the Finance job didn't go through, he'd still have some connection to fall back on." Thereupon, Zeng Songsheng took all the gifts out from his luggage and handed them to Yangchai.

Next day, Yangchai loaded these on his mule-drawn carriage and delivered them in person to Esteemed Elder Bai at the Front Gate customs station. Esteemed Elder Bai was delighted by Yuan Bozhen's thoughtful gesture and quickly accepted the letter and gifts. He left afterward for the prince's residence in the inner section of Beijing city. Seizing a free moment of the prince's time, he asked him earnestly for a job for Yuan Bozhen. The Department of Army Training that the prince had organized was then recruiting staff. After listening to Esteemed Elder Bai, the prince decided to request, in a supplementary memorial to the throne, Yuan Bozhen's transfer to the Department.

For almost a year now, Yuan Bozhen had been given several lucrative jobs in Hubei. He was mindful that his wife living far away in Shanghai was inevitably a target of people's gossip. He therefore wrote a letter to his father-in-law, asking him with great sincerity to persuade Miss Kuan to come back to him in Hubei, so he could save face.

Master Kuan got the letter and, sure enough, did what he was asked to do. He went to Shanghai to talk to his daughter. He mentioned that Yuan Bozhen's current official status had gone up another notch, that Yuan Bozhen had already taken a few cushy jobs in Hubei where the governor-general had shown him special favors. There would no doubt be further promotions to follow soon. His daughter must not be so stubborn as to let all this slip away or, worse, let someone else take her place.[6]

Miss Kuan turned out to be someone who cared only about the outward appearances of reform. She had not yet liberated herself completely from her slave mentality and calculating mind. After listening to her father, she had an abrupt change of heart and decided there and then to put her sponsorship of the women's school and other projects on hold. She accompanied her father to board an Osaka Company steamship the next day to return to Hubei.

At the pier in Wuchang, Master Kuan sent a servant into the city to inform Yuan Bozhen of their arrival. Yuan Bozhen went on board himself to welcome Master Kuan and his daughter and take them home in sedan chairs. At the reunion of the in-laws and of husband and wife, all the earlier ill feelings were blasted out to the outermost reaches of the sky. Nothing more needs to be said about the family bliss that followed.

It so happened that Master Kuan was an old acquaintance of the governor-general's. The following day, Master Kuan put on his travel clothes to pay a visit to the governor-general's office. As soon as the governor-general saw the calling card, he invited him into the reception room. They chatted a bit about old times and each other's life and career since they last met. The governor-general then asked Master Kuan his reason for coming to Hubei. Master Kuan briefly explained the matter of escorting his daughter back to her husband, Yuan Bozhen.

"My, oh, my! Intendant Yuan is Elder Brother's son-in-law!" The governor-general was taken by surprise. "This man is very capable. Just the other day, the superintendent of the Department of Educational Affairs in Beijing sent an official request for me to recommend people familiar with educational matters to go to the capital. I've decided to nominate him. I haven't announced it yet. When you go back, could you please get the word to him?"

Hearing this, Master Kuan thought, "Yuan Bozhen is sure lucky. This transfer by nomination will lead to riches and promotions. I'm so glad I've brought my daughter back. Otherwise, once he's gone to Beijing, he'll cast my daughter aside."

They chatted some more before Master Kuan took leave of the governor-general to go back to the Yuan residence. He went straight into the main section of the residence to look for Yuan Bozhen; he wanted to let him know what the governor-general had just told him. Along the way, he ran into Yuan Bozhen, who had a letter in hand and a grin on his face. As it happened, Yangchai's effort to secure the Finance job for Yuan Bozhen had come off. It was a letter from him asking Yuan Bozhen to quit his mining post to go to Beijing at once. Yuan Bozhen showed Master Kuan the letter, and Master Kuan also repeated the governor-general's words about recommending Yuan Bozhen to work in Beijing.

Yuan Bozhen said, "It looks like we'll be going to Beijing one way or the other. The government here will have to appoint someone else to take care of mining anyway. I don't need to resign."

Master Kuan remarked, "All I can say is that I just got here with my daughter, thinking that I could relax for a couple of days. There was no warning that both of you would be leaving for the north so soon. We've hardly sat down long enough to warm our seats."

"So true," Yuan Bozhen agreed. He then went back into the bedchamber to tell Miss Kuan to start packing her luggage again.

The next turn of events was nothing short of amazing. As soon as the governor-general sent out his reply to the education superintendent by courier, with Yuan Bozhen's credentials attached, an official communication came from the Department of Army Training. It conveyed that the prince had requested Intendant Yuan Bozhen's transfer to the Department and that Yuan Bozhen be instructed to report to Beijing at once. The governor-general read it and was amazed by what he read. He summoned Yuan Bozhen right away and showed him the communication. Congratulating him, he inquired into Yuan Bozhen's connection with the prince. Yuan Bozhen told him everything.

"I see," replied the governor-general. "But my recommendation of you to the education superintendent has just gone out and can't be retrieved. In any case, you'll have to go to Beijing. When you see the prince and the education superintendent, you'll decide for yourself which job you'll take. You're free to explain your reason for accepting one and turning the other down."

Reader, in a matter of just a few days, Yuan Bozhen received three pieces of good news: one from the Department of Army Training, one from the Department of Educational Affairs, and one from the Department of Finance. All three offices were newly established after the imperial court had decided to implement reforms to strengthen the country. A job with any of these three was something coveted by all expectant intendants but really out of reach for most of them. Ever since Yuan Bozhen put on the phony appearance as a promoter of reform, he had managed to rise from an honorary assistant prefect to an expectant intendant. His maneuvers even landed him three of the most lucrative jobs offered by powerful officials. The man was truly a cut above all others. The favors and honors bestowed on him were of a unique, superior kind.

By the time he left the governor-general's office, all those with expectant statuses in Hubei's provincial capital had heard the news. They all commented, "It's a worthwhile tale to tell when one of us gets to be such a hotshot!" Several busybodies took it upon themselves to organize a celebratory function, with expenses paid by those attending. It was a banquet with more than ten round tables, complete with a performance by a Beijing opera troupe. The venue was the Jiangxi Fellow Provincials Club. It was a group invitation to Yuan Bozhen to the wining, dining, and entertainment occasion, partly to congratulate him on his transfer and partly to bid him farewell. Yuan Bozhen could not refuse and showed appreciation of their kindness with his presence.

After three rounds of toasts, Intendant Huang stood up and poured a full cup of wine. He said to Yuan Bozhen, "Congratulations, Elder Brother! Remember the time when I told you that once you become an expectant intendant, you'll have the chance to take on any assignment, whether in domestic or foreign affairs or in agriculture, industry, commerce, or mining. My words have now come true. What's more, the jobs that you've been offered came as a result of the recommendations to the throne by the grandees in Beijing. Truly, as expectant intendants go, you are unique. Take this cup and drink up. Make this farewell party the beginning of your smooth journey of ten thousand miles into the future."

Yuan Bozhen thanked him, took the cup, and drank up. Others watched. Then the guests from other tables took turns to toast him. After drinking more than ten cups of wine, Yuan Bozhen could not help but feel a little tipsy. He stood up and spat out whatever popped into his head. His words turned out to be totally heartless and untrue but also, at the same time, utterly heartfelt and true. And so it goes:

> Vital clues are spelled out for all aspirants in officialdom;
> No one must make light of warnings to benefit these times.

It is not clear what Yuan Bozhen had to say. Read on to find out in the next chapter.

NOTES

1. Rawhide-tanning Li was the nickname of Chief Eunuch Li Lianying, possibly because of his family background of processing animal hides. Both Li Lianying and Cui (Yugui) were well-known eunuchs during the late Qing. Castrated males had been a perennial institution inside the imperial palace. The need for a man's physical strength without threat to the court ladies' virtue was obvious. Possibly because of their problematic gender, eunuchs were generally looked down on in Chinese society, though, occasionally, some seized power for themselves and dominated imperial administration because of their proximity to their masters.

2. Set up after the Boxer Rebellion, it was replaced a few years later (1906) by the Ministry of Education.

3. When it was inconvenient, for one reason or another, to identify a third party by name in a conversation or in writing, the practice was to refer to him as *qiantu*, literally meaning "the road ahead" or "the prospect." Here, "they" or "the other side" best conveys the meaning, with Chief Eunuch Cui understood as the referent.

4. It was an office established to oversee financial reform after the Boxer Rebellion and replaced by the Ministry of Finance in 1906.

5. In chapter 5, Yuan Bozhen knew that Yangchai was serving as a department director in the Ministry of Foreign Affairs.

6. In the original, "her place" is supposed to be the status of a *gaoming furen*, an honorary ladyship conferred by imperial edict on the wife of a high-ranking official who had rendered extraordinary service to the throne. This was Master Kuan's exaggerated projection of Yuan Bozhen's future career to persuade his daughter to go back to him.

$$\cdot \; 16 \; \cdot$$

Once the mask is stripped away,
the tracks of the past are fully revealed;

In a lyrical poem, warm-hearted
but trite, the point of the tale is unveiled.

*A*s we were saying, after downing more than ten cups of wine, Yuan Bozhen was a little drunk as he stood up to speak: "I'm honored by your great kindness and generous reception. I was nothing but a poor scholar before. Looking back on my life, I should be happy with what I've come to achieve. When one gets to Beijing, one's wishes won't go beyond the dual goal of 'promotions up official ranks and making riches.' But 'promotions up official ranks and making riches' have to start somewhere. For this reason, what I've always liked best and hoped the most to see is that our imperial court will implement policies of change and reform. Why do I wish for these so much? It's because every new program started by our imperial court will open up an extra source of income and another round of commendations for us expectant officials.

"Take, for instance, the current situation in Jiangsu province. There are more than three hundred expectant intendants and more than five hundred expectant magistrates hanging around for their chances. Without the new policies, how else would the government possibly take care of so many of them? Therefore, new policies are the life pills for people like us with expectant statuses. Without them, we would most definitely starve to death.

"I do have a piece of advice for you, gentlemen. Though ten thousand mouths today might chant 'reform, reform' in unison, you mustn't take reform too seriously. You should only take on the appearances of reform, not the spirit of it. You must bear in mind that the spirit of reform is the fountainhead of misfortune and disaster. Switch to the appearances of reform, and the shortcut to promotions and riches will reveal itself to you. If you, gentlemen, believe these words of mine, you'll find your own path to riches and prosperity and continue to get them until your old age, without ever having to feel dejected or lost."

Behold! Yuan Bozhen cited his own experiences in his speech as an object lesson to illustrate the hidden tricks in recent officialdom. In concise, succinct language, Yuan Bozhen spelled out at once all that is left on this storyteller's mind, leaving him with nothing more to do except quit writing here and now.

However, there is one final point to make. Where there is cause, there is effect. The current topic of reform, despite its multitudinous strands and threads, can be grouped under three major headings: education, finance, and army. All three must indeed be promoted at the same time, and none should be neglected. This is what reformers, both authentic and phony, have said in common. Since the cause of the phony reformer is double-sided, his goal is also double-sided; since his goal is double-sided, its result is also double-sided. This storyteller has tried to sort out the causes, objectives, and results of Yuan Bozhen's actions and deeds and playfully sums them up in a diagram. Take it, if you will, as a mere passable guide to the current state of our officialdom.

Cause
↓
The desire for promotions and riches

As superintendent of the provincial Middle School	In charge of the Provincial Mining Bureau	As deputy director of the Bureau of Defense and Garrison Affairs
Contributes school start-up fund	Collects dues owed by military households	Sets up police academy
Drafts university regulations	Sets up correctional center	Proposes hiring of foreign drill instructor
	Sets up camphor company	
	Develops the Zhushan antimony mines	
	Purchases copper coin machine	
Promotion of education (Department of Educational Affairs*)	Financial management (Department of Finance*)	Training of armed forces (Department of Army Training*)
To mimic the civilized way	To forestall revolution†	To profit those above at the expense of those below†

Objectives
↓
Result
↓
Phony reform

*As noted in earlier chapters, the Qing court did establish the Department of Educational Affairs, the Department of Finance, and the Department of Army Training in the post-Boxer period. They were replaced by the Ministry of Education, Ministry of Finance, and Ministry of War in 1906. At the time of the author's writing, changes in government structure and institutional labels were very much a part of the ongoing reforms.

†In the original, as translated here, the objective of "Financial management" and that of "Training of armed forces" were printed by mistake in each other's columns instead of under their correct departments.

Thus, people like Yuan Bozhen hold fast to "phony" as the key word and remain phony in whatever they do. Take, for instance, those who start modern schools. They may give the appearance of starting modern schools, but, in fact, they get by simply by changing the names of old academies. Those who set up police systems may give the appearance of setting up police systems, but, in fact, they get by simply by putting uniforms on thugs. Those who establish chambers of commerce may give the appearance of establishing chambers of commerce, but, in fact, they get by simply by changing the regulations and bylaws of old government offices. By the same token, the extortion of money from the people in the name of government bonds and the appeasement of foreign powers in the name of diplomacy all show the contradiction between name and reality. There is no need to cite every example. Indeed, none of this is worth a laugh.

However, readers must not make light of phony reformers. They should keep in mind that in this world of ours, where there is the authentic article, there is the impostor; vice versa, where there is the impostor, there is the authentic article. A few phony reformers make a start, and hundreds of thousands of authentic reformers will follow. At this time, those who promote schools understand the essence of education. Those who talk about troop training emphasize the quality of soldiery. Those who are in fiscal management dare not only extort and embezzle but also learn, gradually, the principle of strengthening the country through agriculture, industry, commerce, and mining. Some of the leading provincial officials have even petitioned the throne in memorials to adopt constitutional monarchy and to send missions abroad to examine political practices in foreign countries. They treat reform with extraordinary sincerity. To trace all this back to its origins, one finds that it is all because phony reformers have paved the way and authentic reformers follow in their footsteps.

Westerners who study human science and the theory of the struggle for survival have said it well. Humans have evolved from monkeys, and monkeys have evolved from dogs. In primordial times, dogs were the only animals that could sit up to look far. With the most developed thinking faculty of all animals, they gradually evolved into monkeys. A long, long time later, monkeys with greater thinking ability evolved gradually into humans. This storyteller is of the opinion that the earlier reforms in China belonged to the age comparable to the age when dogs evolved into monkeys. The reforms in the future would be like the times when monkeys evolved into humans. He has therefore written this novel about Yuan Bozhen with the modest hope that phony reformers will gradually evolve and become, every one of them, authentic reformers.

This novel has been concocted out of thin air and contains whatever came to this author's mind. Both the characters and events depicted did not exist or happen. Readers should not get too serious about them and should take this simply as a leisure read. Yuan Bozhen is not based on verified facts, and Yuan Weixian is only fictitious.[1] He who reads it and gets all stirred up is a fool.

However, there is one additional observation to make: Yuan Bozhen was situated in the transition when some dogs became monkeys and some monkeys became humans, but we definitely cannot say he was fully human with human dignity. To call him a dog or a monkey, however, is something he would never have willingly accepted. In all fairness, he did use reform as a cover for his pursuit of promotions and riches. This novel writer decided, therefore, to give this work a fitting title, *The Phony Reformer*. In addition, he has composed a crudely worded lyrical poem to conclude the book's sixteen chapters. And so it goes:

(To follow the tonal meter of "The Charms of Niannu")[2]

> On a banner hung high
> Across the wide, open stage,
> The two characters for "reform"[3]
> Are boldly displayed.
> A shift in approach to go after riches
> Makes for a keen discernment of the age.
> A mask to deceive and empty words for mischief,
> The shortcut proves the way to succeed.
> Laugh not at them, gentlemen,
> For cold-blooded are half of them.
> In Ueno Garden, so they say,
> And on Rue J.-J. Rousseau in Paris,
> Their bronze statues still stand tall today.[4]
> May heaven pity a China beaten up and wan.
> Let brave men of talent to its rescue come.
> Make changes of substance from within,
> Forge ahead, pave the way, and
> Follow the sages in earnest steps.
> Incense burned and prayers prayed,
> May the new turn of fate begin this very day.

NOTES

1. Yuan Weixian is Yuan Bozhen's other name. See chapter 1.
2. The lyrical poem began as *lyrics* composed to a particular musical tune during the Tang dynasty (618–907) but evolved into an independent form of poetry during

the Northern Song (960–1127). "The Charms of Niannu" is allegedly a tune once favored by the Tang female singer/entertainer Niannu.

3. The Chinese term for reform comprises the two characters *wei* and *xin*. See "Translator's Introduction," note 7.

4. This is a joint reference to the Meiji Japanese leader and rebel Saigo Takamori (1828–1877) and the Enlightenment thinker and writer Jean-Jacques Rousseau (1712–1778). See "Translator's Introduction," note 28.

Bibliography

Bickers, Robert, and R. G. Tiedemann, eds. *The Boxers, China, and the World.* Lanham, MD: Rowman & Littlefield, 2007.

Bodde, Derk, and Clarence Morris. *Law in Imperial China: Exemplified by 190 Ch'ing Dynasty Cases.* Cambridge, MA: Harvard University Press, 1967.

Chu, Samuel, and Kwang-ching Liu, eds. *Li Hung-chang and China's Early Modernization.* Armonk, NY: M. E. Sharpe, 1994.

Cohen, Paul. *History in Three Keys: The Boxers as Event, Experience, and Myth.* New York: Columbia University Press, 1998.

Confucius. *Confucian Analects, The Great Learning & The Doctrine of the Mean.* Translated by James Legge. New York: Dover Publications, 1971.

"Dian shi zhai hua bao" (Dianshizhai pictorial). http://daten.digitale-sammlungen .de/~db/0007/bsb00075644/images/.

Dianshizhai huabao (Dianshizhai pictorial). Bound edition. Shanghai: Dianshizhai, 1884–1898.

Dieming (Anonymous). *Guanchang weixin ji* (The phony reformer). Shanghai: Shanghai gudianwenxue chubanshe, 1956.

Dieming (Anonymous). *Guanchang weixin ji* (The phony reformer). Shanghai: Zhonghua shuju, 1959.

Dieming (Anonymous). *Guanchang weixin ji* (The phony reformer). Taibei: Shijie shuju, 1976.

Dieming (Anonymous). *Xindang shengguan facai ji* (The phony reformer). 2nd printing. Shanghai: Zuoxin she, 1906.

Dieming (Anonymous). *Xindang shengguan facai ji* (The phony reformer). In the combined volume *Xindang shengguan facai ji, Hou guanchang xianxing ji* (A sequel to *Guanchang xianxing ji*, An exposure of the officials' world), and *Lengyan guan* (Observations with an impartial eye), in the series, *Zhongguo jindai xiaoshuo daxi* (A comprehensive collection of novels published in the modern period). Nanchang: Baihuazhou wenyi chubanshe, 1991.

Elliott, Mark. *The Manchu Way: The Eight Banners and Ethnic Identity in Late Imperial China.* Stanford, CA: Stanford University Press, 2002.

Elman, Benjamin. *A Cultural History of Civil Examinations in Late Imperial China.* Berkeley: University of California Press, 2000.

Esherick, Joseph. *The Origins of the Boxer Rebellion.* Berkeley: University of California Press, 1987.

Fan, Tiequan, and Xiangji Kong. "Keming dangren Ji Yihui zhongyao shishi shukao" (Investigation into important aspects of the life of the revolutionary Ji Yihui). *Lishi yanjiu* (Historical research), no. 5 (2013): 173–82.

Feuerwerker, Albert. *China's Early Industrialization: Sheng Hsuan-huai (1844–1916) and Mandarin Enterprise.* Cambridge, MA: Harvard University Press, 1958.

Fitzgerald, John. *Awakening China.* Stanford, CA: Stanford University Press, 1996.

Folsom, Kenneth. *Friends, Guests, and Colleagues: The Mu-fu System in the Late Ch'ing Period.* Berkeley: University of California Press, 1968.

"The Grand Canal." UNESCO. http://whc.unesco.org/en/list/1443.

The Great Qing Code. Translated by William Jones. Oxford: Clarendon Press, 1994.

Halsey, Stephen. "Sovereignty, Self-Strengthening, and Steamships in Late Imperial China." *Journal of Asian History* 48, no. 1 (2014): 81–111.

Hao, Yen-p'ing. *The Comprador in Nineteenth Century China: Bridge Between East and West.* Cambridge, MA: Harvard University Press, 1970.

Hershatter, Gail. *Dangerous Pleasures: Prostitution and Modernity in Twentieth-Century Shanghai.* Berkeley: University of California Press, 1997.

Horesh, Niv. *Chinese Money in Global Context: Historic Junctures Between 600 BCE and 2012.* Stanford, CA: Stanford University Press, 2014.

Judge, Joan. *Print and Politics: "Shibao" and the Culture of Reform in Late Qing China.* Stanford, CA: Stanford University Press, 1997.

Kaske, Elisabeth. "Fund-Raising Wars: Office Selling and Interprovincial Finance in Nineteenth-Century China." *Harvard Journal of Asiatic Studies* 71, no. 1 (2011): 69–141.

Ko, Dorothy. *Cinderella's Sisters: A Revisionist History of Footbinding.* Berkeley: University of California Press, 2005.

Ko, Dorothy. *Every Step a Lotus: Shoes for Bound Feet.* Berkeley: University of California Press, 2001.

Kuhn, Philip. *Rebellion and Its Enemies in Late Imperial China: Militarization and Social Structure, 1796–1864.* Cambridge, MA: Harvard University Press, 1970.

Kwong, Luke. *A Mosaic of the Hundred Days: Personalities, Politics, and Ideas of 1898.* Cambridge, MA: Council on East Asian Studies, Harvard University, 1984.

Kwong, Luke. "The Rise of the Linear Perspective on History and Time in Late Qing China (c. 1860–1911)." *Past & Present* 173 (2001): 157–90.

Liu, Kwang-ching. *Anglo-American Steamship Rivalry in China, 1862–74.* Cambridge, MA: Harvard University Press, 1962.

Liu, Lydia, Rebecca Karl, and Dorothy Ko, eds. *The Birth of Chinese Feminism: Essential Texts in Transnational Theory.* New York: Columbia University Press, 2013.

Lu Xun. *A Brief History of Chinese Fiction.* Translated by Yang Xianyi and Gladys Yang. Beijing: Foreign Languages Press, 1959.

Lu Xun. *Zhongguo xiaoshuo shi lue* (A brief history of Chinese fiction). Beijing: Dongfang chubanshe, 1996.

Mao, Zedong. *Mao Zedong junshi wenji* (Mao Zedong's writings on military affairs). 6 vols. Beijing: Junshi chubanshe and Zhongyang wenxian chubanshe, 1994.

Murphey, Rhoads. *Shanghai: Key to Modern China.* Cambridge, MA: Harvard University Press, 1953.

Naquin, Susan, and Evelyn Rawski. *Chinese Society in the Eighteenth Century.* New Haven, CT: Yale University Press, 1987.

Nivison, David. "Protest Against Conventions and Conventions of Protest." In *The Confucian Persuasion,* edited by Arthur Wright, 177–201. Stanford, CA: Stanford University Press, 1960.

Porter, Jonathan. *Tseng Kuo-fan's Private Bureaucracy.* Berkeley: Center for Chinese Studies, University of California, 1972.

Pusey, James. *China and Charles Darwin.* Cambridge, MA: Harvard University Asia Center, 1983.

Qian, Xingcun (A Ying). *Wanqing xiaoshuo shi* (A history of the late Qing novel). Beijing: Renmin wenxue chubanshe, 1980.

Reynolds, Douglas (with Carol T. Reynolds). *East Meets East: Chinese Discover the Modern World in Japan, 1854–1898.* Ann Arbor, MI: Association for Asian Studies, 2014.

Rowe, William. *Hankow: Commerce and Society in a Chinese City, 1796–1889.* Stanford, CA: Stanford University Press, 1984.

Rowe, William. *Hankow: Conflict and Community in a Chinese City.* Stanford, CA: Stanford University Press, 1989.

Schwartz, Benjamin. *In Search of Wealth and Power: Yen Fu and the West.* Cambridge, MA: Harvard University Press, 1964.

Spence, Jonathan. "Opium Smoking in Ch'ing China." In *Conflict and Control in Late Imperial China,* edited by Frederic Wakeman and Carolyn Grant, 143–73. Berkeley: University of California Press, 1975.

Sweeten, Alan. *Christianity in Rural China: Conflict and Accommodation in Jiangxi Province, 1860–1900.* Ann Arbor: University of Michigan Center for Chinese Studies, 2001.

Tu, Wei-ming. "Cultural China: The Periphery as the Center." *Daedalus* 120, no. 2 (1991): 1–32.

Von Glahn, Richard. "Foreign Silver Coins in the Market Culture of Nineteenth Century China." *International Journal of Asian Studies* 4, no. 1 (2007): 51–79.

Wagner, Rudolf. "Joining the Global Imaginaire: The Shanghai Illustrated Newspaper *Dianshizhai huabao.*" In *Joining the Global Public: Word, Image, and City in Early Chinese Newspapers, 1870–1910,* edited by Rudolf Wagner, 105–73. Albany: State University of New York Press, 2007.

Wagner, Rudolf, ed. *Joining the Global Public: Word, Image, and City in Early Chinese Newspapers, 1870–1910.* Albany: State University of New York Press, 2007.

Wang, David. *Fin-de-Siècle Splendor: Repressed Modernities of Late Qing Fiction, 1848–1911.* Stanford, CA: Stanford University Press, 1997.

Wright, Mary, ed. *China in Revolution: The First Phase, 1900–1913*. New Haven, CT: Yale University Press, 1968.

Ye, Xiaoqing. *The Dianshizhai Pictorial: Shanghai Urban Life, 1884–1898*. Ann Arbor: Center for Chinese Studies, University of Michigan, 2003.

Yeh, Wen-hsin. *Shanghai Splendor: A Cultural History, 1843–1945*. Berkeley: University of California Press, 2007.

Zheng, Yangwen. *The Social Life of Opium in China*. Cambridge: Cambridge University Press, 2005.

Zou, Zhenhuan. "Ji Yuancheng ji qi chuangban di Zuoxin she yu *Dalu bao*" (Ji Yuancheng and the Zuoxin she and the *Continent* that he established). *Anhui daxue xuebao zhexue shehui kexue ban* (Journal of Anhui University: Philosophy and Social Sciences), no. 6 (2012): 106–16.

SUGGESTED READINGS

Studies on modern or late imperial China have greatly multiplied over the last half century. The following are select works that, together with the titles listed above, serve as a starting point for readers who wish to explore historical themes touched on in the novel. The bibliographies and notes in these works should also be helpful. As is well known in the field, the *Bibliography of Asian Studies*, published online by the Association for Asian Studies, has an extensive coverage of articles and books on China. Access requires subscription, which university libraries are likely to have.

General

Historical encyclopedias and biographical dictionaries are useful. David Pong, editor in chief, *Encyclopedia of Modern China*, 4 vols. (Detroit, MI: Charles Scribner's Sons, 2009) provides a quick reference to many of the late Qing personalities, events, and institutions. Although dated, Arthur Hummel, ed., *Eminent Chinese of the Ch'ing period (1644–1912)*, 2 vols. (Washington, DC: US Government Printing Office, 1943–1944) is still a handy tool for basic research. Endymion Wilkinson, *Chinese History: A New Manual*, 4th edition (Cambridge, MA: Harvard University Asia Center, 2015) encompasses the whole of Chinese history and, as such, furnishes an intelligent guide through the interim dynasties to the late Qing. For broad coverage of historical themes of the period, the two volumes of *The Cambridge History of China* for the late Qing, vol. 10, ed. John Fairbank, and vol. 11, eds. John Fairbank and Kwang-Ching Liu (Cambridge: Cambridge University Press, 1978 and 1980), contain highly readable essays based on solid research by an earlier generation of scholars.

For Qing administrative terms in English, often with brief annotations, two works are recommended: H. S. Brunnert and V. V. Hagelstrom, *Present Day Political Organization of China* (Shanghai: Book World, 1912) and E-tu Zen Sun, *Ch'ing Administrative Terms* (Cambridge, MA: Harvard University Press, 1961).

Modern Press, Fiction, and New Print Culture

The essays in Cynthia J. Brokaw and Kai-Wing Chow, eds., *Printing and Book Culture in Late Imperial China* (Berkeley: University of California Press, 2005) discuss Chinese book printing in earlier times and its modern developments. The Chinese transition from wood block to Western-style printing is deftly told in Christopher Reed, *Gutenberg in Shanghai: Chinese Print Capitalism, 1876–1905* (Vancouver: University of British Columbia Press, 2004). Tobie Meyer-Fong attempts an admirable literature review on related topics in "The Printed World: Books, Publishing Culture, and Society in Late Imperial China," *Journal of Asian Studies* 66, no. 3 (2007): 787–817. Also useful are Natascha Vittinghoff, "Readers, Publishers and Officials in the Contest for a Public Voice and the Rise of a Modern Press in Late Qing China (1860–1880)," *T'oung Pao* 87, nos. 4/5 (2001): 393–455; and Henrietta Harrison, "Newspapers and Nationalism in Rural China 1890–1929," *Past & Present*, no. 166 (2000): 181–204.

The essays in Milena Doleželová-Velingerová, ed., *The Chinese Novel at the Turn of the Century* (Toronto: Toronto University Press, 1980) revisit some of the best-known late Qing novels and fiction writers. Perry Link elucidates not only a subgenre of late Qing fiction in *Mandarin Ducks and Butterflies: Popular Fiction in Early Twentieth Century Chinese Cities* (Berkeley: University of California Press, 1981) but also the advances in late Qing printing technology. The many fiction magazines published during the late Qing and early Republic deserve a close examination, as is given of the early years of *Xiaoshuo yuebao* (Short story magazine) in Denise Gimpel, *Lost Voices of Modernity: A Chinese Popular Fiction Magazine in Context* (Honolulu: University of Hawai'i Press, 2001).

Government and Foreign Relations

Many of the novel's episodes unfold at the subprovincial and provincial levels. Kung-chuan Hsiao, *Rural China: Imperial Control in the Nineteenth Century* (Seattle: University of Washington Press, 1960) has a wealth of information on the Qing empire's rural areas. T'ung-tsu Ch'ü examines the prefectures and districts ("the smallest administrative units" under imperial rule) in *Local Government in China under the Ch'ing* (Cambridge, MA: Harvard University Press, 1962). While John Watt concentrates on a vital link in local government in *The District Magistrate in Late Imperial China* (New York: Columbia University Press, 1972), Bradly Reed presents a lucid picture of the power and influence of government underlings in *Talons and Teeth: County Clerks and Runners in the Qing Dynasty* (Stanford, CA: Stanford University Press, 2000).

Further up the power scale, Kent Guy analyzes the development of provincial administration from the Qing conquest to the High Qing in *Qing Governors and Their Provinces: The Evolution of Territorial Administration in China, 1644–1796* (Seattle: University of Washington Press, 2010). For a refreshing if somewhat controversial account of the imperial top and center, see Evelyn Rawski, *The Last Emperors: A Social History of Qing Imperial Institutions* (Berkeley: University of California Press, 1998).

Foreign contact motivated many of the late Qing reforms. The following essays in the two volumes of *Cambridge History of China* delineate an overall framework of the late Qing Sino-foreign intercourse: in vol. 10, Frederic Wakeman, "The Canton Trade and the Opium War," 107–62; John Fairbank, "The Creation of the Treaty System," 163–212; Joseph Fletcher, "Sino-Russian Relations, 1800-62," 318-50; in vol. 11, Immanuel Hsu, "Late Ch'ing Foreign Relations, 1866–1905," 70–141; Marius Jansen, "Japan and the Chinese Revolution of 1911," 339–74.

Two aspects merit special attention. First, the Zongli Yamen (Office for the general management of trade affairs with various countries), created in 1861, attested to a broadening of the Qing approach to foreign relations from the old tributary ties (with lesser neighboring countries) to the treaty system. Two works on the Zongli Yamen remain standard references: S. M. Meng, *The Tsungli Yamen: Its Organization and Functions* (Cambridge, MA: East Asian Research Center, Harvard University, 1962) and Masataka Banno, *China and the West, 1858–1861: The Origins of the Tsungli Yamen* (Cambridge, MA: Harvard University Press, 1964). A more recent study is Jennifer Rudolph, *Negotiated Power in Late Imperial China: The Zongli Yamen and the Politics of Reform* (Ithaca, NY: East Asia Program, Cornell University, 2008).

Second, extraterritoriality (the exemption from the native legal and penal procedures) and consular jurisdiction (the consul's legal oversight of fellow nationals in a foreign country) were the legal pillars of the foreign presence in China from the midnineteenth century until the mid-twentieth century. Both of these are explored in depth in Wesley Fishel, *The End of Extraterritoriality in China* (Berkeley: University of California Press, 1952); and Pär Kristoffer Cassel, *Grounds of Judgment: Extraterritoriality and Imperial Power in Nineteenth-Century China and Japan* (Oxford: Oxford University Press, 2012).

Elite Status, Examinations, and Credential Sales

Ping-ti Ho tackles elite mobility from a deep historical perspective in *The Ladder of Success in Imperial China: Aspects of Social Mobility, 1368–1911* (New York: Columbia University Press, 1962). Another classic on the subject is Chung-li Chang, *The Chinese Gentry: Studies on Their Role in Nineteenth Century Chinese Society* (Seattle: University of Washington Press, 1955). Later researchers have employed more refined and focused approaches. See, for example, the essays in Joseph Esherick and Mary Rankin, eds., *Chinese Local Elites and Patterns of Dominance* (Berkeley: University of California Press, 1990). For a reflective case study of elite women during the late Qing, see Nanxiu Qian, *Politics, Poetics, and Gender in Late Qing China: Xue Shaohui and the Era of Reform* (Stanford, CA: Stanford University Press, 2015).

Benjamin Elman's continued interest in the civil service examinations (see his 2000 work, cited in the bibliography) led to the publication of his more recent *Civil Examinations and Meritocracy in Late Imperial China* (Cambridge, MA: Harvard University Press, 2013). With a catchy title, Miyazaki Ichisada, *China's Examination Hell: The Civil Service Examinations of Imperial China,* trans. Conrad Schirokauer (New Haven, CT: Yale University Press, 1981) is informative. Johanna Menzel Meskill puts together a useful collection of scholarly views on the subject (to the mid-twentieth century) in *The Chinese Civil Service: Career Open to Talent?* (Boston: Heath, 1963). Whatever shortcomings the Chinese might have found in the examination system, foreign assessment was not all harsh or negative, as discussed by Ssu-yu Teng in "Chinese Influence on the Western Examination System," *Harvard Journal of Asiatic Studies* 7, no. 4 (1943): 267–312.

The legal sale of offices and titles afforded opportunities for career advancement but also encouraged abuses. Where money for such sales changed hands, greed and fraud crept in. Two studies published in the 2010s examine the criminal activities of middlemen and low-ranking government personnel along the money trail: Elisabeth Kaske, "Metropolitan Clerks and Venality in Qing China: The Great 1830 Forgery Case," *T'oung Pao* 98 (2012): 217–69; and Mark McNicholas, "Scamming the Purchase-of-Rank System in Qing China," *Late Imperial China* 34, no. 1 (2013): 108–36. Interestingly, the legal sale of credentials was extended to wealthy overseas Chinese during the last Qing decades. See Ching-hwang Yen, "Ch'ing's Sale of Honours and the Chinese Leadership in Singapore and Malaya (1877–1912)," in *Journal of Southeast Asian Studies* 1, no. 2 (1970): 20–32.

Reforms before and after the Boxer Rebellion

For the scope of post-Boxer reforms, see Chuzo Ichiko, "Political and Institutional Reform, 1901–11," in *Cambridge History of China*, 11:375–415; also, Douglas Reynolds, *China, 1898–1912: The Xinzheng Revolution and Japan* (Cambridge, MA: Council on East Asian Studies, Harvard University, 1993). For a wide array of topics pertaining to reform during the late Qing, see the workshop papers in Paul Cohen and John Schrecker, eds., *Reform in Nineteenth-Century China* (Cambridge, MA: East Asian Research Center, Harvard University, 1976). Ting-yee Kuo and Kwang-ching Liu undertake a review of government projects in the second half of the nineteenth century in "Self-Strengthening: The Pursuit of Western Technology," *Cambridge History of China*, 10:491–542. Hao Chang addresses the intellectual aspects of change in "Intellectual Change and the Reform Movement, 1890–98," *Cambridge History of China*, 11:274–338. The problematic time frame in its title notwithstanding, Rebecca Karl and Peter Zarrow, eds., *Rethinking the 1898 Reform Period: Political and Cultural Change in Late Qing China* (Cambridge, MA: Harvard University Asia Center, 2002) contains insightful essays. A broader investigation into the cultural dilemma as educated Chinese during the late Qing and early Republican periods, including fiction writers, struggled to accommodate tradition and modernity in their outlook is Theodore Huters, *Bringing the World Home: Appropriating the West in Late Qing and Early Republican China* (Honolulu: University of Hawai'i Press, 2005). Finally, Joseph Levenson, *Confucian China and Its Modern Fate: A Trilogy* (Berkeley: University of California Press, 1968) emphasizes cultural tensions and is always a stimulating read.

Returned Students and "Old China Hands"

"Returned students" from abroad were agents of change, especially when they were recognized as such and placed in responsible positions by the government. See

Shaohui Deng, "Government Awards to Students Trained Abroad, 1871–1911," in *China, 1895–1912: State-Sponsored Reforms and China's Late Qing Revolution*, ed. and trans. Douglas Reynolds, special issue of *Chinese Studies in History* 28, nos. 3–4 (1995): 35–48. For Chinese students who went to Japan, see Paula Harrell, *Sowing the Seeds of Change: Chinese Students, Japanese Teachers, 1895–1905* (Stanford, CA: Stanford University Press, 1992). A parallel case is examined in Edward Rhoads, *Stepping Forth into the World: The Chinese Educational Mission to the United States, 1872–81* (Hong Kong: Hong Kong University Press, 2011); also, Weili Ye, *Seeking Modernity in China's Name: Chinese Students in the United States, 1900–1927* (Stanford, CA: Stanford University Press, 2001).

Westerners who spent long years living and working in Qing China also played a role. Well-known figures like W. A. P. Martin (1827–1916), Timothy Richard (1845–1919), John Fryer (1839–1928), and Robert Hart (1835–1911) helped shape Chinese attitudes to change, as discussed in Jonathan Spence, *To Change China: Western Advisers in China, 1620–1960* (Boston: Little, Brown, 1969). In particular, Robert Hart, a British diplomat turned Qing official, had worked for more than forty years as inspector-general of the Imperial Maritime Custom Service, taken part in nearly all major diplomatic negotiations on the Qing government's behalf, and assisted in developing, among other things, China's postal service. His correspondence and diary are valuable for his firsthand observations on contemporary events, policies, politics, and personalities. See John Fairbank et al., eds., *The I. G. in Peking, Letters of Robert Hart, Chinese Maritime Customs, 1868–1907*, 2 vols. (Cambridge, MA: Harvard University Press, 1975); Katherine Bruner et al., eds., *Entering China's Service: Robert Hart's Journals, 1854–1863* (Cambridge, MA: Harvard University Asia Center, 1986); Richard Smith et al., eds., *Robert Hart and China's Early Modernization: His Journals, 1863–1866* (Cambridge, MA: Harvard University Asia Center, 1991).

Military, Educational, and Financial Reforms

Yuan Bozhen's claim to fame rested on his supposed expertise in military, educational, and financial affairs. These were three of the major areas in which many of the post-Boxer reforms took shape. For the military aspect, Ralph Powell, *The Rise of Chinese Military Power, 1895–1912* (Princeton, NJ: Princeton University Press, 1955) traces the connections between the new armies and early Republican warlord politics. Against the genteel male ideal (suggestively termed the "silk-fan attitudes") since the Song dynasty, Nicolas Schillinger explains how Chinese military reforms since the late nineteenth century had aimed to fashion tough fighting men out of army recruits in *The Body and Military Masculinity in Late Qing and Early Republican China* (Lanham, MD: Rowman & Littlefield, 2016). "Silk-fan attitudes" is used in Joseph Levenson, *Revolution and Cosmopolitanism: The Western Stage and the Chinese Stages* (Berkeley: University of California Press, 1971), 1, and mentioned in Frederic Wakeman, "Foreword," xii–xiii. Yuan Shikai, a high Qing official and, later, president of the Chinese Republic, was privy to Qing China's programs of military modernization, as discussed in Stephen Mackinnon, *Power and Politics in Late Imperial China: Yuan Shi-kai in Beijing and Tianjin, 1901–1908* (Berkeley: University of California Press, 1980).

For educational reform, William Ayers focuses on a pivotal figure, possibly the inspiration for the novel's portrayal of the governor-general who assigned Yuan Bozhen to educational projects in Hubei province and in Beijing, in *Chang Chih-tung and Educational Reform in China* (Cambridge, MA: Harvard University Press, 1971). Marianne Bastid appraises the role of a "modern gentry," exemplified by Zhang Jian (1853–1926), in promoting gradualist change in *Educational Reform in Early 20th-Century China*, trans. Paul Bailey (Ann Arbor: Center for Chinese Studies, University of Michigan, 1988). Paul Bailey recounts the late Qing efforts that laid the groundwork for future Chinese educational discourse in *Reform the People: Changing Attitudes towards Popular Education in Early Twentieth-Century China* (Vancouver: University of British Columbia Press, 1990).

Finally, Yuan Bozhen's so-called financial know-how was confined mainly to his role in a few projects that might have qualified him as an "official-entrepreneur." Wellington Chan provides a penetrating look at the political and financial nexuses between the imperial government and merchants, in *Merchants, Mandarins, and Modern Enterprise in Late Ch'ing China* (Cambridge, MA: Harvard University Asia Center, 1977). Again, with the governor-general Zhang Zhidong as focus, Thomas Kennedy explores an important project in Hubei, in "Chang Chih-tung and the Struggle for Strategic Industrialization: The Establishment of the Hanyang Arsenal, 1884–1895," *Harvard Journal of Asiatic Studies* 30 (1973): 154–82. John Stanley tells the fascinating tale of Hu Guangyong (1825–1885), whose roles in native banking, military logistics, and foreign loans were legendary, in *Late Ch'ing Finance: Hu Kuang-yung as an Innovator* (Cambridge, MA: Harvard University Asia Center, 1961).

Prostitution and Gender Relations

Matthew Sommer, *Sex, Law, and Society in Late Imperial China* (Stanford, CA: Stanford University Press, 2000) is an important study of Qing regulation of sexuality and sex-related activities, including prostitution. Elizabeth Remick discusses, among other things, the "prostitute tax," which featured in the novel as a financial resource earmarked for the local police, in *Regulating Prostitution in China: Gender, and Local Statebuilding, 1900–1937* (Stanford, CA: Stanford University Press, 2014). For a fine collection of essays illustrating the "historical-social jurisprudence" approach to Chinese legal practice, past and present, with case studies on marriage, divorce, rape, and so on, see Philip Huang and Kathryn Bernhardt, eds., *The History and Theory of Legal Practice in China* (Leiden, NE: Brill, 2014).

Gender studies in the China field have grown significantly in the past several decades. Though over half of its sixteen chapters deals with the post-Qing period, Susan Brownell and Jeffrey N. Wasserstrom, eds., *Chinese Femininities/Chinese Masculinities: A Reader* (Berkeley: University of California Press, 2002) comprises well-argued studies that illuminate the past. Ann Pang-White, ed., *The Bloomsbury Research Handbook of Chinese Philosophy and Gender* (London and New York: Bloomsbury Publishing, 2016) takes a close look at the historical influence of Confucianism, Daoism, and Buddhism on Chinese gender issues. Covering a chronological scope from the eighteenth to late twentieth centuries, Beverly Bossler, ed., *Gender and*

Chinese History: Transformative Encounters (Seattle: University of Washington Press, 2015) is notable for exploring the meanings of gendered encounters. For another perceptive overview, see Susan Mann, *Gender and Sexuality in Modern Chinese History* (Cambridge: Cambridge University Press, 2011). The journal *Nan Nü: Men, Women, and Gender in China* is a good place to locate articles on related topics in recent or ongoing research.

Bandits, Salt Smugglers, Eunuchs

Phil Billingsley, *Bandits in Republican China* (Stanford, CA: Stanford University Press, 1988) is a pioneering work that should be read together with a later, coauthored article, Youwei Xu and Philip Billingsley, "'Out of the Closet': China's Historians 'Discover' Republican-Period Bandits," *Modern China* 28, no. 4 (2002): 467–99. Although its focus is on bandits along the China-Vietnam border, Bradley Davis, *Imperial Bandits: Outlaws and Rebels in the China-Vietnam Borderlands* (Seattle: University of Washington Press, 2017) throws light on the novel's episode involving bandits in the *provincial* "borderlands," where government control tended to be weak.

Where government control seemed tight, as over the production and distribution of salt, smuggling tended to be rampant (see the Li Guobin episode in chapter 10 of the novel). For a study of the wealthy merchants who gained the right to produce and distribute this daily necessity, see Ping-ti Ho, "The Salt Merchants of Yang-chou: A Study of Commercial Capitalism in 18th Century China," *Harvard Journal of Asiatic Studies* 17 (1954): 130–68. Also useful is Man Bun Kwan, *The Salt Merchants of Tianjin: State-Making and Civil Society in Late Imperial China* (Honolulu: University of Hawai'i Press, 2001). For the Qing and, later, Republican efforts to reform the salt administration, see Samuel Adshead, *The Modernization of the Chinese Salt Administration, 1900–1920* (Cambridge, MA: Harvard University Press, 1970).

Toward the end of the novel (chapter 15), eunuchs played a role in Yuan Bozhen's career advancement. The following articles deepen our understanding of eunuchs in general and during the Qing: Melissa Dale, "Running Away from the Palace: Chinese Eunuchs during the Qing Dynasty," *Journal of the Royal Asiatic Society* series 3, 27, no. 1 (2017): 143–64, and "Understanding Emasculation: Western Medical Perspectives on Chinese Eunuchs," *Social History of Medicine* 23, no. 1 (2010): 38–55; Norman A. Kutcher, "Unspoken Collusions: The Empowerment of Yuanming Yuan Eunuchs in the Qianlong Period," *Harvard Journal of Asiatic Studies* 70, no. 2 (2010): 449–95. With sample data on two Ming cases, Jacqueline Eng and her coauthors offer an intriguing view from physical anthropology, in "Skeletal Effects of Castration on Two Eunuchs of Ming China," *Anthropological Science* 118, no. 2 (2010) 107–16.